HOW TO BE FABULOUS

CARMEN REID

Boldwood

First published in 2026 by Boldwood Books Ltd.

Copyright © Carmen Reid, 2026

Cover Design by JD Smith Design Ltd

Cover Images: Shutterstock

A CIP catalogue record for this book is available from the British Library.

Paperback ISBN 978-1-83656-608-3

Large Print ISBN 978-1-83656-607-6

Hardback ISBN 978-1-83656-606-9

Trade Paperback ISBN 978-1-80656-184-1

Ebook ISBN 978-1-83656-609-0

Kindle ISBN 978-1-83656-610-6

Audio CD ISBN 978-1-83656-601-4

MP3 CD ISBN 978-1-83656-602-1

Digital audio download ISBN 978-1-83656-603-8

This book is printed on certified sustainable paper. Boldwood Books is dedicated to putting sustainability at the heart of our business. For more information please visit https://www.boldwoodbooks.com/about-us/sustainability/

Boldwood Books Ltd, 23 Bowerdean Street, London, SW6 3TN

www.boldwoodbooks.com

For each and every one of my wonderful Annie Valentine fans – stay fabulous, babes!

AUTHOR'S REMINDER
ANNIE VALENTINE IS BACK!

For everyone in need of a little refresh, here's an introduction to the characters from the series.

Annie – our heroine, 40-something mother and fashion makeover queen. After many years as the top personal shopper at London fashion heaven, The Store, she's currently star presenter on popular TV show *How To Be Fabulous*. She's the eternal optimist, on a quest to make every day and every outfit just that little bit better.

Lauren – Annie's oldest daughter, now a young adult out in the world, currently working at fashion label, Perfect Dress, in New York. Fiercely opinionated and independent, artistic and so into fashion, Lauren looks like her late father, Roddy, with his raven-black hair and steely blue eyes.

Owen – Annie's oldest son, now an 18-year-old about to set off for uni. Tall and gangly with his mother's lighter hair, Owen has a big sense of humour and is totally into all music. He plays violin, drums, glockenspiel, guitar – electric and acoustic.

Ed – Annie's huge-hearted second husband is sporty, outdoorsy, scruffy, and tragically, couldn't care less about clothes. He's head of music at St Vincent's School, plays violin, guitar, loves every kind of music and is a fantastic dad to all four children.

Minette and Max – Ed and Annie's twins are adorable, when they're not fighting, screaming, or having a complete meltdown, obviously. They're walking, talking, four-year-old pre-schoolers in need of a lot of parental time and energy.

Svetlana Wisneski-Roscoff – the fabulous multi-millionairess former wife of many important men, including oil baron, Igor Wisneski. A former beauty queen from Ukraine, she has her own house in Mayfair, a daughter, Elena, two sons, Michael and Petrov, and a new English barrister husband, Harry. Annie was once her beloved personal shopper, but over the years, they've become close friends. Svetlana owns Perfect Dress and films regular financial advice slots on *How To Be Fabulous*.

Elena – Svetlana's secret love child, who was estranged from her mother previously. She is now all grown-up into an extremely determined and ambitious young woman. She helps to run Perfect Dress in New York.

Dinah – Annie's younger sister. Dreamy, creative, artsy Dinah, who is always lovely to everyone. She gave up her day job to become nanny to Minette and Max during Annie's busy TV filming schedule. She's married to architect, Brian, and they have a daughter, Billie.

Connor – Annie's oldest, 'cashmere sweater' of a best friend. Once her late husband's bestie. He's an actor who has enjoyed TV, film and now West End theatre fame. He's single, yet again, and more than a touch diva-ish, but he's family.

Fern – Annie's mother. A retired podiatrist who brought up her daughters as a hard-working single mum and instilled the love of a quality piece of clothing. She lives outside London now and suffers some health issues, including early-stage dementia. She's well looked after by her daughters and carers.

October 1st: Save The Date!!

My darlings!

We would love to give you an exclusive early opportunity to buy this season's must-have – an invitation to Svetlana Wisneski-Roscoff's Garden Fashion Gala.

A fashion show and auction of dazzling vintage, one-off and pre-loved designer clothes and accessories.

All proceeds will go to a wonderful charity:

Thrive Dressing.

Our confirmed special guest: *TV star and fashion guru, Annie Valentine. More to be announced.*

When: *Friday, October 1st, from 7 p.m. till 11 p.m.*

Where: *The marquee, Balfour Gardens, Mayfair, W1.*

Dress: *Something Fabulous!*

Buy your ticket and register to bid on the night: www.gardenfashiongala.com/tickets

If you have designer items to donate to this fabulous event, gardenfashiongala.com/donate will explain how.

Stay fabulous friends!

PROLOGUE

Annie manhandled the awkward cardboard boxes into the basement storeroom, then put her own heavy tote bag into the doorway to hold it ajar, just in case the unreliable timer light decided to randomly click off. Then she lifted the boxes one by one onto their correct places on the shelf and, well, now that she was down here, would it be so terrible to look for the box labelled:

Handbag stall, Box 7

Just a little peek in there wouldn't hurt anyone, she reasoned. She just wanted to check, she told herself, that all was well, and everything was safe. Spotting the box, she took it down and opened the flaps. Oh! And there it was! The absolutely immaculate, hardly ever been out of the house *Devon* bag, so impeccably made by that very exclusive label, The Row. The bag was smooth, tan, shiny as a conker, with a heavy gold zip that screamed quality and that unmistakable bold shape. She ran her hands over the satiny calf-skin surface. She had tried to resist the lure of this bag, but it was no good, she could recognise the signs, she had fallen in deepest, dreamiest handbag love. It was too late. She was already planning outfits around this treasure; matching the shoes and boots from her wardrobe that would best coordinate with it... and those deep shoulder handles! The bag would look gorgeous slung over a camel coat, a red coat, a navy coat. It would look so smart placed in the crook of her elbow too. It was perfect. The handbag classic. The one and only. Brand new, these bags sold for an impossible amount – around the £4,000 mark. Imagine, £4,000 for a hard-working leather tan tote... *£4,000!* When a perfectly nice and serviceable one could be had for £100. But, oooooh, she slid open the zip to look at the pristine suede lining. It was gorgeous, heart stopping. She knew herself very well; she knew how often she had been involved in a handbag love affair. A bag that promised to make you laugh, cry and change your life. She had thought that she was too sensible and grown-up now for this kind of nonsense. But here she was all over again, with her hands on a bag that she wanted so much, too much, to make her own.

'What shall we price it at?' Paula had asked her and for a moment, Annie had been sorely tempted to say '£400?', whip out her card and take the bag off the market there and then. But she was one of the charity show's organisers. She was here to make sure that every single item so generously donated reached its true value to make as much for the good causes as possible. So, Annie had taken a deep breath and told Paula, 'This is a very valuable bag in pristine condition. It needs to be £2,000 at least. Maybe more if we think we can get away with it.' So, Paula had made the label, tagged it around the bag where Annie saw it now with the figures '£2,400'. Way, way too much for her to be dropping on bags, that was for sure. She took it fully out of the box, deciding she would just slip it over her shoulder to see how it felt, before putting it back in, folding the flaps, saying a mental goodbye and trying to forget about it forever. So, the bag was out, over her shoulder, cradled lovingly between her side and her arm just for a moment, just to let her appreciate its weight, smoothness, and gorgeous craftsmanship. And then... that's when the erratic timer light jumped out of its socket, throwing the storage room into darkness and some internal draft – maybe caused by the lift pulling up higher into the building – caused the door to move, pushing her tote bag out of the way and slamming shut with the automatic click of the Yale lock. *Oh, for crying out loud!*

She was in pitch blackness, without the slightest glimpse of light, complete blackness with boxes on the floor, bags on the floor, quite the obstacle course between her and the door. And there was a £2,400 bag over her arm. Even if she wanted to put it back before she did anything else, she would have no clue how to find the right box. She could feel her breath growing shallow in her chest. *Someone's going to come in and find me and think I was trying to steal this bag!! From a charity!!! A £2,400 bag!! This is going to look terrible! I'm going to be kicked off the fashion show and kicked off the TV and I'll never be able to show my face in public again! For a bag... a handbag! Although, there was no denying the exceptional quality of the leather or the stitching...*

Annie!! She had to get her head together here. She had to calm the heck down and get out of this room before anyone else appeared and jumped to any wrong conclusions. The light was just on the other side of the door, she reminded herself. Yes, the door was locked, but the knob to open the lock was on her side. She just had to find the door in all this blackness, open the lock, turn the light back on and everything would be fine. OK, so where exactly was the door? She turned herself around and very slowly, very gingerly stepped forward, trying not to step or trip on anything that could be in her path. She inched forward, hands out in front of her. And inched... and inched... but there was nothing, absolutely nothing ahead. She stretched her arms out further and felt her toe hit a box. She felt her way carefully around the box. And forward a little further, arms outstretched. *Don't fall*, she told herself. Falling would not help in any way at all. What if she injured her ankle and couldn't get up... or hit her head and... not only would she lie here all night undiscovered, but the show might be jeopardised and then her name would be trashed by hundreds of London's most influential fashionistas.

Annie!! She told herself off. She was spiralling, she had to get a grip. She could feel something in front of her now. But it wasn't the smooth plaster of the wall... or the reassuring wood grain of the door... no, this felt like cardboard and now she could feel the metal of the shelves. She'd walked into one of the shelving units that lined the room. But that was OK, she told herself. If she followed the shelving unit all the way round the room, she would eventually get to the door, wouldn't she? But follow it to the left? Or to the right? She tried to picture herself in the room. Where was she exactly? She couldn't tell. *Never mind,* she told herself, if I follow the shelving in one direction, I will get to the door. That's logical, completely logical. So, she inched along keeping her fingertips on the cardboard and trying to steer clear of all the boxes, bags, and now something metal underfoot. *Totally logical, just keep going,* she told herself. But the room felt enormous, and she had completely lost her bearings. It was so dark. Even straining her eyes, she could see nothing in front, utter darkness. Very unhelpfully, she now started thinking about Agent Starling in *Silence of the Lambs* groping her way around that hideous basement while the murderer stalked her in night vision goggles.

Annie!! She told herself off again. That was definitely not helping. Good grief, how did she get herself into these ridiculous situations, time after time?

'If I got myself in, I can get myself out,' she said out loud to give herself a little boost. She tucked the bag more tightly under her arm, running her fingers over its smooth surface. 'We're a team now,' she told the bag. 'I know you can help me to keep it together. You're a totally together kind of handbag. And *when* we get out of here... even if it's tomorrow, I will just pony up the cash and make you mine.'

1

Annie for cocktails:
Mid-blue silk blouse with deep cuffs and neck bow
Flared blue velvet trousers
Long, purple faux fur coat
Pink patent leather handbag
Black suede ankle boots

'Babes! I am here! I made it!' Weaving past tables, chairs and the late afternoon crowd, Annie, laden down with handbags, tote bags and shopping, hurried across the beautiful antique wooden floor of the cosy London bar to where one of her oldest and dearest friends, Connor McCabe, was sitting waiting for her at their favourite corner booth. And bless him, there were two elegant cocktails on the table because he'd already got the drinks order in. He looked up, ran a hand over his luscious blue-black highland warrior style locks, and gave her something of a glare. His drink was already two-thirds of the way down she saw now.

'I'm sorry, I'm sorry... I didn't think I was so late...' A quick glance at her wrist watch told her she was seventeen minutes late, which was a bit of a social faux pas, especially when you were meeting one of London's – no make that one of the UK's – big-name, actually recognisable, stars of stage and screen, even if you had known him for decades and way, way before he was famous. She kissed him on his chiselled cheekbone, hustled herself into the banquette opposite his, then picked up her drink, chinked it against his and said, just before she took a long mouthful, 'Nobody puts McCaby in the corner.'

The *Dirty Dancing* joke did at least make him smile. 'I am grovelingly sorry I'm so late,' she said, once a second sip of the drink had gone down and she was ready to speak again. 'And this is delicious... so fruity and *mm, mm* packs the kind of punch I'm sure you'd like to give me right now.'

'Thank you. Our favourite barman, José, is in today and he made it especially for us. He's named it the "TV Dark and Stormy".'

'Very clever,' she took another sip. 'We're both on TV, you're the dark one, and I'm obviously stormy.'

This made him smile again. 'Ah, the legendary Connor McCabe smile. All is right again with the world when I am basking in the Connor McCabe smile, made famous on TV and now available all over the West End, but I knew you first. Never forget that. I have the photos you never want published,' she teased because laughter, jokes and plenty of teasing was the bedrock of their long and happy friendship, which had deepened in the very darkest of times following the death, many years ago now, of Annie's first husband, who had also been Connor's best friend.

'*Why* are you so late?' he asked, not quite ready to let her off easily.

'I am seventeen minutes late!' She protested. 'It's not like I'm forty minutes late or had—'

'Forgotten me altogether, which can I remind you has happened before.'

'No, don't remind me...' Annie turned to the two handbags, one large, one small, the umbrella and the large shopping totes, which she'd dumped onto the rest of the banquette, in fact her multiple bag-carrying habit was part of the reason why Connor now always snagged the booth for them, instead of a showy table in the centre of the room. 'You didn't speak to me for about two months after I forgot our date. I seem to remember I had to lure you back with cashmere,' she teased.

'I should think so too. And 4-ply, nothing nasty from the back of an Amazon van,' Connor retorted.

'As if you would wear anything from the back of an Amazon van... I am late because of... so many reasons. It's the first of September and September is a killer month in our household, let me tell you...'

Annie leaned back in the booth, took another fortifying sip and tried to corral all that was happening this month into some sort of sensible list in her mind.

'Ah,' Connor nodded. 'Ed goes back to school, you are on a TV shooting schedule, and what about the twins?' Connor asked, arching one of those devastatingly attractive eyebrows.

'The twins have started kindergarten with... mixed results,' was Annie's take on this latest stage for her four-year-olds. 'Minette very excited, Max crying to break my heart every morning.'

'Poor Max, he's obviously a non-conformist who loves his Mummy.'

'Yes... and then Lauren is still in New York,' she updated Connor about her eldest daughter. 'And that seems to be going OK... thank goodness. And Owen...' even as Annie prepared to say these words about her now eighteen-year-old son, she couldn't really believe they were true. 'Owen is about to start university in Glasgow.'

'Oh yes! Of course he is... Away to bonnie Scotland,' Connor added in his best version of a Scottish accent, even though he grew up in Lancashire. 'How is his wee mammie going to cope with that?'

'Oh... it'll be fine,' she said to try and convince herself. 'Owen... he'll make friends anywhere and he'll be up and down on the train and it's... it's only a seven-hour drive...' she'd googled it, but that was probably only if you went in the middle of the night and didn't stop even for a wee. In truth, she couldn't really think about it too much. Wasn't it bad enough that Lauren was in New York? Now Owen going to Scotland! He would be fine, but Annie wasn't so sure about herself. Owen... Owen was her little boy and the spirit of fun at home and the family member who made everything light-hearted.

Honestly, what was the matter with her children? All her other friends seemed to have offspring who were perfectly happy to stay in London – and why not, it was one of the greatest cities in the world. Her children would both be back, she told herself quickly. They were having an adventure, they were travelling and experiencing other places, other cultures and then they would *definitely* be back.

'And what about you, Connor babes?' She took another bolstering sip of that outrageously strong cocktail, sure she was breathing out flammable fumes by now. 'What is happening with you?'

'No, no. Not so fast, Annie. I need to hear about the new series of *How to be Fabulous* and how it's shaping up.'

Her reply to this was to sigh and say, 'Exhausting babes, exhausting. You know how it is. Whatever you've got, you've got to give, give, give. And TV will only ever take, take, take. By the time we wrap, I'll be ready to lie flat on my back... preferably in a soothing Italian spa, but more realistically on the floor of my bedroom, barricaded shut against the twins in the middle of a rampaging row. But instead, what have I agreed to do as soon as shooting stops? I have agreed to help Svetlana put on a huge, glitzy, charity fashion show.'

'Whoa! That sounds ambitious.'

It would be fair to say that Connor looked an exact mixture of astonished and intrigued. 'A glitzy charity fashion show?' he asked. 'With your Mayfair multi-millionairess friend at the helm. So, when is this? And where? And who is coming? Details, details, Annie, that's what I want to hear.'

Honestly, Annie was a little surprised that she hadn't already told Connor about the Garden Fashion Gala. This show had been in her head for months on end and, surely, she must have mentioned it to him. But then when she thought about it, the idea for the show had only come about early in the summer when Svetlana had decided to purge her vast designer wardrobe and sell a significant proportion to raise money for charity by hosting a lavish garden party fashion show and auction. So, really it had only been a few months of planning and prepping and in that time, there had only been one or two get-togethers with Connor and they had involved the whole family, so maybe she hadn't mentioned it to him. 'It's on October 1st... in exactly one month's time,' she told him, a little startled at the thought. One month... when there was still so much to do.

'And when do you finish filming?' Connor asked.

'Due to wrap in fifteen days, but let's be realistic and say seventeen days.'

Connor pulled a face. 'Oooooh,' he sympathised. 'That's going to be tight.'

'No kidding,' Annie replied. 'No lolling about in Italian spas for me.'

'Definitely not. And your son is heading to uni, don't forget, and your baby is crying about kindergarten and I've not even asked how the long-suffering Ed is doing.'

'Ed who?' she joked. 'Yes, I do occasionally run into my husband in the kitchen. He gets up extra early to make me a coffee before I head out of the door to TV-land.'

'He's a very nice man. You are too lucky.'

This, she had to agree, was very true. She and Ed worked as a team to hold it all together. Nothing about her busy, stressful life would make sense if he wasn't by her side helping her. She needed to remember to take some time now and then to tell him how much she appreciated him.

'No sign of a very nice man in your life, then?' she asked Connor.

He shook his head before adding cheerfully, 'But there is the joy of still searching.'

'True.'

'Annie, you have got people helping you with this show, haven't you?' he asked now, sounding a little concerned. 'Svetlana must have... minions.'

'She does and this fabulous woman, Paula, who used to work with me at The Store is our right-hand showrunner. But ulti-mately... this is our show, our big moment, our chance to pull off something impressive, so—'

'The buck stops with you,' Connor said, understanding perfectly. 'And how is it coming on?' Annie was torn for a moment or two between being relentlessly optimistic or being honest.

'I'm going to get in another round of these bad boys before I can tell you,' she admitted and went off in search of José, the magical mixologist.

* * *

When a second round of TV dark and stormies were in front of them, she felt she could properly offload some of the heavy weight of angst she'd been carrying around with her over the last few days.

'Spill,' Connor commanded after chinking glasses with her once again.

'The caterers are booked, the flowers, same, drinks, same, glasses, chairs, waiting staff, coat check, all done, marquee, like-wise,' she said. 'Donations are coming in – beautiful clothes, amazing accessories and hard cash, so that's all good. The starry guest list – both high society and fashion – has been compiled, the tickets designed...'

'But...' Connor leaned towards her, sensing there was a major speed bump on the fashion show road that Annie was hurtling towards. 'I'm definitely sensing a "but",' he said, then added, 'And this is no time to make jokes about my butt sensing skills.'

'Very funny,' Annie said immediately, but she could feel her tension headache easing. Somehow, nothing was ever so bad when you shared it with Connor. He'd lived through so many of her crises, major and minor, that he would definitely be able to remind her that maybe she could pull through this one too. 'I've not printed the invitations and sent them yet because... because I... well, maybe I'm just being paranoid...'

'I doubt it,' Connor said.

'Because, well, I just have a funny feeling that something isn't quite right. Something hasn't been done. Something is going to derail the whole project.' Annie shook her head. 'I can't explain it. It's probably just nerves, but I can't bring myself to print and send invitations with my name on them as the guest star to all these important people, especially the very important fashion people, until I know that it's going to be a brilliant show that it is definitely going to happen. I mean... I may not work in TV forever. In fact, I know I won't work in TV forever. I need to make more fashion world connections. I need to think about my next move,' she tried to explain. 'So, this show needs to be amazing and put me on the fashion map. Not turn into a disaster that makes me a laughing stock forever.'

'This doesn't sound good, Annie,' Connor sympathised. 'So what are you going to do?'

2

Thea at hand:
Slouchy, navy cashmere V-neck
Silver taffeta pencil skirt
Navy sueded high-heeled pumps
Silver chain bracelet
Silver tassel earrings

It was 6 p.m. when she finally hugged Connor goodbye because they both had places to be, other people to see and anyway, they had downloaded all their current issues and given each other thoroughly good advice. 'Isn't it amazing how much easier it is to solve other people's problems!' Annie had laughed. And she promised to follow at least some of the good advice that Connor had offered.

Now, she was back on the busy pavement in her favourite part of central London, still basking in the glow of warm early evening sun at the very tail of the summer. She walked with a brisk step on heels a little higher than they should be for pavement walking followed by a long journey on the Tube. But it was her thing, her mantra, her *raison d'être* even, if you were going to go all French about it, to be always a little overdressed. Interesting things happened when you wore interesting clothes and that was a fact. Hadn't the late, great Dame Vivienne Westwood herself decreed that: '*You have a more interesting life, if you wear impressive clothes*'?

And Annie had seen these words in action both for herself and for the hundreds, maybe thousands, of people she had shopped for, styled, made over during her long career as a personal shopper, now a TV fashion guru and in future... *in future*...

Those words seemed to get a little caught in her mind. In future. Realistically, she wasn't going to be on TV forever, was she? Realistically, every season felt as if it was in danger of being the last because the show might not be recommissioned or she might be replaced by someone much more excitingly new and nubile. This was fashion after all, if she was going to live by the sell-by-date then she would also die by the sell-by-date. And then what?

Increasingly, she was giving this a lot more thought. She had ideas, of course – become a much more private, exclusive personal stylist, maybe to a starry list of clientele; or set up her own channel online, giving advice, selling lovely things, counting on the continued loyalty of her very own fans. But she also loved the idea of being just a little closer to the real, beating heart of fashion. What did she mean exactly? She didn't even know. She was just a little obsessed with the idea of fashion shows and new collections... advising designers on whether their ideas were amazing or too off-the-wall... being able to have a say in what was in, what was out, knowing exactly what colour was going to be all over the socials eighteen months from today. She wanted to be much more a part of the fashion industry, that was the truth. TV was not lighting her creative fires. The TV show was about looking for nice clothes on the high street and wearable separates and affordable, practical things... and sometimes she could hardly remember that she used to pore over *Vogue* as a teenager and had taken herself off to art school because nothing else would do. And, in truth, even though she wasn't quite sure what it should be, she wanted a *proper* career.

Her husband, Ed, had been at his school for many years. He had risen up the ranks to become head of department, maybe one day in the future he'd been deputy head or even head or move to another illustrious London establishment. Whereas, all that faced her at the end of many successful TV years was a boot in the bum and a 'sorry, no thanks, we've found a foxier number.' To add insult to injury, while Ed had paid holidays, sick pay, a pension plan, Annie swung from short-term contract to short-term contract, always beset with the worry that the next contract would be her last and she wasn't going to get renewed. In her time between TV contracts, she scrabbled about, working for Svetlana's dress company, personal shopping for some long-term clients, buying and selling on Vinted and scrambling to pay her share of the bills. This had once been exciting and filled with potential and ultra-flexible for her life as a mother of young children, but... Annie had lately come to realise that she was a growing weary of all the insecurity and the pressure of having to sing for her supper every moment of the day. She wanted something more solid. She wanted to be part of something bigger and more... reliable.

But she seriously doubted this was a problem that she was going to solve today. So, she let her tense shoulders drop a little, despite the weight of the many bags. Then she deliberately smoothed out the worried crease that she knew was settling in between her eyebrows and she tried to look around, at the people, at the lavish shop windows, and enjoy the fact that she was strolling in beautiful shoes and a well-loved summer dress, through the beating heart of fashionable London. She admired a tall woman with flame-red hair strolling past in an elegant charcoal linen jumpsuit. Copper and charcoal, gorgeous. And there was a Serena Williams lookalike, artful braids caught up in an impressive bun, rocking the kind of shocking pink satin blouse that had launched designer Elsa Schiaparelli to fame almost 100 years ago. Annie was just intending to glance at the graceful, wooden framed windows of the Ralph Lauren shop, you know just turn the head, glance, nod with approval and keep on walking, but, oh, now... that was catching her eye. She was going to have to stop and walk over and take a closer look at that completely stunning pale gold dress. Just one month from now, she was supposed to be a major part of what she still hoped could be *the* charity fashion event of the season. It had occurred to Annie more than once that she *needed* something new and fabulous and of this exact moment-in-fashion to wear. And this dress... it was silky, slippy, fluid and drapey. It had a very flattering V-shaped neckline, a twisted front and, oh, she loved, make that, *adored*, the built-in cape effect. She could twirl and swish and she would have her very own, almost-to-the-elbow cape. Gold *with a* cape – she could be the show's very own super heroine if she had a gold, caped dress. To be honest, she did already feel like the show's heroine – all those mountains of clothes she had sorted from Svetlana's wardrobe, persuading her what to sell, what to have re-tailored, what to donate. Then all the clothes she had sourced from past clients, friends, pretty much everyone she'd ever known. She'd also lined up models, brought Paula on board, done the guest list, written commentaries for the compères to read out... She loved to be a fixer, but this show, she was just about all fixed out and there was still one whole month to go. So much could still go wrong... that's what her gut was telling her. That was the endless niggling feeling.

Ideally, the show still needed some show-stopping items of clothing. Ideally, another three professional models would also make a huge difference. Ideally, there were a lot of other things required between now and October 1st to make sure that this really would be the hottest ticket in town. And... never mind, she was going in to see about that dress. Because a gold dress with a cape would definitely make everything better for Annie. This she did know.

* * *

In the changing room, she took a long, appraising look at herself in the dress. It was very, very good – this dress. The twisted design that let fabric drape very flattering over offending lumps and bumps at the front. If you'd had four children, despised the gym and really if it came to a choice between svelte and pastry, would go pastry every time, you did appreciate some flattering drape. And she had the perfect shoes and bag to go with this beautiful friend, no doubt about it. The cape! She gave a little swish and a swirl in front of the mirror. She would go out and talk it over with the shop assistant. In a store like this, the shop assistant would want to be consulted. And Annie would enjoy talking about shoes, bags and whether to wear tights and Spanx or not with a trusted expert. From her own days as a personal shopper in The Store, she knew that it could be a long and quiet day in a high-end shop, so when a customer was trying and buying, then most assistants loved an in-depth chat. 'What do you think?' she asked as she swished open the curtain and stepped out of the changing space.

'Absolutely loving that on you,' the assistant gushed. In fact, her face split into a smile and she actually clapped her hands together.

'It's so beautiful, so flattering and I love, love the cape,' Annie told her. 'I'm Annie by the way.'

'I'm Thea. Nice to meet you and we all love this dress. As soon as we put it in the window, we've had so many people come in and ask to try it on. It is so statement-y but flattering and so comfortable to wear.'

'I have bright pink strappy heels, so that's what I'm thinking,' Annie confided. 'And bag choices... another colour? Gold? Or maybe something darker.'

'I can suggest some options, just to hold, just to get you thinking,' Thea offered.

So, Annie followed her out of the changing area and towards the handbag collection. They were comparing clutches when the store's front door opened and Annie was sure she could feel a hush descend. Seeing Thea look up and remain fixed on whoever had just come into the shop, Annie also turned to have a look.

And there was no mistaking the crisp, jet-black pageboy haircut, the huge gold-framed glasses with a yellow tint and the severe black trouser suit. This was one of the most famous women in fashion – PaigeP, editor-in-chief of fashion bible *Stylesetter*, the international magazine, available in thirty-five languages, *Stylesetter Daily*, the fashion trade daily newsletter, and not forgetting Stylesetter Publishing, which produced ten to-die-for fashion-themed coffee table books on July 1st and December 1st every year. You couldn't buy them in the shops or anywhere mainstream, you had to apply for a place on the waiting list for these limited-edition babies. Annie was the proud owner of six of them and at £150 a copy, that was no small investment. PaigeP had been at the top of her game for well over a decade now because she was so influential, so authoritative. When *she* said something was over, it was dead and buried. Where *she* pointed, everyone flocked to follow.

Many conflicting questions were rushing into Annie's mind at the sight of this most fashionable of all the fashionistas. First of all, what was she doing in Ralph Lauren? That seemed way too mainstream for PaigeP, who was known to champion tiny and completely unique labels. Could Annie dare approach her? Maybe to ask about this dress, was that a good idea? Which bag should she carry with it? *No, no, don't be ridiculous!* Or what about, could she send her an invite to the Garden Fashion Gala? Had they already sent one? Had they dared to include PaigeP on their invitation list? And then came the completely outrageous thought... could Annie somehow work for *Stylesetter*? Would that give her the influence, the fashion access, the kind of status that she had recently begun to hanker after? But instead, despite all of these ideas rushing around her head, Annie remained frozen to the spot, unable to think of even one sensible thing to say.

PaigeP strode towards the nearest assistant. 'I've come to collect my order,' was all she needed to say to send the assistant flying towards the back of the shop. Then PaigeP was left standing, waiting, and she inevitably cast her eyes around to take in what was on display and what was happening in the store today. Her eyes fell on Annie. And stayed on Annie. If Annie had felt frozen before, now she was transformed into a statue. A bunny in a golden dress in front of PaigeP's highly critical headlight glare. The silence seemed to grow, enlarge and draw in every other person on the shop floor. Until Annie couldn't stand it any more and blurted, 'It's the cape. That's what makes it for me.'

More silence... Annie was transported back to school, to being under the eyes of the glacial headmistress and wishing she could dissolve, disappear. PaigeP continued to look at her, but lo and behold, the bold wine-red lips were parting and out came PaigeP's words of wisdom. 'Yes,' she said, 'shades of LaCroix. Unusually bling for Ralph.'

Annie felt frozen to the spot once again. Was that good? Bad? Was LaCroix in? Or out? Should Ralph be doing bling or not? Like the ancient oracle of Delphi, PaigeP had spoken and it was up to the world to try to decipher her meaning.

'Your order, madam,' an older woman, who was obviously the senior manager approached PaigeP with two bulging carrier bags. In a bid to stop staring, Annie turned back to Thea and wordlessly took the clutch from her hands. Dared she walk over to the mirror to gauge the effect? Or would that be rude? Oh, for goodness' sake, this woman wasn't the Queen... but then again, she was definitely fashion royalty.

'Not that bag!'

Annie turned in some horror because PaigeP had spoken once again and this was clearly directed at her. In fact, PaigeP was approaching the handbag display now.

Annie could see the look of fear on Thea's face. No doubt terrified she was going to be in trouble for even suggesting this choice. 'All a bit pedestrian,' was PaigeP's verdict as she cast her eyes, still behind those flashy, yellow-tinted frames, over the selection. 'That one maybe,' she pointed, 'but ideally,' she looked Annie up and down, 'something very shiny from Jacquemus... or snake-skin, vintage Jimmy Choo.'

Annie nodded mutely, once again feeling like a schoolgirl, but this time, a schoolgirl with a hopeless crush.

'I only come here for the cashmere,' were PaigeP's final words and with a turn of her heel, she was out of the door, into the waiting silver car and with a discreet electric purr, she was gone. Annie looked at herself in the mirror. The dress was perfect. She was buying it. Then, of course, she would go and hunt down the exact bag that PaigeP had specified, no question. But the first thing she would do, she scrambled inside her handbag for her phone, was make sure that PaigeP's people got a follow-up message 'from the woman in the caped gold dress in Ralph Lauren' about her invitation to the Garden Fashion Gala.

3

Maria on duty:
Pink linen blouse, starched and ironed
Stretchy black trousers
Black lace-up, rubber-soled shoes
White cotton apron, starched and ironed

Annie stood on the steps outside Svetlana's highly polished Mayfair front door and waited for her bell ring to be answered. She took a moment to turn and look at the beautiful residents' garden which, in less than a month now, would be hosting what they both wanted to think of as *the* fashion event of the season. All summer long, Svetlana had been working with the residents' committee and the gardeners to improve the space and it was much greener, lusher and more flower-studded than ever before. On the night of the show, there were plans for lanterns in the trees, a lit-up walkway to the marquee and industrial quantities of fairy lights all around the sombre black railings.

It was an additional expense, but everything was going to be set up the day before, for a full dress rehearsal, to make sure that the plans were going to come to life just as Svetlana and Annie had imagined. Annie glanced back at the door, at the luscious pot plants on either side of it and at the blooming window boxes at each one of the antique windows on this four-storeyed town-house. Svetlana, who was quite insanely wealthy now – having made a series of spectacularly good marriages, divorces and investments – had grown up in a tiny Ukrainian village and some essence of being a countrywoman, of enjoying growing things, of needing plants, flowers, even vegetables to grow, remained. The door opened and Svetlana's long-standing maid and house-keeper, Maria, opened it, crisp dress, white apron and broad smile in place.

'Welcome, Ms *Valentina*,' Maria said, stepping back and extending an arm to show Annie into the house. '*Madame* would like you to come upstairs to the smaller sitting room.'

'Thank you, Maria. And how are you?' Annie asked as she followed Maria through the hall and up the staircase, taking in the beautiful lights, paintings, family portraits, gorgeous wallpa-per, and all the elegant touches that made Svetlana's house feel somewhere between a palace, a luxury hotel and a real home.

'I am very well, thank you, Ms *Valentina*. The boys will be here next weekend, so I am excited to see them again.'

'Of course, I bet they can't wait to be home to be spoiled by you.' The boys were Svetlana's sons, Petrov and Michael, at boarding school in Scotland now, which was a little heartache for Maria, who had cared for them ever since they were babies. Maria tapped on the sitting room door and a cheerful 'Come in,' rang out from the other side.

She held the door open and Annie walked into the beautiful room, all gleaming cream and gold with properly impressive art on the walls. There at an antique table at the window was Svet-lana – the woman who had once been Annie's favourite customer in the personal shopping suite but who now was both a business partner and a real friend. 'Hello, my darling *Annah*,' Svetlana gushed, as she stood up and they approached one another for an affectionate hug.

'Let me just admire the "Svetlana does casual" look,' Annie said with a smile, taking in the pale beige cashmere jogging bottoms and hoody, accessorised with ropes of gold jewellery, huge diamond and pearl earrings and the tousled blonde bob that Svetlana was currently sporting.

'Maria will bring us some coffee and we will sit down at my table here and talk about the show and everything we still need to do,' Svetlana instructed.

'Perfect.' Annie took herself over to the table and, still with half a mind on the sumptuous room, the paintings, the flowers, the delicious scents in the air from candles, from Svetlana herself, then she pulled her laptop from her bag, opened it up and focused on the business of today.

'First, we go through the checklist, yes? Then we talk about what still needs to be organised,' was Svetlana's suggestion.

'Checklist coming right up,' Annie told her, clicking through to the relevant file. She read through their long list. The marquee was booked, the lighting, too, the catering, the flowers, the tables and chairs. There was a DJ and a draft playlist. Three models, two semi-professional and one professional – an old friend of Annie's – were confirmed, ideally three more still needed to be 'sourced'.

'I'll look after that,' Annie told Svetlana. 'I have some ideas.' She was thinking about Ed's school and wondering if she could maybe entice some of the athletic team's girls to enjoy a night of fashion-glamour. 'The other special guests... including our compère?' Annie read out from her list. 'You were going to find us a starry presence to be the main host... it's three weeks and six days, my love. Is there any word?'

'Oh yes.' Svetlana fixed Annie with the megawatt smile created by probably the finest dentists in the world and framed by soft, pillowy, perfectly lipsticked lips. She waggled a manicured finger. 'I am not going to tell you yet. No, I leave as big surprise for you.'

'Excellent,' was Annie's response, but in all honesty, she would rather have known because then it would be official. She could put it on the invites and make it public and there would be much less danger of the 'mystery guest' backing out. So that would be one less thing to worry about. Plus, sometimes Svetlana's surprises were too surprising – and not in a good way. 'So... shall I print and send the invitations?' Annie asked. 'Are we all set, ready to go? Is it time to officially invite people now? I'll put "mystery guest star compère" or something. But we're good to go, Svetlana?' Annie gave her friend a long, searching look. 'The permit from the council...' she added. 'You took care of that and I've ticked it off the list, but the marquee people want a copy of it.'

'Oh yes, yes...' Svetlana flicked her hand dismissively. 'I will go to my office and find it. It's in the files. I have been so busy, crazy busy. We bought a holiday house. Up in the north of Scotland, near the boys' school. So we can see them more often, have their friends to stay and let Harry play plenty of golf.'

Svetlana looked through the pile of papers on her table and slid a glossy brochure towards Annie. 'Is beautiful but needs a lot of *vuerrrrk*!' Over her many years in London, Svetlana had almost completely mastered the troublesome 'w' that peppered the English language, but occasionally one got the better of her, especially where *work* was concerned. And she was always doing work, or more accurately having work done – to her houses, to her cars, and to herself. Annie glanced through the brochure, eyes on stalks. She had expected something pretty lavish, but this highland 'lodge' was something else – chandeliers made of antlers, swathes of wooden panelling, wooden bannisters, acres of tartan carpet. The grounds were also extensive – a one-acre garden with rolling lawns and an additional twenty-four acres of 'native woodland'.

'Is very beautiful,' Svetlana informed her, 'but needs new bathrooms, new kitchen, new decoration, new heating, heating, much more heating and then will be very comfortable. You will come and visit.' Svetlana's invitations always sounded like commands.

'Of course,' Annie said. 'Remember when we went hill walking in heels in the highlands?'

They both laughed at that crazy memory.

'It was disaster,' Svetlana laughed, 'a fun disaster. But we not do this again. Insurance company would not refund my handbag.'

This made Annie laugh again as she imagined Svetlana terrorising the agent on the other end of the phone about why she had cut up her Hermès handbag to make shoes when they were lost on a hillside at night. 'OK, so back to the list,' Annie said. 'I do the invitations, find three more models, start planning the dress rehearsals... and do some more clothes organising. You get confirmation from our guest compère and keep persuading starry guests to turn up on the night.'

'And we need more clothes, very special ones,' Svetlana insisted. 'More, more. I call all my friends and harass them again. We want clothes on the catwalk, clothes on rails in the marquee and a stall of very special handbags. I *vant* to make over £1,000,000.'

'Gulp... that's a lot of money, babes,' Annie warned her. 'Even big TV stars don't make a millions on their charity drives.'

'Yes, but we will do it,' was the simple verdict. And Annie could not help but admire the complete conviction coming from Svetlana. If the woman was going to do something, she always went big.

Just then Maria came in with the coffee tray. So, steaming cups of glossy black coffee were poured out into elegant bone china. There were also crystal glasses of water and a little silver milk jug for Annie, as well as a delicate plate of freshly baked miniature cookies. Annie already knew Svetlana wouldn't touch one, and she would eat at least three, to make Maria happy and to satisfy the intense sugar cravings that her to-do list was inducing.

Once there had been a little lull in the conversation to allow them to sip the coffee, drink some water, and in Annie's case chomp down a biscuit, she asked about the latest Perfect Dress news. 'It is all good,' was Svetlana's update on the dress company. 'Many good regular customers, the business is growing steadily, nothing exciting, steady. But we need something more "show-stopper" for the next collection. I have asked everyone to think about this. Exciting design, something to talk about, make publicity.'

'Yes, that's a good point,' Annie agreed. 'I'll have a think, throw some ideas into the fire.'

'And what about your girl Lauren?' Svetlana asked now, leaning forward, an expression resembling troubled crossing the perfect features. Annie felt herself give almost something of a little start at this question. What about Lauren? Was there something she didn't know? As far as she knew, Lauren was happy in New York, happy at Perfect Dress, 'dating' a boy she liked a lot, and all was well. But she would be the first to admit, with the show and Owen about to set off to uni in two weeks' time, maybe she'd not given as much thought, or been as regularly in touch with Lauren, as usual.

'I thought everything was fine with Lauren,' Annie said, but Svetlana shook her head and fixed Annie was a serious look.

'No, *Annah*,' she began, 'Elena says Lauren is not happy and Elena does not know why.'

'Oh no... I didn't know...' Annie said, feeling a fresh wave of anxiety. Not that she needed to do it, she would remember, but still, at the top of her to-do list, she now put:

Call Lauren

4

Dinah visiting:
Navy denim shirt
Blue cord blazer
Blue, grey and brown checked midi kilt
Tall lace up brown boots
Brown beret
Flower earrings
Vintage bangles
Khaki green floral quilted velvet tote bag

Annie was not a morning person. She was always the one lolling in the bed for just a few more minutes while Ed got up at the first tweet of the alarm, showered, got the twins up and was down in the kitchen brewing strong coffee while Annie struggled with emerging from under that gorgeous, warm and enveloping duvet.

'Get up!' She could hear Ed shouting at her from the kitchen. 'Annie! Go and have your shower! It's the morning... And maybe you shouldn't have spent the entire night researching handbags on your phone!'

Annie just groaned. The late-night handbag googling was getting completely out of hand. There was no denying that Ed was already convinced she was a crazy woman and maybe he did have a point. But could any husband truly appreciate the need for exactly the right bag at the right time? He had one briefcase-meets-messenger bag, which he'd used faithfully for years. He didn't seem to ever need anything else apart from maybe a ruck-sack for hiking trips. Her current handbag looked just a little shabby and over-loved. Like a favourite cuddly toy, it was fraying at the edges, worn and just a little tatty. There was absolutely no buying a new handbag – not with having just bought the gold dress and the Jacquemus evening clutch it *needed* – and now that she no longer had a staff discount, and not to mention the incred-ible price inflation of all the luxury bags—

No! So all this scrolling and searching was to find the bag she exactly wanted, but pre-loved and at the price she could – at a pinch – afford. But buying pre-loved was a minefield. There were so many fakes out there. And there were so many sad, saggy old bags that had lost all their life and their lustre. Back in her Ebay-ing prime, she'd had a list of trusted sources, but now, she was out there on handbag safari, hunting high and low, scouring reviews for clues, scrutinising photos for giveaway clues, in her quest to find the exact right bag at the exact right price. And so far, it couldn't be found. She dragged herself to the shower, where zingy citrus gels and shampoos were on hand to try and zap her back to life.

A little more awake now, she headed towards the kitchen where the prospect of coffee was reviving her spirits as she began to mentally go through her schedule for the day. No filming... no TV commitments today, she realised with a little surge of relief. The new episodes of *How to Be Fabulous* were almost all 'in the can' and for the next couple of months there would be time to do the two things she did between bouts of filming – one, catch up with everything in her life that had been put on hold during the gruelling filming weeks and two, begin to panic about whether the series after this one would get commissioned and would she still be in it, not replaced with a pouty twenty-four-year-old, and would her pay still be at the same healthy rate as before.

Everyone always imagined that now she was on TV, she was fabulously loaded. But this couldn't be any further from the truth – TV presenter pay, now that they were on a mainstream channel, was generous in term of the hourly rate, but she only worked for twenty weeks in the year. So really, she earned a much more ordinary amount over the year as a whole and in the time between filming, wondered what she should be doing with herself to contribute more to the family finances. And did life not get more expensive by the minute? Not a day passed without either a child needing something new or replaced, or the house requiring another bill and/or repair – Yes, the new handbag idea, she was going to have to put that right out of her mind and get on with the day.

'And good morning to my lovely wife,' Ed said as she arrived in the kitchen, hair still damp, dressing gown still on, as she really could not make decisions about hair styling or outfits until the breakfast coffee had been downed.

'Mummmmmmmeeeeeee,' both of her twins chorused in delight, clambering down from their chairs, toast still in hand, to give her a morning hug.

'Hello, hello, darlings,' she replied, pulling them both in close, kissing the jammy faces and smelling the warm, morning skin of two delightful little four-year-old humans.

'Daddy says it's a nursery day.' Max looked up her and she could already read the wobbly lower lip. Ed passed her the coffee cup and she took a bolstering mouthful.

'Yes, it is a nursery day,' she said calmly. At this, Minnie began to wave her hands in the air and cheer. 'I love nursery... we are doing painting and I love painting.'

'That sounds lovely,' Annie enthused, perching herself on the chair next to her children. Unfortunately, Max was already gearing up for a heartfelt sob about nursery, so Annie took another slug of coffee and prepared to comfort him. 'Oh, Maxie, buddy, it's just for a few hours... and I'm not at work today, so I'll be there to pick you up and we can go to the park and even the café on the way home.'

Max looked up at her through eyes threatening tears. 'Can you pick us up before lunch?' he asked, voice full of tragedy.

'No!' Minnie shrieked immediately. 'I love lunch!'

'Let me have a think about that, Maxie...' She didn't want to overpromise, she didn't want Minnie to think that Max had 'won', she didn't want it the other way around either. Oh, everything would be a lot easier if Max loved nursery too... everything would be a lot easier if the twins could just agree on something, anything. But that wasn't likely to happen any time soon.

'OK, my lovely family, I need to get going,' Ed announced as he put dishes into the dishwasher, gave the counter a quick wipe down and pocketed his phone.

'Can I just say, you are looking very hot...' Annie told him, as he bent down to kiss her and then the children.

He was sharply dressed for school in blue shirt, tan chinos and tie. The face was clean shaven, the steely, curly hair was well cut and he smelled just the right level of fresh and ferny. He was also fit and muscular, and really Annie needed to put 'pay attention to Ed' on her to-do list.

He wished her good luck with the nursery run. 'I'll need it,' she replied with a glance at Max's welling eyes. She struggled with the Mummy guilt – when at work, she worried if the children were OK and if they were missing her. When at home with them for long periods, she worried if her career and future earning potential were passing by and could never be regained.

'Has everyone had enough toast?' Annie asked. 'OK, let's go and get dressed then,' she added brightly.

The tears that had been threatening began to burst out of Max. *This will pass... he'll settle in...* Annie told herself, determined to remain positive and cheerful about nursery, even if her little boy crying broke her own heart.

* * *

Annie was just exiting the Tube station on the way back from the traumatic nursery run when her sister, Dinah, called. She barely broke her stride to pull out, answer and clamp phone to ear, but she did in the process notice the woman walking in the other direction. This woman was so beautifully put together and Annie always had a moment to appreciate someone who had spent care and attention on their look. The woman had a smooth steely grey bob, dramatic dark glasses, possibly Chanel, and she was wearing long black suede boots and the kind of sculptural black dress you didn't see very often – a high neck, architectural sleeves, complicated, teeny pleats, intricate cutting and Japanese fabric, Annie guessed. Then there were angular silver earrings, a slash of plum lipstick and a chic black bag accessorising this look. Very good. This was a woman who knew her stuff.

'—Annie? Are you there? Are you listening to me?' her Dinah asked.

'Yes, of course, course I'm listening. But I just passed a masterclass in sixty-something sophistication and had to admire it. I'm walking back from the Tube station and she walked past in, possibly, Yamamoto.'

'Lovely,' Dinah said without sounding too interested. 'How is everyone? I'm not quite sure what to do with myself now that I don't look after the M&Ms very much. Can I come round and see you?'

'Only for an hour,' Annie warned, 'I'm putting the timer on. I have a lot to do... filming has finished and now there's a fashion show to plan. Do you want to help with a fashion show? We have tasks for everyone.'

'No and you're insane,' Dinah warned her. 'Anyone who knows anything about fashion shows knows they're a nightmare because you're dealing with wall-to-wall divas, egos, flakes, creative types, and basically everyone who you would never want to help you with organising anything.'

Annie sighed. There was a little too much truth in what Dinah was saying there. 'You have a point, but that's not going to stop me trying,' she told her sister. 'If it goes well, I think it will be amazing for my fashion CV.'

'And if it goes badly?' Dinah asked.

'This is me and Svetlana,' Annie insisted. 'We will make it brilliant.' That was the aim, that was definitely the aim. She and Svetlana could pull this off. Would pull this off. One million pounds Svetlana had said with her usual determination.

'Come round.' Annie added, 'I'll get the coffee on for me and the saintly herbal teabag brewing for you.'

'See you soon,' Dinah promised. As Annie stalked up the hilly road of lovely townhouses towards the Leon-Valentine residence, she thought as calmly and logically as she could about the fashion show. Although the big ticket items were all in place – the venue, marquee, flowers, music, catwalk, chairs, invitations, team of helpers – she knew there were still a lot of important gaps to fill. They didn't have enough models and she'd said she would sort that. They didn't really have enough clothes, not for a one-hour show and sale rails of items to buy on the night. There wasn't much PR or wow factor, or marketing buzz happening yet and most of the starry names hadn't replied to their invitations to confirm they were coming. In short, there was 'A Lot To Do', but yes, she would put the kettle on and listen to Dinah and tell Dinah about all the things on her mind, too, because that's what sisters were for, after all.

* * *

'So, first of all, Lauren,' Annie began, as she boiled up water in the kitchen. 'Apparently, she's not happy; I've heard this from Svetlana, but I cannot get her to reply to my calls. She will send messages, but they are just the usual and not telling me anything.'

'A bit worrying,' Dinah agreed.

'Exactly... guess I just have to keep trying. And if there's still not much more than texts and smiley face emojis, maybe I'll have to get on a plane.'

'Oh dear!'

No, maybe that was a bit drastic at this stage, Annie thought to herself. She was a little worried, but she wasn't in full-on panic mode. She would message Elena, she decided, Svetlana's daughter and Lauren's boss. Elena could hopefully put her mind at rest or at least get Lauren to return her calls.

'I'll keep trying,' she said to reassure Dinah as much as herself.

'OK, so what about the twins, are they settling into nursery?' was Dinah's first question, once the hot drinks were made and they'd settled into the sofa in Annie and Ed's very comfortable sitting room – lots of shades of pale on the walls, in the curtains, the rugs, cushions and shelving, but grounded with a wooden floor and sofas in a washable and forgiving denim blue. The arrival of twin babies had seen Annie give up for once and for all on her white sofa dreams. Now, her styling goals were confined to arranging frames and ornaments beautifully on the shelves and curating a lovely coffee-table collection of glossy books with a beautiful bowl. Although Annie did notice that one of the twins had put some plastic dinosaurs and a small bouncy ball on top of the smooth white pebbles in her bowl.

'Nursery? Minnie loves it and Max hates it, or so he says, but to be honest, I wonder if that's just to be different to Minnie. The nursery staff are lovely, and doing everything they can to try and help Max fit in. But it's a trial leaving him there.'

'Oh no,' Dinah sympathised. 'I'm around... if you want me to step in and babysit, until he gets used to the idea?'

'No, I worry that will make things worse. In fact, I do have a slightly sneaky idea...'

Dinah smiled. 'Go on, then.'

'Well... I thought I'd just tell Max, "OK, if you want to stay at home with me, that's fine," then I'll get him to tag along with me, doing nothing special, in fact having the most boring time possible. After a day or two, he'll maybe think maybe nursery isn't so bad, after all.'

'Yeah,' Dinah agreed, 'sometimes, they just need to be allowed to choose. So if he's been at home and then he's choosing to go back to nursery, it could be fine... or it could go horribly wrong and you'll have him by your side for a whole year and then have to go through all this again for school.'

Annie threw her hands up at the thought of that. 'I will have to make life very boring for Max,' she said.

'And I was also thinking, Annie...' Dinah began, 'what are you doing for your wedding anniversary...? I mean, isn't it, Oct 1st? And you two romantics, you always like to do something special.'

'Oct 1st?' Annie gave her sister a look, her heart sinking. 'That's the day of the fashion show and I didn't even twig.'

'Oh—'

'Oh my God...' Annie couldn't believe she hadn't realised. And hadn't she just resolved to pay more attention to her husband?

'We'll just have to agree to celebrate the next day... or maybe the day after that. I will probably need some time to recover from all the fashion drama.'

'Yup, realistically. A couple of days I'd have thought.'

'Siri!' Annie shouted at her phone, 'set reminder for later today to discuss wedding anniversary with Ed.'

Siri repeated the request and confirmed.

'Siri! Set reminder to call Elena at 6 p.m.'

Siri confirmed and Dinah tried not to giggle.

'Is *he* running your life now?'

'I wish he was. Bring on the robots,' Annie joked, 'me and everything else around here will work so much better.'

'So... what about Owen?' was Dinah's next question.

'Yes! Exactly, what about Owen?' Annie repeated. Good grief it was nearly 11 a.m. and still there had been no sign of her school leaver, about to become a university student son. 'Don't tell me he's still in bed? Honestly, I'm going to install a klaxon outside his room and have it set up to go off at 9 a.m. every morning.'

'You can talk,' Dinah reminded her. 'I've never met anyone who could sleep in like the teenaged Annie.'

Annie had to admit her sister had a point. 'If I could just sleep in until 11 a.m. every so often, I would probably be a completely different person – so chill, so relaxed.'

'I want to give Owen a present, for going away to uni,' Dinah went on.

'That is so nice of you, perfect Auntie.'

'You are a perfect auntie, too, so let's not compete. What would he like? Should I ask him? Or Siri? Or do you have ideas...? Because it must be soon.'

'What do you mean soon? He's not going till October. That's when uni starts.'

'But not in Scotland...' Dinah countered. 'I looked Glasgow uni up and it starts the first week in September. Fresher's week starts next week.'

This news was even more astonishing to Annie than the wedding anniversary clash.

'What!! Next week!!' she exclaimed. 'Why did I not know this?' she wondered out loud. Did Ed know this? What about Owen? Did Siri know?

Annie was hit with a wave of overwhelm. She'd thought worrying about the fashion show, the twins and Lauren was quite enough to be getting on with, but now here was Dinah, who was supposed to be her shoulder to cry on, bringing news of wedding anniversaries and surprise university start dates!

'But he's not ready...' Annie protested. 'I'm not ready. Next week?! It can't be! Owen!' she shouted, jumping up and heading for the hallway. 'For God's sake, you have to get up!!'

5

LAUREN, NEW YORK

Pizza-ready Noah:
Soft brown cord trousers
Soft brown cord jacket
Mustard yellow T-shirt
Mid-blue and brown thick, textured scarf
Vegan-strapped watch

To say that Lauren had made a big effort for tonight was putting it mildly. She had pulled out all the stops. Her long dark hair, with its glamorous puffy fringe was washed, dried, and straightened to within an inch of its life. Her understated make up made the most of her pale blue eyes, porcelain skin and cherry lips. Her dress, a crushed silvery grey slip of a thing, was new. But her black boots and her trusty denim jacket were old, comfortable favourites that she loved to wear. She'd slung some simple chains around her neck and threaded her favourite slim, silver hoops through her ears. One generous blast of the luscious perfume she'd got for her birthday and she was set for dinner in Greenwich village with Noah.

Noah, Noah... they had been together for just over four months now and Lauren was in a jumble of emotion about it. She really liked him, no doubt about that. She found him interesting, maybe even fascinating. She also found him fun and intriguing. Of course he was handsome, almost everyone in this city was the 'best version' of themselves. Their hair was expensively cut, their teeth straight and whitened to perfection, they worked out, ate 'clean' and dressed well. So, Noah was no exception. Well, except to her, he was. He was tall, olive-skinned, with dark, tightly curled hair, which he wore just above the shoulder. He had one of those rangy frames, all shoulders and long legs, so his coats and scarves flapped around him, making him look a touch windswept and poetic.

Yes, she was really into him. When he held her, kissed her and looked deep into her eyes, she was fluttery and close to believing that maybe this could be love. But... when they went out with friends, when they partied, then he was such a social butterfly and so attentive to all their female friends that she wondered if he cared for her as much as she cared for him. And then there were the gaps – those aching days, even weeks, when he barely messaged, barely seemed to have time for her, made her heart ache but said he was too busy with work. And he always swept her off her feet when he breezed back into her life again. She'd seen other young couples up close – Elena and her boyfriend, Sye, for example – Sye was away for work *a lot*, but somehow, he never seemed to drive Elena into any kind of pit of despair the way Noah drove her.

Was it her? Lauren would wonder. *Am I being too needy? Obsessive? We're both twenty-four... it's still dating, waiting to see what will happen, taking it slowly. I can't rush in and declare undying love for the guy, he'll run away.* So, Lauren was trying to rein it in, play it a lot cooler. She didn't rush to answer his messages. Sometimes, she even turned a meet-up or a party down. *Who am I? What do I want?* These were the questions she was trying to answer for herself. She didn't want to be 'that girl', clinging to her phone, needing a message from Noah to make everything OK again. But tonight sounded as if it was going to be different. He'd sounded so upbeat, asking her to his favourite 'cosy little place', telling her he had 'exciting news to share', flattering her that 'I want to tell you first'.

So, there was a new dress and careful hair and make up and now, she was approaching the restaurant and she knew he was already there, because he'd messaged a moment ago to tell her: 'I'm in a booth near the back, best seats in the place.'

'There you are!' were his words of greeting and as the cheerful smile flashed over his face, she smiled too. They kissed hello and she liked the way he held onto her jacket and pulled her towards him, so that she was all caught up in his hair, skin and smell.

Earlier her room had been beautifully tidied, with fresh bedding and flowers in a glass on her bedside table because she wanted him to come to hers tonight. She wasn't going to let him argue that he needed to be up early, or on the other side of town, or whatever. She wasn't going to his boyish flat share; he was sleeping over at hers. Just thinking of that gave her butterflies of excitement.

'Hey, Lauren,' he said, in his smooth, laid-back voice as they surfaced from their hello kiss. 'Good to see you. You look beautiful.'

'Hey, Noah, you too.' She settled into the seat opposite his and they smiled a little goofily and took each other in. They hooked their legs around each other and held hands over the tabletop, her pale fingers contrasting against his darker ones.

'I feel like it's been ages,' he said.

'Yeah, almost two weeks.' Not that she'd been counting, of course.

'Wow... a lot has happened in two weeks. A lot...'

'Yeah?'

'Yeah. Right, look at the menu,' he said, 'then we'll order, and I will tell you all about it.'

So, they looked, ordered and the waiter brought them big glasses of iced water and a diet root beer for Noah, which made Lauren shudder. She'd lived in New York on and off for three years now, but she still couldn't understand root beer. It smelled the same as Germolene!

Noah began by reminding her of how he'd been searching for a different job because doing social media marketing for a major shoe retailer had never 'aligned with his values' and he was desperate to do something with 'meaning' and 'purpose', so he could show up for work every day 'excited by what I'm going to do for the world'. Which did, to be honest, all sound a little idealistic to Lauren, but she loved his enthusiasm and the way that he truly believed this was going to be possible. Truly gorgeous-looking pizzas were set in front of them, which the waiter instructed them to 'Enjoy!'

'So...' Noah began, cutting into his enthusiastically. 'OK, I'm just going to take a bite before I tell you what's happened.'

OK, Lauren thought as she was cutting into hers, but kind of steeling herself. Whatever Noah's big news was, it was obviously something to do with a new job. Not anything exciting about them... or their social life... or friends, or a holiday... or well, what was it that she had expected, really? Maybe something about the two of them going on holiday together would have been very nice. She would like to think that Noah wanted to go away with her, spend time with her, that they were going to plan something exciting... together. Or, maybe it was that he was moving much closer to her part of town. That would be amazing to hear – that he wanted to make it more convenient for them to spend time together. It would be proof that he did actually want to spend more time with her.

'I have a new job,' he said, as soon as he'd swallowed down his mouthful of classic New York pizza. 'And it is so exciting...' His smile was bright, in fact, his whole face was lit up, eyes shining. He looked so happy about it, that Lauren couldn't help smiling too.

'That's amazing, Noah,' she said, mirroring his enthusiasm. 'Tell me all about it.'

'So... I'm going to be the head social media manager – like head, like in charge of all of the social media campaigns, all the output, the design, the look, the feel, everything—'

'Wow, that's going to be a lot... you are going to be very busy. Do you have a team?'

'No, I am the boss, I *am* the team – it's all going to be me, which is great because I can be in charge of every little thing and my inner control freak is going to love it.'

'What's the company?' Lauren asked, wondering if they made vegan shoes, or biodegradable shoes, or maybe clothing you could cut up and compost or something equally useful and admirable. Noah shook his head, making his wild hair bounce about in front of his face. There was a little pause as he tackled another chunk of pizza, so she decided to embark on another mouthful herself. She was properly hungry and the pizza was excellent.

'Not a company,' Noah continued once he'd chewed his mouthful down and could speak once again. 'I'm going to be working for a non-profit – a zoological society.'

'Oh my goodness, that's pretty different from selling shoes.'

And she was genuinely pleased for him, because he was

following his heart, following his dream... but didn't working for a non-profit usually mean very low pay? And New York was super-expensive. He probably wouldn't even be able to stay on at his flat share in Williamsburg... he would be moving even further out.

'This organisation is amazing,' he waved his hands expansively. 'I mean they run a zoo, but it's all about research, conservation and protecting habitats. I'm so proud to be working with them.'

'Sounds so worthwhile,' she agreed. 'Do you like the people you'll be working with?'

'Oh, I love them!' he replied and went on to explain at length what the three people he'd met so far were like and all about. 'So, so on my wavelength, it's incredible. I just got this feeling as soon as I met them. They were so pleased I'd had all this commercial media management training, of course. But they could see that wasn't my path, wasn't in my soul.' He put his hand on his heart and Lauren found herself looking a little too long into his deep brown eyes and wishing that she occupied a little more space in his soul.

'So... is the pay OK? I mean charities are not known for having lots of money,' she ventured.

'Yeah... well...' Noah seemed to falter at this question and for a moment, she was worried he was going to round on her for caring more about money than about doing good. Instead, he paused, took something of a breath and began with, 'Well, I am taking a pay cut to work there. Like a twenty per cent pay cut.'

'Oooft...' she sympathised.

'But the society isn't based in New York. So, they have cheaper offices, cheaper staff, a lot of land and they can put so much more money towards their work.'

'Oh, so where are they based?' Lauren's knowledge of upstate

New York was sketchy. She knew it existed but she hadn't spent any time exploring it.

'Well...' There was another pause and suddenly she wasn't so sure if she was going to like what he was about to say.

'It's in Cleveland... in Ohio.'

'Cleveland!' She had to struggle for a moment with her gasp reflex as there was a danger that she might either choke on this chunk of pizza or let it drop out of her mouth in surprise. 'But that's—'

'A long way away,' he agreed.

Lauren could not have been more surprised. No, upgrade that to shocked. Noah had invited her here to tell her he was moving to Cleveland. Nothing about this was good. She felt completely jolted. She was beginning to think she might throw up. She liked him so, so much. And clearly, she meant nothing to him, despite the hello kiss and the handholding.

'Have you – have you been to Cleveland?' she managed to ask, sounding weak and confused.

'No, in fact, I haven't, at all. We've done two rounds of interviews online. They've offered me the job, which is amazing. And they are paying for me to go out and meet them all next week.'

'Right...' What did this mean? He was moving to Cleveland? Was he going to come and visit her? Did he want her to go and visit him?

'Cleveland is a long way away. I mean, you're going to move there, right?' she asked. 'You're not going to commute to the office a few times a month... or work remotely?' This was her last shred of hope.

Noah shook his head and looked at her with something that at least approximated sadness.

'This is such an amazing opportunity for me. I can't wait to start with them. It's going to be life-changing for me and for the animals. They're breeding extremely rare rhinos!'

'Noah... it's going to be a bit life-changing for me too,' she said. 'I thought you were my boyfriend, I thought we were a couple and now you're moving to Cleveland and you've not mentioned one word about it.'

He shrugged and mumbled something about 'all really fast' and knowing this was what he had to do and a purpose-filled life etc., etc.

But really she wasn't listening, she was mainly concentrating on not bursting into tears. Because he was so happy about the thing that was going to take him away from her and seemed completely clueless about the fact it would impact her, impact them.

'So, what about us?' She decided to just come out and ask as he clearly wasn't going to make it simple for her to understand. 'Are we going to try and see each other... do long-distance?'

Noah had the decency to look down at his plate and then she just knew.

'No... it looks like we're not,' she said.

'I don't think it would be fair to you.' Noah glanced up at her now and for a moment, she lost herself in those warm brown eyes again. He would still come back and forth to New York, wouldn't he...? She could go and visit him in Cleveland... did it have to mean the end of everything between them? As if he was reading her thoughts, he slipped his hand over hers.

'It's not like I'm never going to be back in town,' he said, 'and it would be so nice to stay over...' This came with a little arch of his eyebrow.

But that, *that* just killed it for her. Was he hoping she was going to be some sort of 'friend with benefits' here? Maybe she was already just a friend with benefits. In fact, was she even a friend if he'd done all this planning and plotting about his new job without even mentioning it to her?

'No, I don't think so, Noah,' she said managing to summon up some last shreds of dignity. 'Friends tell each other about stuff. They share their thoughts, their hopes and dreams. They don't go, "hey, meet me for pizza, by the way, I'm changing jobs, cities and dumping you" – completely out of the blue, without any thought as to how the other person might feel.'

Maybe if he'd picked this moment to say something, anything really, that showed he was sorry, or he cared, or he was in some way upset for her, it could have ended on a better note. But instead, he just repeated his line about needing to follow his path.

'Yeah... well... if it's OK, I'm going to follow my path too. And it leads to my home. Goodnight,' she said, fumbling for her purse in her handbag. 'Goodbye and have a very lovely life.'

She knew she had some actual cash in her purse, because a girl with a thrift store habit always gets a better deal with cash, so best to be prepared. So, she dumped $30 on the table, which more than covered her pizza and water.

'No, don't pay,' Noah protested. 'I'm sorry it's ended like this. I'm sorry you feel like this.'

'Yes, I'm paying,' she said firmly. 'You can always donate it to the bloody rhinos.'

And with that, she picked up her jacket and somehow, despite the rage and the tears building and threatening to spill, she managed to walk out of the restaurant, head held high.

6

Ever-cool Paula:
Shaggy black, sparkly, short-sleeved sweater dress
Knee-high, rubber-soled plum-coloured boots
Super-sized gold hoop earrings
Stacked gold, silver and semi-precious rings
Neon nails

'One more size 6 Chanel-alike skirt suit is going to send me over the edge,' Paula declared, dropping something candy-pink and nubbly with bright golden buttons onto a knee-high pile of scarily similar items.

'I know, babes,' Annie sympathised. 'It's like the 1980s has opened her wardrobe and vomited the contents into our laps. Is this how long people hang onto old clothes for? I mean the eighties! That is a long, long time ago now. And they haven't even sent us ra-ra skirts, they've sent us the kind of suits Melanie Griffiths wore in *Working Girl*. Can anyone make any use of these? I mean, I know eighties fashion is having a moment, but that's for the twenty-somethings and I don't think we will have many of them shopping at our high-end luxury show.'

'I think we just keep searching through everything we've got,' Paula said, although they had now been in this small warehouse unit for four hours and the piles of clothes on the tables marked 'sale rail' and 'donate' were looking a lot larger than the table marked 'fashion show'. And there weren't too many bags left to go through.

'All Svetlana's things are still in her house,' Annie reminded herself as well as Paula, because spirits were definitely starting to flag. 'And everything that she is putting into the sale is amazing. I've personally weeded it from her wardrobe and it's all fantastically good – and almost all post-2005 too.' As she said these words, Annie realised with astonishment that 2005 was twenty years ago now... How could that have even happened?! How could something from 2005 now be 'vintage'? And how could Paula, who had once been her twenty-something assistant at The Store, now be a sophisticated woman of the world who ran her own events company? When realisations like this struck, Annie felt about a hundred years old.

'The fact is,' Paula began, 'we could do with many more quality items, Annie, the really good stuff – properly headline items. There is hardly anything in the whole show so far that is going to attract attention, chat, tweets, buzz! We need some fashion buzz.'

'There is still time,' Annie assured her – sounding more confident than she perhaps should – 'c'mon, sit down for a moment, let me have a rummage through my bags and see what I can find to revive us.'

'It's a bit late in the day for coffee,' Paula told her.

'I was thinking we might need something a bit stronger than

coffee, babes. And... here we are...' Annie had had an inkling that this evening in the clothes warehouse with her old friend might get stressy, so from the depths of her tote bag, she pulled out the two cans of fizzy wine she'd packed earlier. 'Still chilled,' she told her friend.

'Do you usually go around with cans of wine in your bag?' Paula asked, looking a little concerned.

'No! Not usually, so no need to worry about me. But I thought we might appreciate a little reward.'

Cans in hand, they both pulled up a chair in the midst of the explosion of clothes and bags and sat down for a drink and a break. Paula, several inches over six foot tall, long black braided hair, legs that looked as if they could pole vault, dewy walnut skin, made quite the contrast to her friend, Annie – who was creamy pale, unless wearing fake tan, plumper than she wanted to be, bright blonde, and twelve years older, but nevertheless they had been friends for years and years, ever since Paula had joined Annie at The Store's personal shopping suite as a trainee. Neither of them worked there now, Annie had her TV career and Paula was an event organiser.

As soon as Annie had realised how serious Svetlana was about this fashion show, she'd hurried to get Paula involved. The girl knew everything there was to know about fashion and she now ran seriously cool events all over London. This turned out to have been a good decision. Over the years, Paula had morphed from the fun-loving, fashion-obsessed youngster she was at The Store into a slick, highly organised, totally sussed operator. She had already come up with all kinds of clever ideas and solutions that Annie and Svetlana could never have, plus, she had contacts.

'So what else is going on in your life?' Paula asked Annie as she cracked open the can and took a sip from the top. 'Mmmm, not too bad, even if I am a champagne girl myself.'

'Of course you are!' Annie laughed as she opened her own can. 'So... there's the TV stuff, just finished shooting the new series.'

'Nice,' was Paula's comment, 'looking forward to watching that.'

'There's a lot of Paris featured,' Annie said. 'You'll love it. Then there's this fashion show, obviously. This is going to use up all my attention for the next...'

Annie didn't even want to think about how few days were left between here and showtime.

'The clock is ticking,' Paula said. 'We need more fab-u-lous clothes for this fashion party.'

Annie took a breath and another mouthful of wine. 'We can do this, babes. We've pulled off all kinds of minor miracles under much tighter deadlines.'

'Yeah, keep telling yourself that... and how are all the children?' was Paula's next question.

'You don't want to hear about the children,' Annie protested. 'You're still a carefree young woman about town, you don't want me banging on about how Max doesn't like nursery and Owen is about to head off to uni in Scotland.'

'Uni!! Owen?!' Paula sounded horrified. 'But he was just this little guy when you were at The Store. It can't be that long—'

'Yes, it is. Owen is eighteen and off to Glasgow, God help us... can I trust him to turn off a hob, Paula? Or have a regular shower, not lose his phone, keep up with his athlete's foot treatment?'

Paula pulled a face at the last one.

'He'll work it out,' Annie decided. 'He'll have to. But it's a worry. To add to all my other worries.'

What would life be like when all the children had left home, she wondered. And what was she going to do when the fashion show was over? What was the next big move going to be for her?

Paula interrupted her thoughts with the question, 'Why don't we look through those boxes over there? Those ones haven't been touched yet.'

She pointed to four big cardboard cartons. 'You never know,' she added hopefully. 'Could be a long-lost cache of Pucci dresses... or a bundle of Missoni knitwear... what about you, what would you love to find in here?'

Annie's hand hovered over the tape. 'Handbags,' she began. 'Really beautiful, class handbags, Mulberry, a touch of Chanel, or Loewe even... imagine finding a few vintage Loewe bags in here.'

'Oh yes, that would be very nice... and what clothes would you like to find?'

'Prada,' Annie decided. 'You just can't go wrong with some gorgeous vintage Prada, or Dolce, Paula!' she experienced a wave of déjà vu. 'We always got so excited when the new Dolce deliveries arrived at The Store.'

'Oh, we did!' Paula agreed. 'Come on, let's cross our fingers, open up and see what we can find.'

'I've downgraded from Dolce,' Annie complained, gesturing to the pretty, but very much high street dress she was wearing this evening. 'Mrs blooming M&S, that's who I am. You're the only person that I will admit my M&S habit to. The fact is, they have some nice things when you know how to look.'

Paula rolled her eyes and hissed something that sounded a little like 'never!', then she set her amazing orange nails to work ripping along the tape and with two final pops, she pulled back the cardboard flaps. 'Oooh,' was her first reaction, 'this could be interesting.' Putting her hands into the box, she carefully lifted out a bundle of silky chiffon in the lighter shade of pale that made it obviously a wedding dress. 'It looks like a whole box of them...' she said, burrowing down. 'Wedding dresses, bridesmaid dresses, maybe even wedding guest dresses.'

'We could end with a bride... like at all the big fashion shows.'

'Annie, with this collection of dresses, we could have the whole blooming ceremony.'

'But are any of them any good, Paula? Is there anything worth showing here? Or is it all sale rail or donate.'

'Let's keep looking... see what we find,' Paul said, bringing out dresses two at a time for Annie to smooth out over the table and examine.

'I take it you know who the "mystery" compère is by now,' Paula asked, as she brought out the next armful of tulle.

'No. I think I've missed the update on that one. Do you know?' Annie asked.

Paula nodded.

'And why do I get the feeling that you're not very happy?' was Annie's next question. At this, Paula raised her eyebrows and gave Annie a look. 'Uh-oh... who is it?'

'The cheesy star of daytime ITV... the one and only super-tanned and oddly Botoxed Vince Hastie,' Paula said, and now it was Annie's turn to raise her eyebrows and give a look of horror.

'Oh no, not him!' Annie declared. 'But he's not right for a fashion show. He's not stylish, not at all classy.'

'Good friend of Svetlana's apparently,' Paula added. 'Well, passing acquaintance who offered to do it for free, more like.'

'And doesn't he sometimes make bad taste jokes, really bad ones? And have rumours that he's a bit too "hands on" not been swirling about him?'

'Hmmm mmmm.' Paula nodded vigorously.

'Oh. My. Lord. So, now what?' Annie said struggling to get her words out.

Paula shrugged. 'Try talking to Svetlana?' she suggested.

Not enough models... not enough 'showstopper' clothes... and now Vince Hastie... Fashion VIPs were coming to this event.

Her name was emblazoned on the invitation. She could feel herself cringing inwardly. She had to get this event back on track or she would never get any work in fashion ever again.

7

LAUREN, NEW YORK

New York night-time passer-by:
Stretchy red minidress
Ankle-length classic trench coat
Quilted Chanel bag
Chunky white trainers

Lauren had been walking and walking. Not ready to go back to the flat, but not wanting to go anywhere else yet either, she had found the walking soothing. Walking helped her to keep going, to not cry, and it did feel good to have this cool, crisp breeze against her face. Oh, just everything about this evening had been upsetting. That stupid boy! So selfish, so inconsiderate. And how stupid of her to think she meant much to him. *Stupid, stupid.* She was on the very edge of Manhattan Island now, the Hudson River was in front of her, dark and cool, gleaming with the lights of the city at night. She crossed the lanes of traffic so she could go right up to the railings on the edge. The wind properly in her face now.

Without Noah, or maybe that should be without her imagined version of Noah – she felt very alone. Yes, she had Elena,

Gracie and the handful of other friends she'd made in New York so far, but it wasn't much to show for all her time here. This was a superficial place, you breezed into people, you hung out with them for a while, then you or they moved on. Looking at the river in front of her and the tall buildings behind, feeling the endless roar of the city on the move 24/7, Lauren felt small and insignificant, just a speck on the map of this vast place.

Everyone was always so excited about the fact that she lived here and worked in fashion. But really, life in New York was mainly lonely and so expensive and at times like this, she felt one million miles away from the people who knew and loved her best. It would be lovely to call her mum now and tell her about Noah and listen to her mum's cheerful and no-nonsense advice. But as it was approaching 10 p.m. here in New York, it was the small hours of the morning in London and this wasn't enough of an emergency to wake her mum and Ed up. And... there was something else about Noah's big move that had stirred Lauren. Yes, him finding his purpose and following his path had sounded a little bit much, but she had also been impressed by it. And now, standing here, alone in this huge city, looking out over the river, Lauren wondered if she'd ever really thought about finding her purpose and following her path. She had thought she loved working in fashion, but lately, it had all seemed frivolous and pointless. Did the world need another Perfect Dress? Not really. The world needed people like Noah, who were prepared to take a pay cut, move to Cleveland and work to save endangered animals.

Whatever she might have thought of him, or said to him, she knew she was still going to miss him. Miss thinking about him... miss planning their next meeting, even if he had been all unreliable and mercurial and had made her feel she didn't really know who she was to him. She was still going to miss him being her 'sort of' guy in this town. What to do next? What to change?

What to aim for? These questions churned over in her mind as she turned and walked the blocks to her cramped flatshare. As soon as she walked into her room and flicked on the light switch, she saw her freshly made bed, with the little glass of flowers, all set for the romantic evening that had never happened. And she fell onto the bed and burst into tears.

* * *

The next morning, it was tempting when Lauren opened her puffy eyes to replay the tragic events of the night before and feel oh-so sorry for herself. It was also tempting to get her mum on the line and have a great long moan about it all. Yes, she was longing to wallow, because she did feel a lot of angst. Was she ever going to meet someone who cared for her as much as she cared for him? And what about finding her purpose? Following her path? Was she ever going to be able to do that? And... another big question... did she want to stay in New York? Yes, it was almost impossible not to call her mum and download all this worry onto her and listen to her cheering advice.

But... Lauren held the phone in her hand and thought about it. Did she need another pep talk? It would be lovely. She would hear all about the twins and Owen and whatever was going on with her. But her mum would probably tell her how lucky she was to have this job and to be in New York and promise her there were so many more lovely guys out there... and it would be good to hear. Cheering and loving and kind – that was her mum. But it wouldn't help Lauren move on one inch from where she was right now. Instead, she had a strong feeling that she really had to get on with her life now. She had to channel all the good advice and words of wisdom her mum and Ed had given her over the years. She had to get on with things and work this out for herself.

Yes, she told herself again, *I have to take things into my own hands*. She was the one who had to work out what she really wanted from here on and make it happen.

She went to the tiny bathroom and gave her face a careful wash, holding handfuls of cold water against her eyes until they looked brighter and clearer. She decided that she couldn't possibly start such an important morning looking all scrubbed bare, she had to put on her game face.

She rubbed in tinted moisturiser and dotted a little pink blush over her cheeks, then she stroked her favourite tawny grey shadow over her eyelids, before outlining them with a darker grey pencil. Mascara and a swoop of lip stain completed the look.

'Nice,' she told her reflection and began to brush through her hair to try and restore it to the tumbling loveliness she'd achieved pre-date yesterday evening. A bolstering squirt of the favourite perfume followed. Then she went back to her room and picked out a sober navy day dress that hadn't had much action but was perfect for the seriousness of today. And hearing her mother's words in her mind, she told herself that 'no dress can go out of the door without accessories', so on went slim silver necklaces, her favourite silver hoop earrings, a long, silky scarf, then her baseball boots and trusty denim jacket. She shook her hair till it was more rumpled about her shoulders.

'Nice,' she said to her reflection again. 'Better than nice. Pretty damn hot,' she told herself. She drank down the glass of water she'd poured and then packed up her big-city-girl tote bag. In went her wallet and phone obviously. Next came her hard-working laptop. Later today, Lauren was meeting Gracie for brunch at their favourite little brunch spot.

But before that, Lauren was going to get to the café early. She was going to choose a quiet corner, load up with coffee and get to work. If she rolled up her sleeves and took a good look out there on the internet, she was going to find the answers to all the questions that were rattling round her head. She would find out what kind of path she wanted to be on and how she could get onto it. She would work out if she wanted to stay here in NYC, or if she wanted to get back to London. She would create a sparkling resumé, she would fire off enquiries, ask to speak to people. She was a smart girl with plenty of abilities who wanted to do good and useful things. Someone, somewhere, would be able to make use of her. She too could work with the kind of purpose that had sent Noah off to Cleveland. The right path was out there waiting for her. She just had to get on the case and track it down. Lauren reached into her make up bag and chose a brighter lipstick. Yes, this was a day for a much bolder shade of lipstick.

8

Svetlana bossing:
Camel pencil skirt
White big-lapelled shirt
Snakeskin heels
Gold and diamond bangle stack
Diamond rings
Diamond earrings

'So, just talk me through the food you can actually make. Please, just put my mind at rest so I can at least hope you won't be eating takeaways and junk all of the time. I accept you will eat it some of the time, but please tell me what you can actually make.'

Owen smiled at his mum from the back seat of the car. He gave her that shrug that she knew meant: *you're making a huge fuss, but if this will help to calm you down.*

'OK... let's see,' Owen began, 'the easy stuff first – beans on toast, fried eggs on toast, avocado on toast, tuna and cheese on toast...'

'That is a lot of toast,' Annie worried. 'You need to choose bread that's good for you. Brown bread, nice thick slices.'

'OK, Mum. So, moving on to pasta – pasta with red pesto, pasta with green pesto, pasta with cheese and ketchup, which I know disgusts everyone but it is one of my favourite meals, especially covered in black pepper.'

'Did you pack a pepper grinder?' Annie asked, causing both Ed at the wheel and Owen in the back to dissolve into laughter. 'OK, fair enough,' she admitted, 'maybe a pepper grinder isn't an absolute student essential... maybe your flat will have one.'

'I can also make rice and fry things – bacon, sausages, salmon steaks, chicken breasts, mushrooms, red peppers, carrot batons... I can also boil potatoes, frozen green beans, sweetcorn and peas. I might eat cereal with milk, or Pot Noodles, or sausage rolls some of the time, Mum, but I will not eat them all of the time.'

This was reassuring.

'Food is really important, Owen. It makes you feel good. It keeps you healthy. Not eating well can make you ill very quickly. And you have to eat yoghurt, Owen, for your microbiome.'

More snorts of laughter from the back seat. 'Mum, you literally exist on coffees, raisin Danishes and those cinnamon buns. And you seem fine.'

'I do not!' she countered. 'I eat salad and vegetables and fish and even quinoa...'

'But you do especially like a big noodle fry-up with lots of hoisin sauce,' Ed reminded her.

'I do... you have me there.'

'That is a good one,' Owen said. 'Maybe you should send me the recipe for that one, Dad.'

'Will do,' Ed replied. Annie looked out of the window. They were taking Owen to uni... they were taking her precious boy Owen to university... in *Scotland*. She knew this was happening. It was in her mind as a fact, a date, a road trip they'd had to prep for, but somehow, she still couldn't quite believe it. *Owen? University?* She suddenly could only think about him as ten years old, had that image firmly in her mind, but quickly glanced towards her grown-up boy in the back seat, because otherwise, the wave of nostalgia was going to wash right over her and it wouldn't be good. Owen looked all smiley and relaxed back there, as if this was nothing, 'no biggie' as he liked to tell her multiple times a day. But his hair was freshly cut and washed and he was wearing his absolutely precious and cherished vintage The Clash T-shirt – the iconic one with the bassist smashing his bass guitar on the floor. So, she knew that he'd given today lots of thought. This was definitely a carefully considered version of Owen. And of course, he was excited to be setting off on this big adventure, but maybe there was a little nervousness behind his smile.

She was much more nervous, emotional and just, well, in danger of being overwrought by this day, much more than she had thought she would be. She couldn't help thinking he was woefully unprepared for coping even slightly on his own. She'd completely spoiled and mollycoddled him and now he was going to bear the brunt. Random bits of advice kept spouting out of her mouth. Owen and Ed were beginning to find it funny... she knew they were. But she couldn't help herself.

'You've got to look after your feet,' she was telling him now. And why? Even she knew she sounded a little bonkers. 'You can catch things from communal showers. Did you take flip-flops up with you? And make sure your towels get hung up to dry properly. Hopefully, they've thought of that and there's a towel rail in your room, ideally heated. It's just... a damp, dirty towel, it smells and you can get skin infections.'

'Mum!' Owen protested again. 'You'll be telling me how to put laundry powder into a washing machine next!'

'And look, you're to take an Uber home whenever it's late. I don't care how expensive it is. You can message me for the money, if you need to—'

'You're going to regret that,' Ed couldn't help interrupting.

'No, seriously, you've got to be safe, Owen. Really, I don't care about sausage rolls, athlete's foot and manky towels nearly as much as I care about that. It's the most important thing.'

'Gotcha, Mum. Loud and clear. Be safe, dry my towels, eat fried chicken and green veg... keep my feet fungus-free. Anything else? Are we going to have to endure a sex talk?' was Owen's next question.

Annie and Ed exchanged a glance. 'No,' Ed said in his calm way. 'We've had all the sex talks we need for now. The important thing for you to know, Owen, is that you can ask us any time about anything you need to ask us. It's just sex. Let's just try and keep things normal and open and keep talking about stuff. Don't bottle up any worries or any questions. But we respect your need for privacy on this too.'

'Phew,' was Owen's response. And Annie couldn't help agreeing. Wasn't it quite enough to be worrying about him feeding and caring for himself, without adding thoughts of his *sex life* into the mix? 'Anything else you'd like to go over with me, Mum? Nail care? Ear wax removal... how to wash a kitchen floor, how to clean a toilet?'

'What about drugs?' Annie asked next, in a panic at this thought.

'Have you got any?' was Owen's cheeky response.

'It's OK, we've talked that over a lot too. Shall we just try and enjoy the journey?' was Ed's suggestion from the front seat.

As they were currently surrounded by juggernauts on a particularly unglamorous stretch of the M1, this wasn't exactly going to be easy. 'I just feel like there's so much I want to say,'

Annie blurted out. 'We've taken such good care of you, Owen, for all this time,' she turned to meet his eyes. 'I want you to carry on doing that.'

Owen seemed to understand that he needed to be serious now, so he gave his mother a solemn nod.

'It can be hard,' Annie heard herself bursting out with more unplanned advice, 'settling in somewhere new, making new friends, studying. I know you're a big, handsome, friendly guy, who loves music, so you might find it easier than most – but you'll have your days, my lovely boy.'

She reached over and Owen let her take his hand. 'You can always, always call us. Or even get on the train and be with us. You can always do that. Don't be lonely. We are always here for you. It doesn't matter if your worry is huge or just a small, silly thing, you can tell us. It's normal to make mistakes and mess up and make a tit of yourself. Everyone does it at your age. You can tell us. We are always on your side. I promise.' She squeezed at his hand. But somehow still felt that she hadn't said enough, or done enough, or taught him enough. She wasn't sure if Owen was ready and she was pretty sure that she wasn't ready for this.

'OK, got it,' he told her and it sounded casual, but the smile that came with this was warm, genuine and went straight to her heart. 'Now, please can we put some music on?' he asked. 'And we have to stop soon to get Mum her next coffee and Danish fix because I think she might have low blood sugar levels or something.'

'Ha, ha,' Annie took another long look at her son, as if she couldn't get enough of him, as if she had to store up much more in the memory bank before he went away.

'Nice T-shirt,' she said.

This seemed to cause him a look of worry, because if his mum liked it, maybe it wasn't a good T-shirt. Maybe all his potential new friends would hate it. He shrugged. 'Yeah... comfortable.' As if that was why he was wearing his carefully considered The Clash top.

Annie's phone burst into life and she could see it was Svetlana. 'Models, Annie? We need more models!' were her opening words, followed by: 'Are you doing something about this?'

'Yes!' Annie insisted and it wasn't a complete lie. She was going to turn to Ed, just as soon as this call was over and ask him if any of the school athletics team had agreed to be in her show.

'Let me know,' Svetlana said. 'And let me know when you find some items we could put on a catwalk and impress people with,' she snapped and then, clearly in full tough-boss mode, hung up.

'Charming,' Annie said and then made her request about the school's athletics team.

Ed's answer was the simple but completely unhelpful, 'No.'

'Oh for crying out loud!' she complained.

* * *

By the time they arrived in the Glasgow street that was going to be home for Owen during his university terms, The Clash T-shirt had already been swapped out for another one and then, at the last minute, swapped back in again.

'Try not to worry about it,' Ed reassured him from the passenger's seat – Annie had driven the last stretch to give him a rest and because he was not the best at following the satnav. 'The Clash is a very dependable touchstone. Either people will have heard of the band and there's absolutely no denying the essential coolness of this 1980s punk iteration, or people won't have heard of them and they'll just think it's interesting that a man is smashing up his guitar on the front of your T-shirt. And it is just a T-shirt, so most people won't notice it at all.'

'What will they notice then?' Owen was pretty openly nervy by now.

'That you're a boy, tall, white, good hair, big friendly smile – if you give them a big friendly smile obviously. That all comes well before T-shirt.'

'I just thought the T-shirt would be... a talking point.'

'It might be... but you and everyone else around you are brand-new. There's going to be a lot to talk about. I promise. You'll do fine.'

Annie glanced over at her husband and couldn't help thinking how sexy he was when giving out heartfelt parent advice. The satnav guided them to the modern block, five floors high, with a small car park round the back where there was mercifully a space.

It took quite some time and effort to get Owen's guitars (plural!), his mini drum kit, his many bags and the shaggy beanbag he had insisted on bringing with him from the car and up to his new shared student flat on the second floor of the building. The place was teeming with mums, dads, new students, bags, boxes, clutter, nerves, tense smiles, and minor meltdowns were happening at every turn.

'What do you mean you didn't bring my hair straighteners?'

'Jake, I told you not to put that there!'

'I can't believe this flat doesn't have an air fryer... I mean that's like a kitchen essential.'

Owen's flat came with a reasonably sized communal space with two sofas, a TV, a dining table and a practical looking wall of kitchen. Owen's room was, to be honest, a bit cramped, especially when all three of them were standing in it.

'Do you mind if I help you to unpack... just a bit?' Annie wanted to know. She suspected that if she didn't do this, Owen would probably still be living out of his bags by the time they came to collect him in December. Not that he was particularly messy, just that he might not see organising his room as a 'priority'.

She sighed at the thought of what this flat could look like after a few weeks. Five boys, all brand-new to looking after themselves. Ed, sensing the tension, suggested he make a little tour of the neighbourhood while Annie and Owen unpacked. The unpacking didn't take long. Much, much less time than the packing which seemed to have gone on for days. Annie filled Owen's new, much smaller wardrobe, putting pants, socks and T-shirts into the drawers, then hanging trousers, sweatshirts and his jackets up on the rail, and finally, stashing the selection of trainers at the bottom of the space. As she did this work, she realised how well she knew all these items. She'd washed, folded and packed them away many, many times before in his cupboard at home. It felt odd to be storing them here in a strange wardrobe in a strange room in a strange city.

'And, you and Ed can go, honestly. As soon as you like,' Owen informed her breezily, as he lined his guitars up beside the window, then began to assemble his drum kit – priorities, she couldn't help thinking, priorities. First install instruments, then get rid of parents.

'Oh... we thought you'd want to come and have dinner with us,' she said, trying to sound as chirpy as her son and not at all hurt. 'You know, your last night... we'll try and fill you up for the week ahead...'

'Thanks, Mum, but we have made an arrangement to go out for dinner together.'

'*We*?' she wondered out loud. 'We who?'

'Everyone in the flat.'

'But... how? You haven't even met them yet.'

'We've got a little chat group. They gave us contact details in advance.'

'Oh... I see...'

'So, we thought it would be nice to go out, get to know who we'll be meeting in the kitchen every morning.'

'Yeah, well, I suppose so... no, that makes sense, sounds nice,' she corrected herself. 'We can come back in the morning and take you to the supermarket.'

Owen looked at her with the eyebrows raised and for a dangerous moment, she wondered if he was going to say no to that too and if they were actually going to be saying their big goodbye in a moment. But then Owen's look softened. Maybe he realised how worried she was about leaving him here, maybe he wanted one last trip around the supermarket at his parents' expense. So, with a slight shrug, he agreed. 'That's fine... great... come round tomorrow and we'll get my food sorted.'

'Do you want to do anything in town with us tomorrow? Go for lunch? Go see some of the sights?'

Owen gave her a smile and shook his head.

'We'll do that next time, when you come to visit,' he said. 'Right now, I want to settle in, get to know my new flatmates, hang out, go exploring in town with them... if that's OK?'

She put a big smile in place to cover up for the fact that she thought her heart might crack. Her plans for tomorrow... the places she'd picked out to go to because Owen might like them, she tried not to think about that because it was going to overwhelm her with sadness. Of course he was right, of course he was excited to get on with his new life. Why on earth had she thought he'd want to hang out with them tomorrow? Just because she had wanted to spend some last special time, focused on him, for her sake, she realised. And now, it was already too late.

'Of course, no problem,' she insisted cheerfully. 'Lovely to hear you so enthusiastic. I'm so proud of you.'

9

Hotel Annie:
Wine and plum patterned blouse
Plum wide-legged trousers
Wine patent Mary Jane heels
Gold clutch bag
Gold and orange earrings
Gold chunky chain necklace

'What do you think?' Ed asked her as they walked into the lobby of the exceptionally nice hotel he had booked for them to stay in tonight.

'Babes, I am pleasantly surprised,' she admitted. 'Very pleasantly surprised. You were in charge of booking, so I was expecting a stinky studio apartment with a fold-down bed,' she joked, as she was ever the splurger while Ed was always saving.

'I thought you might need a treat tonight, because you might be feeling a little sad, so this is your treat, darling wife,' Ed explained. 'Now, that is a very nice-looking bar...' he pointed in the direction of the hotels' very own dark, snug space, already cheerfully lit up against the late afternoon gloom. 'Maybe before we lug the bag upstairs and start unpacking our toothbrushes, maybe we should go in there for a little relaxer.'

This was one of the best ideas she'd heard all day. So, she threaded her arm through his and together they walked into the bar, took a seat in one of the comfortable booth seats and scanned the delights that the cocktail bar had to offer. 'I was out with Connor for cocktails not that long ago,' she confided, 'we snuggled up in a booth seat too.'

'In danger of turning into a total lush then,' Ed warned her.

'Yes... that is my worry. What about the West End Negroni?'

'Now, do you want me to have the same? I could because it sounds very nice. Or do you want me to have something different, so you can try mine? And then consider swapping, then regret it halfway down and want to swap back?'

Annie looked at her husband fondly. 'You know me so well, it's honestly frightening. Let's get the same thing.'

A few minutes later, a smiling waitress was ferrying their drinks over to them. 'Cheers,' Ed offered and gently clinked his glass against hers. With a smile, he offered his toast: 'Here's to Owen getting on just fine without us. And here's to us getting on just fine without him.'

'Do you think he will? Do you think we will?' she asked, feeling twitchy at the thought of them leaving Owen here in this city that she hardly knew at all. This was only her third visit here.

'I know it's my job to be reassuring and say of course he's going to be fine but I'm human, I love Owen... I feel sad too and it's normal for us to have a few worries.' Ed admitted.

'Now I feel worse...'

'We've given him love, advice, money, a phone, a safe place to stay... now, it's over to him,' Ed said. 'And I'm sure there might be a scrape or two, but overall, he'll be fine, Annie. I'm sure he will.

And if he's not, he'll almost definitely call and ask for help. Because he loves and trusts us.'

She rested her hand over Ed's on the table and for a moment, she thought she might cry, so instead, she took a little sip at her drink. 'Oooof,' she declared, after the unusually strong mouthful had made its warming way down towards her stomach. 'That is delicious and comforting and could be the way to iron out all my little worries about leaving him here.'

'Maybe you have to think of it as *bringing* him here to start his new adventure... not leaving him here,' he added gently.

'Good advice,' she said and took another fortifying sip. In her head, she knew Owen was eighteen and street-smart and a people person and loved music and was going to absolutely love being here studying music and economics and making new friends, becoming his own, independent, grown-up person. But also in her head, Owen was all the boys she'd known in those eighteen years, the colicky baby, the adorable toddler, the lost little boy who'd hardly been able to talk above a whisper for months on end when his first dad had died. 'First Dad', that was an Owen invention. Whenever he referred to Roddy, Annie's first husband and father of Lauren and Owen, he said 'First Dad' because Ed had been his dad for so many years now and he never wanted one to overshadow the other, when both were so important to him.

'It's going to be so quiet without him,' Annie said, 'the drums, the guitar, the music playing full volume... the Owen gang.'

'You'll get all that back in the holidays,' Ed reminded her. 'Uni terms are short. He's only going to be away for about half of the year. And Max and Min will only get noisier. It's going to be a long time until they're leaving the house.'

'Thank God for that... and surely someone will stay in London, won't they?' was Annie's next thought. 'Owen will come back, won't he? Everyone won't disappear off to New York like Lauren... or somewhere like Australia?' She had to take a gulp of her cocktail just at the thought of this. 'I don't know how parents can stand it. When they're all grown up, my children can live wherever they like, as long as it's within a ten-mile radius of me. And that's final.' This made Ed laugh.

'You're a brilliant Mum,' he told her. 'And no matter where they live, all the children know that. Now, I think we should stop talking about Owen and start thinking about our lovely hotel room upstairs and the very nice restaurant that we are going to later.'

'I am a little disappointed Owen's decided not to come out with us,' Annie had to admit.

'Yes, me too,' Ed agreed. 'But let's focus on having a very nice time. You do remember it's our wedding anniversary coming up?'

'Yes...' she said cagily, wondering if he knew she was not going to be free that day.

'I already know you're going to be busy. But we'll celebrate afterwards, OK?'

* * *

Once they were in their room, Annie spotted the little minibar tucked in under the counter when she was setting out her toiletries and make up. 'We could start with a little anniversary celebrating right now,' she suggested. 'You just lie back on the bed and get comfortable and I am going to mix us up a delightful little cocktail from the bar.'

'A cocktail?' Ed sounded doubtful. 'From the minibar? I don't think a tiny Pepsi with a thimbleful of Jack Daniels counts as a cocktail.'

'No, no,' Annie assured him. 'They have quite the collection in here. Pimms... orange juice, lemonade, erm gin...' she squinted at the label. 'I could definitely rustle us up a little pre-dinner surprise,' she said, setting the little bottles out along the countertop.

'OK, you do that,' Ed told her, folding his arms under his head. 'Then bring them over here and let's see if we can rustle up another kind of pre-dinner surprise on this extremely comfortable bed.'

'I hope you're meaning a nap.'

Annie poured from a range of little bottles and mixed until her drinks looked suitably pink and sparkly. Then she carried them over and sat on the edge of the bed beside her husband. 'Nice to see you, babes,' she said, putting a glass into his hand. 'It's lovely to be here with you. An oasis of calm in the daily life storm,' she said with a smile.

He held up his glass. 'Cheers to that,' he said and their eyes met and held. *I absolutely love this man,* she thought to herself. No need to say it aloud because he definitely knew.

'Cheers to us,' she said.

Ed took a drink, swallowed, made an astonished face, then burst out in a spluttering cough. 'Don't drink that—!' he warned.

'Too strong?'

'No! Shampoo! There's shampoo or body wash or something totally wrong in there.'

'What!' she exclaimed, horrified at her mistake.

'Annie, you have to get a pair of reading glasses and that is final!'

* * *

'Mum, I honestly think this is enough. More than enough,' Owen insisted, looking down at the basket stuffed full of the food Annie had picked from the shelves on this trip around the Lidl super-market across the road from Owen's accommodation. 'I'm not going to be able to eat all of that in a fortnight!' he protested. 'It will go off! We should probably put some of it back.'

'No... I want to buy you plenty of food,' she insisted, feeling the most overwhelming maternal protective instincts. 'I don't want to think of you being hungry, or eating badly... you will look after yourself, won't you?'

'Yeah, of course,' Owen said, looking at her with something of a surprised expression. 'Mum, I can make burgers, cook chicken, pasta, baked potatoes... I'll be fine. Honestly.'

'Let me buy you this basket,' Annie insisted. 'You can put some of it in the freezer if you like.' Because it suddenly seemed so important to make sure that he had enough, more than enough and that she could stock up his fridge before they left.

'OK,' Owen shrugged, 'we'll buy this and put some of it into the freezer. If you insist.'

'Yes, please.'

When they were back in the kitchen of his flat, they put things into the fridge, the cupboards, the freezer compartments. Annie spent another few moments straightening out his room. Lining shoes up neatly against the wall, smoothing down the duvet on the bed, tidying away the shirt he'd worn yesterday into his new laundry bag.

'Can we take you for lunch?' she suggested. Owen and Ed, who'd been sitting quietly at the desk chair in Owen's room while all this tidying had been going on, seemed to exchange something of a glance at this.

'Annie...' Ed began gently, 'I think we should probably be hitting the road. It's a long old drive back to London and we can always stop for something to eat on the way.'

'Yeah...' Owen agreed. 'I've got some plans with some new

mates for the afternoon anyway. And we want to go exploring...
check out this new town.'

So, here it was rushing right up at her, faster than she could
possibly want, the moment when she really would have to say
goodbye and leave Owen. It was much, much harder than she
could have imagined. She hugged him hard, running her hand
over the back of his frizzy, sandy hair – the hair he'd inherited
from her.

She issued more instructions and endearments and was
grateful that Owen let her, without shrugging her off or making
too much of a fuss. He came downstairs and watched as they got
into the car. He gave both Ed and his mum one more big hug.
Then, Ed behind the wheel, they drove off. Annie put her head
out of the window and craned around to look at her tall, handsome boy waving her cheerfully goodbye. Until her eyes were so
blurry with tears that she couldn't see him any more. Then they
rounded the corner and he was out of sight. It was all so much
harder than she'd expected.

10

The ballet girl:
Purple leggings
White trainers
Baggy brown sweatshirt
Cropped grey puffer jacket
Pink beanie
Oversized Stanley bottle

Phone in one hand, beaker of coffee in the other, Annie was leaning against a wall trying to look casual, as if she just hung out leaning against walls every day of the week. In fact, this was a strategic position. The show needed models and since the athletics team was a no, she'd now had a better idea. She was thinking she would go about this the old-school way – scouting out on the street. Not any old bit of street though, she was currently standing close to the entrance of the local dance school because she had this idea that girls who were used to being on stage in costumes might like the idea of being in the show. And dancer physiques were fit, flexible, muscular, and would know how to move well to the music. Unlike the major designers, she didn't need coat-hanger thin girls for this show because the donated clothes were in all kinds of sizes, so a mix of physiques would be the way to show these clothes off to their best advantage. And she had even checked on the dance school website to see when the advanced classes were scheduled to make sure that she was scouting amongst the oldest girls, not bumping into knee-high toddlers in tutus... though maybe some toddlers in tutus might be adorable for the show's grand finale.

It was incredible to her to think that this show really was going to happen in less than a month now. That she and Svetlana had created this living, breathing, major event from literally a handful of ideas and a major burst of enthusiasm. They had enthused and organised it right into being. Yes, there was still plenty to do... more than plenty to do, but if she, Svetlana and Paula could all keep their effort level dialled up to the max, then on October 1st, they could be putting on the show they had dreamt of, the show that could raise an incredible amount of money for a very good cause and a show that would maybe lead to headlines, buzz, and, fingers crossed, exciting new opportunities.

So, taking a big gulp of coffee, Annie reminded herself that she just had to keep focused, keep working. Oh, a group of girls was coming out of the studio doors now, and with their hair bundled up, grinning and giggling, they looked very late teens – exactly the kind of girls she wanted to talk to. Then she suddenly felt worried... this wasn't the old days. Could you just go up to females in the street and say *'hey, would you like to be a model?'* It might come across as weird and stalkerish. She poked about in her handbag to see if any of her TV business cards could still be found. Ah yes, here was a little bundle of them. They at least had her name, phone number and the address of her TV production company printed on them, so that was more respectable than nothing. OK, time to get over there before they dispersed and disappeared.

'Hello... hello, girls,' she began with a big smile. 'Could I just ask a question?'

The group of five paused in their tracks and looked at her. She wasn't quite sure what that look in their eyes was – curiosity mixed with a good old pinch of dismissiveness and even disdain. 'I hope you don't mind me stopping you like this...' Annie went on as her eyes scanned the group. They were all lovely, fit-looking with the clear eyes and glowing faces of youth. A good range of skin tones and hair colours – she could work with any one of them. Really all five girls would be amazing. And they'd be friends, they'd encourage one another, travel to and fro from rehearsals together. Yes, getting every one of them who wanted to be in this show would be perfect. 'I'm organising a big charity fashion show and I'm looking for girls who might want to be models... and before you think this might all be dodgy. I'm going to give you my card and you can go home and talk to your Mums about it and then call me back to get more info.'

There was a sort of stunned silence. The girls looked at one another as if waiting for someone to make a decision first about how they should react to this.

'Can I give you the cards?' Annie asked.

'Yeah!' one of the girls nearest to her enthused. 'What kind of fashion show? And when is it?'

So, she gave them some of the basic details. But first of all, 'Does that date work for you?' was the most important question. 'No use me talking to you about this if you've got an important dance performance that night.'

'No, it's good. We've got some dance exams coming up in October and maybe auditions, but no shows,' the girl replied.

'So what's this fashion show?' another one asked. 'Is it for a designer?'

'No... it's for charity, but it's a big show, in Mayfair with a big audience, so I'm looking for people who are used to performing, who wouldn't be frightened of going on stage.'

'But we've never modelled,' another girl told her.

'Oh, don't worry about that. If you can dance, you can defi-nitely model – we can teach you all the things you do on a catwalk, but mainly it's about being able to get in and out of your clothes quickly and then being bold and confident as you stride out in front of the audience. You can all do that, can't you?'

'Will we get paid?' one of the dancers asked.

'Well, this is for charity, so we're giving our models money to cover their travel, we'll give them something to eat and drink on the night and, as a big thank you, we'll let everyone chose an item of clothing from the £100 and under donation rails. Does that sound OK to you?'

The girls all looked at one another, some grins breaking out and a sense of excitement building. 'Sounds good.' One girl nudged another. 'Shall we go for it?'

The shy girl at the back, very pale-skinned, very blonde, a little too gangly and tall to be exactly dance physique asked quietly, 'Even me?'

'Oh, sweetheart, definitely,' Annie said. 'I'd love all of you to volunteer. It would be great if we had a group of friends, because you could support each other, look out for each other, practise your twirls together.'

The smiles broke out at these words and soon the group was completely convinced.

'Let's do it!'

'Yes!'

'OK, well, first of all, everyone needs to go home and ask for permission,' Annie told them. 'I'm more than happy to talk to your mums, your parents, and we can even have a mum or two backstage to look after you and help out. The show has a website, so your parents can check that out and make sure they're happy. So, will you promise to be in touch?' she asked them. 'I need to know in the next day or two if you're going to say yes. If not, I'll need to start looking for some other volunteers.'

The girls assured her they would be messaging. So they parted, the group giggling, arm in arm, heading in one direction, Annie in the other while she thought of the tall, very shy girl – the one who didn't think much of herself, who thought she'd be left out, but who's makeover would be the most dramatic, because Annie always poured her makeover magic into the people who couldn't even see themselves properly. She could imagine brushing out the girl's hair, letting the halo of ethereal frizz take over, crimping little under sections even and then allowing that porcelain skin to just be, with dark, glossy, cherries in the snow lipstick slicked across her slight lips. Tall and angelic looking, she would be transformed into the grand finale bride. They would find something in that rummage box of wedding dresses that would be perfect for her. She could carry an enormous bunch of wispy flowers... and finally see all that was unique and wonderful about herself.

Now that the show date was drawing closer, Annie was beginning to feel extremely focused. She knew this was how it had to be. Pulling it all together into the event she wanted it to be, knew it could be, was going to mean total devotion from now until curtain up. OK... as much total devotion as could be given by a mum with four children and all their dramas.

But she wanted to do it. She wanted to walk down the catwalk with Svetlana at the end of the show and take her bows as the fashion crowd cheered. Surely, if it was a success, it could lead somewhere interesting?

She glanced along the pavement ahead of her and saw that woman again... the steely white bob, the enormous shades and the complicated head-to-toe black, Japanese fabric. She was almost in disguise. Annie gave her a nod and a smile as they passed one another. But she got nothing back. *I wonder what her story is?*

11

Florence tidying:
Black sweatshirt dress
Black tights
Black ballet shoes
Diamond earrings

Florence Perkins was on her knees in front of an over-stuffed bookcase in the attic room at the very top of the three-storey villa that she'd grown up in and where her mother had lived for almost sixty years of her long life. Like every other room in this large and attractive home, the attic room was packed, no, a better description would be *rammed* full. In fact, the rooms upstairs were the worst. Up on the first and second floors, where visitors never came, Florence's late mother, Emily, had given her passion for 'collecting' full rein. Florence was Emily's only child and now that her mother had died, peacefully in her nursing home bed at the age of ninety-four, Florence – not at all peaceful, still some way from a nursing home (fingers crossed) aged sixty-five – was somehow going to have to sort all of this muddle out before she put the beloved Perkins family home on the market.

The huge task ahead filled her with fear and sadness and dread. It was an enormous task. Monumental even. In those last weeks when her mother had become properly ill and could no longer be looked after at home by the rota of carers, Florence had been far too wrapped up in visiting, making arrangements, spending time with her mother, trying to cope with the knowledge that there wasn't much longer left, to even think about the house.

And now, in this quiet, empty time, when her mother had been lovingly buried next to Florence's father in the graveyard of the village where they'd both grown up, before setting off for London as young and adventurous twenty-year-olds, now the task of the house was here, rearing up to meet her. If it had just been junk, that would have been so much easier. If Florence had been confronted with rooms full of rubbish, old newspapers, heaps of discarded clothes, matted takeaway boxes, the kind of things you see on house cleaning videos, that would have been a far simpler task. She could have swooped in with rubber gauntlet gloves, a face mask and heavy-duty bin bags, scooped it all up and sent it out to a waiting skip at the front door. But instead, her mother and father's decades of accumulation was the proper collecting of valuables, mixed in with a confusing amount of vintage treasures, untidiness, a tendency to keep almost everything, as well as the inevitable junk.

With almost every item there was a danger that she could be throwing away something that the auction house, or even a museum would be desperate to have. Florence could be throwing away history, important historical records, not to mention important art, antiques and collectables. So, the task came with a heavy responsibility that was weighing down on her shoulders and making her feel close to hopeless.

And she was not a hopeless woman. In fact, quite the opposite, Florence Perkins was very bright, capable, accomplished and knowledgeable. She'd been working in law for forty years until her recent retirement. She lived in a beautiful, riverside penthouse flat that was – perhaps in reaction to her parents' love of clutter, layering and keeping – an absolute temple to minimalism. Florence was very inspired by the traditional Japanese way of life. She had the bare minimum of possessions in her airy, cream-coloured eyrie. But everything that she owned was exquisite and the very best of its kind. When people came round, she could see their eyes out on stalks. She had one sofa (Le Corbusier), one chair (Eames), three important modern paintings and several beautiful lamps. Her wardrobe ran along similar lines. Three work suits (Westwood, Armani and Jil Sander), one handbag (Hermès), one black dress (Chanel), her casual clothes were mainly Japanese. The antithesis to her parents, she saved, she held back, she waited for exactly the right thing and then she tried to only ever buy once. For her, the only reason to buy something was if something she owned had been completely worn out and needed to be replaced.

Anything that came into her life that she didn't need, she immediately sold or donated. Her favourite gifts to give or receive were flowers, luxury food items, or tickets to an event and an outing – not things that would clutter up your life until you had a three-storey townhouse knee-deep in all the objects that had come into your life and somehow got stuck there. She had told herself early this morning, when she'd set off from her calm and beautifully organised home that she just had to start somewhere in her parents' house and make one small corner better. Then carry on from there. And maybe the smallest of the three attic rooms would be exactly the right place to begin, she'd thought to herself as she sat in the quiet of the early morning Tube.

* * *

Now, Florence had bin bags and a selection of labelled boxes and the radio on, so she was just going to start. *Divide and conquer,* she told herself. She would look carefully through everything – pile by pile, shelf by shelf, drawer by drawer – and she would decide, then place things in the relevant bag or box: bin, recycle, keep for me, keep for charity, keep for auction, keep for... it was the final category that was troubling her. She suspected she was going to come across things that should be kept for, well, *history*, or posterity perhaps.

Maybe she should ask the local museum, or would that be ridiculous? And then there was the question of making bequests – there had been a vague instruction in her mother's will about bequests 'to family and friends to be arranged by my daughter, Florence'. But that was all she had to go on. When she'd organised the funeral, she'd gone through her mother's old address book and not found any living friend. There were some children of friends who expressed their sympathy but politely declined the funeral invitation. And family? Florence was an only child, with no children of her own, and, as far as she knew, both her mother and her father had lost touch with their siblings, cousins, nephews and nieces years and years ago. She had put an obituary in both the local London paper and the local paper for her parents' home village a week ahead of the funeral with details of the service, but still the only atten- dees were her and several kind friends of hers who'd insisted on coming along. So, who had her mother meant? Was Florence supposed to track someone else down? And then decide what to give them? It all felt like a mountain of effort ahead.

* * *

Come on, Flo, jolly well pull yourself together. Just pick up this pile here and let's get going.

There was a knee-deep pile of books and papers stacked before the bookcase that she would have to go through before she even got to the books. So, taking a first handful of stuff, she began to look through one old electricity bill, another electricity bill, a pile of random grocery receipts – easy enough to put these items into the recycling box. The programme for a play, that went into the recycling too. Now she was getting into the kind of nitty-gritty where it was more difficult to decide. Here were two carefully cut-out obituaries from a newspaper, the paper tanned light brown with time. She'd never heard of these people – one an actor, one a career diplomat by the sounds of it. Well, they were deceased, she so couldn't contact them or gift them some of her mother's belongings, so she decided to put the notices into the recycling.

Now she was looking at photographs of children, quite modern judging by the colour and the clothes, taken in the last twenty years or so. She turned one of them over to see the words:

Happy Christmas from Oz Aunt Emily. Lots of love from the Lynx family xx

The Lynx family? She had no idea. Her mother's maiden name had been Gardener. So, was this a relative? Or the children of a family friend? Reluctantly, knowing that she had to keep going and couldn't stop to worry about every possible connection, she put the photos into the bin bag. Next in the pile was a small sketchbook. Flipping through it, Florence saw it was almost completely full of her mother's pen and ink drawings and quick, fluid watercolours and she couldn't help sighing. Her mother had not been a professional artist, like her father, but she had loved to draw and paint, filling up much of her spare time with it, so the house was going to be packed with her mother's work. Florence already knew she was going to have to be brutal and keep only the very best of both her mother and her father's work, otherwise her home would be as full as theirs. So, without looking through the sketchbook again, she threw the decorated pages into the recycling, but it wasn't without a pang.

More receipts, more programmes for plays and concerts that had happened years and years ago, she put them all without too much examination into the box. She tried not to think about how slowly she was progressing. She had time, she reminded herself, she had all the time she would need. Even if this work took her months, she would do it properly and it would eventually come to an end and be done. A long, white envelope was next, with her mother's name and address handwritten on the front in black ink. The top had been sliced open and Florence brought out the letter inside. It seemed to be from a rather grand address in Paris. The gist was 'we believe you have in your possession valuable items that were intended for our collection. We would like to talk to you about the restoration of these items.'

Florence felt a wave of concern. Had her mother ever resolved this? Surely... she looked at the date of the letter – April 2005. This must have been sorted out by now. And why not say what 'the items' were? As she put the letter into the box marked:

keep for me

she couldn't help thinking that it was strange.

12

Annie on the doorstep:
Baggy black trousers
High heeled ankle boots
White silk blouse
Rust-red waistcoat
Grey woollen coat
Lashings of bangles and earrings

It was Annie who had come up with the idea of creating beautiful flyers to post through the letter boxes of the biggest houses in her Highgate neighbourhood to tell the owners about the fashion sale and ask for donations. It could be a clever way to find more designer vintage stuff to boost their sale. It had sounded clever and classy at the time – create a glossy leaflet, deliver it round the best streets, bring vintage fashion flying in. But now, going up and down the streets in the rain, up and down pathways, lifting letter boxes, dodging the snouts of inquisitive or even growling dogs, Annie just felt like any other deliverer of leaflets. In fact, she could see her pink, black and white flyer landing on doormats on top of the flyers for pizza deliveries, handymen and taxi services.

And what about all those doors with the strict 'No junk mail' notices? They were always on the nicest houses, so if she didn't post her flyer, she risked losing out on a valuable haul. But if she did post it, she risked getting the fashion show and maybe even the charities into trouble. She hedged her bets. If, by taking a quick glimpse through the window into the sitting room, she decided the house was particularly stylish and a designer-label type person might live here, then she posted the flyer, despite the junk mail warning. But if it looked ordinary, then she skipped it. No need to get entangled with any ordinary Mr or Mrs Angrys. Now she was approaching that intriguing house on the corner. The large, looming townhouse with a top attic floor. The paint was flaking on the window frames, but the front door was painted a pretty grey-blue and was in good condition. The front garden also looked as if it had once been well-maintained but was now overgrown. The roses had sprouted up on long, waving stems, the hedge was overdue a cut and the flower bed had a handful of luscious dandelions growing alongside the garden plants. She'd seen this house many times before on her walks around the neighbourhood and it always caught her eye because it was so much bigger than many houses here and so much prettier. There were many signs that it had once been beautiful and well looked after, but it was beginning to fade. There weren't often many lights on and she suspected that an elderly person lived here who wasn't up to much maintenance work and had maybe stopped caring for the beloved place as much as they once had. This was definitely a good place to drop off a flyer she thought and lifted the letter box to push one in. To her surprise, through the slot, she could see that someone was standing on the other side of the door.

'Oh, hello!' she blurted, letting the flyer fall through the opening. She could hear the rattle of the lock being opened and now here she was standing face to face with a familiar woman.

Most often with Annie, recognising someone wasn't just about looking at their face, or their hairstyle, it was usually about the clothes. She had an acute memory for how people dressed, especially if it was unusual or standout in some way. Svetlana in £1,000 heels with those sculpted calves peeking from a swishy skirt or fitted dress – Annie would be able to spot her halfway down a street. Ed and the saggy elbows of his favourite tweed jacket, again, Annie would recognise him from a mile away. So, this woman, head to toe in black, but a very special kind of black, not saggy, but sculpted, with all those tucks and folds... in a rush Annie realised two things. This was the woman she'd spotted now and then in the local high street, or in passing at the Tube station, and, the woman was wearing vintage Yohji Yamamoto.

'Can I help you?' the woman asked, severely enough to make Annie take a step backwards.

'Hello – I'm so sorry if I startled you,' Annie began. 'I'm putting out leaflets about a charity fashion show. We're looking for designer clothes donations. It's for a wonderful cause,' she added quickly, as she could read the '*I don't think so*' expression more easily than most. 'Now, that is a beautiful tunic,' she added with a real fan's enthusiasm. 'I'm going to guess it's vintage Yamamoto. He really is a genius. Exquisite tailoring meets exquisite fabric. Sorry, I'm being nosy.'

'No, it's all right,' the stern expression softened just a little. 'Most door-to-door salespeople aren't able to spot a Yamamoto.'

'Oh no... I'm not selling anything,' Annie rushed to explain. 'Just spreading the word about a major charity fashion show. If there's anything you might want to donate, we have a donation address just a few streets away. It's all in the leaflet. You'll get a gift aid receipt and it's all absolutely above board. You can even buy a ticket to the show... there are a few left.'

'I see, well...' The woman cast her eye over the leaflet in her hand. 'Nice design,' she added. 'My mother loved that shade of pink.'

'Oh... have you just moved in?' Annie asked, wanting to eke out the conversation just a little longer. 'I live around the corner and I've spotted you at the Tube station a few times. Sorry, I don't want to sound like your stalker...' she added quickly. 'I just have a habit of noticing beautiful clothes.'

She got something of a gentle smile in reply to this. 'No,' the woman replied, 'not exactly. My mother lived here. Well, I did too but that was a long time ago now. She died recently.'

'I'm very sorry.'

'Oh... it was... well, expected is probably the wrong word. You never expect it really. She was ninety-four and in a funny way, she'd lived for so long and recovered from so many things that I thought she'd be around for many more years to come. So, it's fallen to me to clear the place out, which could take months, and then I'll put it on the market.'

'Sounds like a big job and I'm sure it's a difficult one too.'

'Yes... well...'

During these few sentences, Annie had warmed hugely to the woman in the Yamamoto and would have quite liked to invite herself in and listen at much greater length about who her mother was and what Highgate was like decades ago and how was she getting on with the clearance and could Annie help at all... but, she was aware that this woman looked quite like she'd like their conversation to wind up.

'So... well, I'll leave that with you,' Annie said reluctantly. 'Anything you'd like to donate goes to a very good cause. Lovely to meet you and... I'll wave at you the next time we cross paths at the Tube station.'

'Of course, thank you.'

The heavy grey-blue door closed and Annie could hear the lock turning. She turned and began to walk down the path her thoughts about the ninety-four-year-old lady who lived here for sixty-plus years interrupted by a shrill blast from the phone in her handbag. When she saw 'nursery' flash up on the screen, her heart skipped a beat. 'Hello, it's Annie Valentine here, is everything OK?' she asked in a rush.

'It's Max,' the voice at the other end told her.

'What's happened?' Annie asked, feeling the hair on the back of her neck stand up with fright.

'He's just so upset. We think you'll have to come and collect him.'

13

Minnie set for nursery:
Dress with pink, yellow and white flowers
White knitted tights
Red wellies
Pink raincoat
Pink woolly hat
Straw basket

'So, I don't have to go to nursery at all, ever again and that is final?' Max asked as Annie came into the kitchen the next morning. Ed didn't say anything, he just wordlessly handed Annie her morning coffee.

'Muhhhhhmmy, no nursery, you said. Remember you said,' Max was telling her now in his bright, loud and cheerful morning voice.

And this was true, Annie recalled, as the caffeine began to clear the fog from her brain. She had told Max that he could stay at home with her, but maybe she hadn't planned for this experiment in reverse psychology to begin today... exactly. There was So Much To Do.

'Yes,' Annie decided, even if she wasn't sure how this was going to work yet. 'Yes, Max, you can be at home with me. We're not going to do anything exciting; we're just going to do boring Mum stuff, but you can stay at home with me and the boring stuff.'

As Max's hands went up in the air in a cheer, Annie could see an expression of slight doubt cross Minnie's face. *Oh no*, Annie needed to get onto this immediately, or she was going to have both twins on her hands. 'Didn't you say it was pottery class in nursery today?' she asked her little daughter. 'I hope you can make something lovely for me that I can keep on my bedside table.'

'I will, Mummy,' Minnie said, eyes widening and smile back in place. 'What would you like?'

Annie gave it some thought for a moment or two, more soothing mouthfuls of coffee going down. 'What about, a little dish to keep my rings in, at night when I take them off.'

'I love that idea!' Minnie's eyes widened. 'Pink and white, because you love those colours. Or even gold, because they might even have some gold paint.'

'That's perfect!' Annie enthused.

'But that's not fair if Minnie gets to make something for you today,' came Max's protest as he looked up at her and stuck out his bottom lip in a perfect pout. 'I want to make something for you too!'

'Well, Minnie is going to nursery,' Annie reminded him, 'where they have clay and paint and all those things.' *Maybe you could go along to that bloody expensive nursery too, Max!* She was tempted to add.

'We could get clay to have at home,' came Max's immediate

suggestion. Annie held the coffee cup up to her mouth and took a long sip to give her some time to think. She had to be careful here. The idea of keeping Max at home was to make sure that he was bored. He was supposed to start missing Minnie and missing having interesting things to do and friends to play with. The idea was definitely not for Annie to run a mini nursery school for one. Putting her cup down, she told him, 'We're going to be very busy today. You are going to be helping me do all the things I need to do. So, first, we need to get Minnie ready and then we have to take her off to nursery.'

'Yes!' this instruction seemed to warrant another punch into the air for Max, who maybe still couldn't quite believe that he was being let out of nursery so easily, and once again, Annie could see the flicker of doubt cross Minnie's face. Annie drained her mug, and tried to summon up all the energy and enthusiasm she would need to power through her day.

'C'mon, everyone, time to give Daddy a huge hug and let's get this show on the road!' As these words stirred general movement and activity in the kitchen, Annie took a quick glance at her phone to catch up on what she'd missed in the past half an hour or so.

Hey Muuuum! Happy Tuesday!

Followed by two smiley faces.

I am up early today to get some practice in before class. It's all good. Love ya Xxx

Annie could feel her shoulders drop by several centimetres. So, all was well with Owen, fabulous. That meant that for a few hours at least, she could relax on that front and direct her thoughts to all the many other fronts.

'OK, kiddos, let's hustle!' Annie instructed. A jam-packed ten minutes of busyness followed as bodies hurtled up and down the stairs in search of shoes, cardigans, water bottles... then finally they were all set to get out of the door. Annie suspected it wasn't going to go well but took a glance at herself in the hallway mirror anyway – noooo, she wasn't impressed. This was far too Mum-on-the-run and way less woman-of-international-fashion-mystery than she would have liked. She delayed proceedings for just a few moments to use the items that were kept on the shelf beneath the hallway mirror for exactly this purpose – she brushed through her hair, applied morale-boosting red lipstick, added a generous squirt of perfume and a slick pair of sunglasses. There was a blink of sunshine out there, just enough to warrant sunglasses. And in a total rush out of the door like this, when really, this coat was too short for that skirt, then sunglasses made everything better.

'OK, kiddos,' she told the twins, as she made these last-minute adjustments, 'let's go!'

* * *

'I have run out of things to draw!' Max hissed in an urgent whisper because he sort of knew he wasn't supposed to talk to his mummy when she was On The Phone but he also really urgently needed something else to do. Annie gave him a slight scowl but managed to scour the kitchen and find both another scrap of paper and a new crayon without interrupting the animated conversation she was having with Svetlana. 'I've even been door-to-door leafleting my neighbourhood,' she told her friend. 'Because I know how much we could do with some more items – more everything really. We need volume and we need more items of real interest too. Everything you've donated is gorgeous, babes, absolutely gorgeous. And your friends have been so generous too. But Paula and I were trawling through a bit of a box of frogs the other evening. We don't need any more frogs, we need showstoppers, so I've been up and down my streets putting lovely flyers through the doors. Maybe, I'll get more printed up and do some other chichi neighbourhoods too.

'Then models,' Annie went on, not pausing for breath or for Svetlana's take on her leafleting efforts. 'I was hanging about outside the dance school up here doing a little bit of talent-spotting and I think I've got us a group of three dancers... two of their mums have been in touch, so I think it's a yes from them. I think these gorgeous, poised, not at all performance-shy girls are going to join us for rehearsals next week. I'm so looking forward to styling them, teaching them how to walk the catwalk and I'm excited, darling, because our fabulous, grown-up model girls will take them under their wings and I just know the end result is going to be fantastic...

'And another thing,' Annie went on, because this was a really good thought she'd had sometime between 1 a.m. and 3 a.m. last night, 'because there is so much retro clothing going on, maybe we need to really embrace it, not shy away from it. We need to style the girls, noughties style, nineties, hey, even eighties style if we have enough eighties clothing. It could be so much fun and... we need to get in touch with the TV and film companies. They're bound to have wardrobe departments, wardrobe stylists all desperate for retro clothes,' she enthused. 'All those TV shows that are set in the eighties and nineties, where do they get those fantastic vintage clothes from? Probably amazing charity sales that are just like ours!' Hardly pausing for breath, she went on, 'I'm going to get our amazing assistant at the TV production company on the case. She'll know loads of TV and film companies and wardrobe people. I will get her on it.'

Max held up the scribbles he'd made all over his latest piece of paper. 'More paper,' he insisted, pouting once again. Annie held up a finger to convey *'just one minute. I'll be right with you.'* But that didn't work.

'More paper!!' Max demanded again with emphasis. This time she held the finger to her lips as a shush. But now Max decided to stomp about the kitchen angrily.

'So, what do you think? And what else should I be doing?' Annie asked, surprised at how quiet Svetlana was. Usually, Svetlana had an opinion about everything and was never shy about giving it.

'*Annah...*' Svetlana began and her voice was low. '*Annah...*' she began again.

'Yes? What is it? You don't sound happy, my darling. You sound as if you don't like any of these ideas, but honestly, the dance girls are beautiful – all muscle, grace and flexibility – they'll make amazing models. Scouring the neighbourhoods for more fashion goodies is a great idea and... bringing in TV companies is all good too. I know it. We've got to get the buzz going. We need to have press coverage for this show... pre-show as well as on the night, believe me, I'm already thinking about that.'

'*Annah...* all of these things are good,' Svetlana declared. 'You are always so hard working, so full of ideas, it is all good. But I have bad news...'

There was a pause. The kind of unexpected, loaded pause that was making Annie twitch slightly with anxiety. Once again, she held up the warning finger to Max who sighed at her and wondered off.

'So... what's the bad news?' she managed. Her head was full of all kinds of possibilities, but she didn't raise them, just gripped the phone tightly in her hands and tried not to care too much that Max had found a biro and had just scribbled right over the edge of the paper and onto her pale wooden kitchen worktop.

'*Annah...*' Svetlana seemed to falter, again so totally unlike her that Annie's heart was now beginning to beat a little too hard. *Must drink less caffeine, as Ed keeps telling me.*

'It's OK, babes, just tell me. Just rip the Band-Aid off, whatever it is, I'm sure we can cope with it,' Annie encouraged her.

'I did not get the planning permission for the show,' Svetlana said. Just like that, straight up. Like an icy shot of vodka. Annie could hear herself gasping slightly for air as the words and their meaning settled down on her.

'You – didn't – the planning permission—' she managed. 'No planning permission?' her voice had gone a little high and squeaky.

Annie was trying to put together what this meant. No planning permission meant no marquee... and did that mean no show? Really? No show?! *Really?*

'I don't know *vat* to do...' Svetlana said.

'Are you sure?' was Annie's next question. 'Are you sure you didn't get it? I mean we talked about it often. And you said you'd got it. Have you lost it? In your files somewhere?'

'No, *Annah.*'

Annie felt as if there was something she wasn't understanding here. Did Svetlana mean the council hadn't given her permission? Did this mean she needed to appeal? Was there time? Could she go and speak to the council about it?

'Did they say no...? Did they turn it down?' she asked.

'No... I did not apply. I thought it would be fine. But now Harry...'

This was Svetlana's husband, the legal bigwig.

'He says we must have planning permission in place. And now there is not enough time to get it.'

Wait... she did not apply... *she did not apply!* As this took its time to register, Annie struggled... struggled to speak, to think, to even breathe. All this effort. All this time. All the plans... the people already involved... the people already invited. And her hopes that this would be a big important event, putting her on the fashion map. It was all going to be ruined because for some baffling reason, Svetlana *hadn't applied* for planning permission, then *hadn't admitted* until now that she hadn't applied.

Annie took a deep breath in, hoping that it might calm her, but no. She was coming to realise that she felt shocked, but she also felt *furious!* Hadn't she been going on and on to Svetlana since the show was first mentioned about the importance of telling the council, signing off the paperwork, setting it all up properly? And now this... this woman... this, quite frankly, silly *cow!* In her fury that was the only word that would do. This silly cow was going to ruin everything! Just the thought that all her work, time and effort could be in vain, and that there really might be no show at all was stoking Annie's anger even higher.

'I– I can't believe it!' Annie gulped. 'I can't believe you've done this! Or *not done* this... No planning permission!!' And then the floodgates seemed to loosen and she began to speak to Svetlana as she had never done before. 'Now that I think about it – why am I not even surprised, Svetlana? I mean this is so, so like you! You never think the rules apply to you. Face it, you think you are above them! Do you have any idea how hard Paula and I have been working on this show? And you couldn't even be bothered to fill out a form! What does it matter if we're all rushing around, busting a gut for you? We're just the little minions. No doubt you have far more important things to do.'

Annie came to an abrupt halt, shocked by her outburst. She had never, ever spoken to Svetlana like this. But this was the final straw. No planning permission! For a show that was due to happen in three weeks. For a show that hundreds of people had already been invited to. For a show with catering, chairs, flowers, models and a DJ all booked!

This was just crazy, completely crazy. And far from her reputation being boosted and enhanced by this fashion gala, Annie was now looking at some serious reputational damage. This thought gave her anger another boost. 'There are only two things you can do now, Svetlana,' she declared. 'Find the relevant person at the council and beg, beg, beg them to rush through a permission for you or find another venue, within the next few days – otherwise, that's it. The show is over.'

'I don't know if I can do this. You need to help me, *Annah...*' Annie heard those words and thought of all the times she had responded to Svetlana's calls for help and gone absolutely above and beyond for her. She had driven over the Alps for this woman, been chased by thugs, given Svetlana her own daughter as an employee, swooped in on countless crisis moments. But now it was time to set some firm boundaries.

'No. I am not doing it, babes. This is your mess,' she said very firmly. 'For once, I am not jumping in to fix it. I am not rushing about London like a headless chicken because you messed up—'

'I need to explain,' Svetlana tried to interrupt.

'No!' Annie cut her off, although this was also directed at Max who had found a big marker pen and was threatening to do even more irreparable damage to the worktops. 'No explaining, just get out there and fix this, Svetlana. Fix it! And call me when we're back on.'

14

Ed in school mode:
Light blue cotton shirt
Beige chinos
Leather-strapped watch
Brown lace-up ankle boots

'That woman! That woman! This time she really is going to tip me over the edge,' Annie was complaining to Ed that evening once he was back from work. Some of her annoyance was being taken out on the Bolognese sauce that she was smacking and pounding at in its big pot on the stove.

'Oh, boy... I guess this is right out of your hands now...' Ed tried to be reassuring. 'Do you want it to be out of your hands?' he asked. 'I know how much you love to fix things, rush in and solve problems. Maybe you're the one who needs to do the planning application, go down and beg for permission at the town hall... maybe you're the one who needs to find an amazing new venue at a moment's notice. Face it, Annie, if I needed the impossible done, I would come to you.'

She turned from her slightly grudging attempt at rustling together a family dinner to look at her husband. 'That's a very nice thing to say,' she told him. 'Do you really mean that?'

Ed smiled at her. His proper smile, the one that spread wide across his face and emphasised his cheekbones. She particularly liked the pale blue shirt he was wearing today and the fact that his hair was a little overdue a cut.

'Of course I do... come here.' Then they were hugging in front of the stove, until Ed couldn't resist looking over her shoulder at what was happening on the stove. He picked up the wooden spoon and from still over her shoulder, gave the Bolognese a stir. 'Have you added the herbs?' he wondered.

'Not yet,' she replied. 'C'mon, stop interfering this is my supper, I'm sure I can manage. So... which herbs would be the best ones for this?' she tried to sound casual, as she scanned the spice rack.

Ed ran his eye over the little bottles and pulled out his top three recommendations. 'A good teaspoon of these... maybe even two teaspoons of the oregano,' he suggested.

'OK and thank you, now go and say hello to the twins. They're in the sitting room where they have been allowed an hour of telly to let me cook.' *And I will add ketchup to the blinking Bolognese.*

'Aren't we calling it "screen-time" these days, not telly. How was Max's day away from nursery?'

Annie pointed to the biro scribbles on the kitchen island by way of reply.

'Oh, damn... you know that's going to involve sanding back and re-oiling?'

She nodded, then added, 'Or we could leave it until they're both old enough not to scribble on the worktops... maybe another five or six years. But then we might be sad that they're about to be teenagers and we won't have their scribbles any more.'

'It's a problem. And talking of teenagers who don't scribble any more, how's Owen, any word from him today?'

'Yes, all good. Up early rehearsing before class today.'

'Music to my ears – no pun intended. And what about Lauren? Feels like ages since we've heard from her.'

'I know,' Annie agreed. 'There have been messages, pics, Insta things, but I haven't spoken to her for over a week. No windows, apparently, I think she's rushing about in a work and social whirl.' And it was true, Annie had been trying to talk to her oldest daughter, a little spooked by what Svetlana had mentioned, but so far, no success.

And that did make her wonder if maybe Svetlana had picked up the wrong end of the stick and Lauren was absolutely fine. Hope so, fingers crossed. She gave the Bolognese another vigorous stir. Over the bubbling sauce, the chatter of the kitchen radio, the laughter coming from the sitting room where Ed was no doubt joking about with the twins, Annie could now hear the faint chiming of the doorbell.

'Ed, can you get the door?' she shouted because the sitting room was closer and if she left the sauce now, it might catch on the bottom of the pan. She was a bad enough cook to have learned that lesson plenty of times. The bell chimed once again.

'Ed! Door!' she bellowed.

'OK!' she heard him reply, followed by the door opening, some chat she couldn't make out and the door closing again.

'Who was that? Delivery for next door?' she asked. 'I'm not expecting anything.'

'Annie not expecting anything... how unusual...' Ed said as he came into the room with two of those upmarket bags for life that the supermarkets sell you, absolutely packed full.

'Groceries?' Annie sounded surprised. 'But I've not ordered anything. Are they for next door?' Ed shook his head and set the bags down on the kitchen island. 'Not groceries,' he said, 'clothes... for your show. Someone was responding to your flyer apparently.'

'Oh! Did you get their details?' she asked, because she was supposed to do a gift aid form and all that kind of paperwork type thing that *certain people* never seem to bother with.

Ed nodded. 'Details are all in the bag, apparently.'

'Ooooh, sorry, but I need to have a quick look, just let me make sure there isn't a trace of tomato sauce on my hands,' Annie replied, unable to resist the temptation to check out the latest offerings for the show... even if it wasn't entirely clear if there was still going to be a show.

Ed went over to the hob once again, and glancing down at the sauce with some concern, he told her, 'You look, I will stir... and maybe even tweak where necessary.'

* * *

Hands now scrupulously cleaned of any tomato flecks, Annie went over to the bags. In fact, she didn't want these items within any kind of radius of sauce, cooking or the biro scribbles, so she took them to the other side of the room where the table and chairs were set out. Here, she set the bags on the floor and began to carefully unpack the first one. The item on top was already giving her hope that this was going to be a properly interesting haul, as it was made of softest black velvet. As she lifted it out and it unfolded, she could see that it was a delicate evening jacket. Vintage, 1960s maybe, or even older, designed to be worn over your going-out clothes. Amazing condition, she couldn't help noticing, and a French label that she didn't recognise.

Many more lovely vintage sixties and seventies items followed: a plum velvet bolero jacket embellished with lavish designs worked in gold thread, and a silver beaded evening dress. Everything was incredibly beautiful. This was such a generous donation. She could see all these things walking down the catwalk and making numbers in the high hundreds, maybe even four figures. Even though the labels weren't ones that she recognised. Carefully, she folded the clothes back together into the bag and then decided she would just take a quick look before supper at the top one or two items in the second bag.

First, she lifted out the white silk jacket at the top of the bag, then what she saw underneath this made her give something of a double-take. Pale cream silk but with a startlingly bright orange design... was that... the claw of a lobster?! She put her hands on the dress and pulled it out of the bag. Oh my God... someone had made the most glorious homage to one of the fashion world's most famous dresses. Casual followers of fashion might think that the most famous dresses are perhaps – Chanel's little black dress, or Marilyn Munroe's white halterneck, but for real fashion insiders, the original version of the lobster dress by Elsa Schiaparelli, that was fashion collector's gold. And what an incredible homage to those legendary dresses this was. Beautiful silk, bright colours, gorgeous details around the hems, the covered buttons, oh my word, it was glorious. A dazzling white summer dress, decorated with beautifully hand-painted lobsters. Annie laid the dress down on the table so she could undo the zip and look at who had made such an amazing job of copying this legend. Surely, they had to have left a label of some kind in the back of the dress? She slid the zip down, looked for the label and could hardly trust her eyes when she saw a hand-sewn tag with the words:

Elsa Schiaparelli, Paris

She stared at it for a moment... had the copier copied the label too? That was the first question to come to mind. Because the alternative, that she was holding a genuine, Schiaparelli lobster dress in her hands, that someone had come to the door and just casually dropped it off for a charity sale – well, that wasn't going to have happened, was it? That couldn't possibly have happened! She folded the dress tenderly and laid it across the chairs, then had to see what else was in this bag. Quite genuinely, her hands began to shake as she pulled the next item out. Could this really be... another Schiaparelli dress and a Schiaparelli evening jacket of black silk velvet with a sun embroidered in gold on the back?

'Ohmigod, Ed!' she called out. 'Ed! You need to come over and take a look at these... but stand back, keep your distance, we can't risk any kind of tomato sauce stains.'

Her husband came and stood close enough to look at the dress in her hands but not anywhere near enough to harm it. 'That looks very lovely,' he said carefully, obviously understanding that this was a beautiful thing and judging by Annie's face, an important, maybe even wondrous thing, but he didn't exactly know why.

'This is like fashion gold dust, fashion plutonium... whatever is the rarest possible thing you can think of in the real world, this is the fashion equivalent,' she said. 'I just can't believe someone has dropped it off at the house without any kind of explanation. And currently we have no show... no show, Ed. Yesterday we had a show and no showstoppers. Today we have three of the most incredible showstoppers I could ever have hoped for. And no show!'

'That is a bit of a problem,' Ed had to admit.

'That's putting it mildly... and so far, I haven't found any details,' she realised. 'There's nothing in the bags – no name, no address, no way to register for gift aid.'

'Really?' Ed sounded surprised. 'But she said she had put everything on a sheet of paper inside.'

'She? She?' Annie asked, emptying out the bags once again with care but with speed this time and double-checking for any sign of details. 'There's nothing here! And who was she? Where did she come from? Have you got any clues for me at all?'

Ed just slowly shook his head.

15

Bedhead Annie:
White cotton embroidered pyjama bottoms
Pink vest top
Layered overnight serums
Pink silk sleep cap

Sometimes when something bad has happened, or is in the process of happening, it can be the worst in the morning. First thing in the morning, as your brain is just coming back to consciousness, the terrible thing that has happened comes to mind and for one hopeful little moment you can almost convince yourself that it was a bad dream. You might even smile with relief, just as Annie was doing at this very moment, as her brain told her that falling out with Svetlana... not having a venue... the show being on the brink of collapse... was all a dream. She was going to open her eyes and it would all be over and back to the way it was before. But then, she woke up properly, really opened her eyes and realised with a thud of weight on her chest that no, it was all real. Svetlana had not got the permission they'd needed, they'd had very strong words on the phone, and for now, at least, there was not going to be a show.

Was it time to cancel things, she wondered. Should she be phoning caterers, chair suppliers, models, the gorgeous dancers, the DJ? Should everyone be told? Or was it too soon? She tried to imagine sending out emails cancelling all the invitations and the enormous fuss it was going to cause. VIPs with carefully planned diaries would have gaps! Dates and dinners would have been rearranged to accommodate Svetlana's big event. Limos might have been booked, new outfits bought. She did not want to be on the receiving end of all this disappointment and even anger, when none of this was her fault. She had asked Svetlana over and over about the permission and Svetlana had absolutely reassured her that everything was in place.

Annie had known Svetlana for years, and in recent times they'd grown much closer, *real friends* was how Annie had thought of them – and it had taken a long time for the client/adviser hierarchy to break down. But now, it felt as if their friendship had been torpedoed too. For whatever reason, Svetlana hadn't been able to be honest with Annie, her friend. And honesty, well, that was the key ingredient. If you couldn't be honest with your friend. If you couldn't say, 'I haven't done the paperwork', or 'please help, I've dropped that ball', or whatever reason there was for this epic fail, if you couldn't say what was on your mind, then where were you as friends? And Svetlana had put Annie's name on that invitation. She knew – or should have known – how much the success of the show meant to Annie and meant for her future, *her friend's* future.

'Hello, Mumma.' It was something of a surprise to have Max pop up at her side of the bed. He must have crawled very quietly over the plush carpet, into the room and round the side of the bed to pull this trick off.

'Hello! Am I late?' she wondered, glancing at her bedside clock. 'Did Daddy send you up to tell me to go have my shower?' Although it occurred to her that without the show, what did she have to get up for? What did she have to shower for even? What did she have to hustle along and do today?

'No...' Max told her, pushing his squishy little face right up in front of her. She couldn't resist giving him a kiss.

'What's up?' she asked. 'Is Minnie driving you crackers?'

'No.'

'Do you hate your breakfast this morning?'

'No!' this came with a giggle.

'What are you thinking about then?'

'Minnie said they were making pizza at nursery today.'

'Ohhhh... pizza?' Annie had an inkling of what this could be about. Max nodded.

'And you like pizza A LOT!' she said, which was putting it mildly. Tantrums had been had, cars had once been turned around back towards pizza restaurants, in fact, the meal was all but banned at home because once he'd had pizza, Max was reluctant to go back to eating anything else for days. Max nodded again enthusiastically.

'Do you think Minnie will bring you some pizza home?' Now there was a vigorous shake of the head.

'No! She said she was going to eat all her pizza and there would be none left for me.'

'Oh dear, what a shame...' *Do not offer to make pizza with Max at home today, do not do it,* Annie warned herself. The idea was to make sure Max was so bored he wanted to go to nursery, the idea was NOT to run a tiny nursery at home for Max. *Hold the line.* A critical moment was approaching and she knew she had to play this right.

'Mumma? Do you think…' Max began carefully. *Do not offer to make pizza*, she reminded herself.

'I'm very busy today, Max,' Annie added quickly, although what she would be busy doing wasn't entirely clear – maybe quietly crying in her bed. That was a strong contender for top activity today.

'Could I go to nursery for the morning, when they are making the pizza and you could come and get me afterwards?' Max was suggesting going to nursery! After just one day! Although on the other hand, maybe she was a very bad mother. Just one day of Mummy day care and Max had swapped sides. This was what she wanted, of course, but did Max have to want to go back to nursery quite so much?!

'If you go to nursery, Max,' Annie began carefully, determined not to blow this, 'you'll have to go for the whole thing because, the pizza will get made in the morning, then it will get baked and you'll want to stay and eat it for lunch and then you'll probably need to have a little nap because you know how everyone gets tired after pizza.'

'No, they don't!' Max protested.

'Anyway, by the time you've had lunch, there's story time, then playing outside – and you like both of those things – and then it's time to come home.'

'OK, I'll go to nursery with Minnie. Otherwise, she will get all the pizza,' Max declared.

This was so surprising that Annie was frightened to say a word in case she ruined it. 'Well, I better get my skates on and have a shower,' she decided that was safe enough. 'Can you tell Daddy I'll be down in five minutes and can he please make my coffee?' This made Max burst into laughter.

'What's so funny about that?' she wanted to know.

'Because you always say that. And do you know what Daddy says?'

'No...'

'He will say "five minutes? Ha, ha... I don't think so... more like twenty-five minutes. So, I'll make the coffee later."'

'Well, he's a very cheeky daddy!'

This made Max laugh again.

'OK, go have some food, put on some clothes. And I'll get scrubbed up.'

* * *

In the shower, under the spoiling, fragrant foam, she remembered the astonishing trove of legendary clothing that had arrived at the door last night. She'd quizzed Ed closely about the woman who had dropped it off. 'A grey bob...' he'd recalled. 'And dramatic spectacles, I think they were purple...'

'Was she wearing black?' Annie had asked.

'Yeee-ees,' he'd hesitated. 'I think so. She was small and she was wearing a dark, quilted coat, with a very distinctive collar... like a big, squishy doughnut, but in a good way. Even I could tell that it was stylish.'

'Oh. My. God... very well spotted, excellent work! I think I know who that could be.'

So, this morning, just as soon as M&M were at nursery – *would Max honestly, willingly go, without wailing?* But if that happened, she would come back to Highgate and as there was nothing to do right now for the show, Annie would track down the woman whose door she had turned up at when she was distributing flyers. The fascinating lady in the Yohji Yamamoto...

16

Florence at the door:
Black pleated fabric tunic
Black leggings
Grey felt slippers
Silver and gold pendant
Gold watch
Silver and gold earrings

Lauren picked up her phone but wasn't sure if she had the courage to open her email. The last few days had just been too hard. She had sent out all those resumés, all those speculative enquiries, offering her services, offering to volunteer even, and so far, either deafening silence or polite 'thanks, but no thanks' messages had come back. It was going to be even harder than she'd thought to change from working in fashion to doing something much more worthy and worthwhile. It felt as if no one cared about what she had done or what she could do. And the feeling that she was just a speck of person in a great big city was weighing her down. This wasn't how she thought grown-up life would be. It had all seemed so much more exciting, a life in fashion, when she was at school and flicking through the pages of fashion magazines, watching clips from backstage at the fashion shows... she'd thought it would be about travel and events and meeting glamorous people... creative and...

OK, sometimes life at Perfect Dress had been like that. There had been fashion shows and rushing about finding inspiration in thrift shops and tracking down unique fabrics, but it hadn't been like that for some time. It had become much more office-y and same-y and boring. And she couldn't help feeling that she'd lost the fashion joy. She didn't care if red was in and plum was out, or bangs were short or long, or if skirts were slim or floaty, not the way that she once did. She opened her email and saw two new messages had come in, both from organisations she would have loved to work for. With a sigh, she opened the first one and read the polite, standard lines of rejection that she had come to completely expect.

Before she opened the second, she felt just that slight flutter of hopefulness. She just needed one person at one organisation to come back to her with a positive reply. Just one foot in one door... that was all she was hoping for. Her heart in her mouth, she opened the email and read the lines. Oh, it wasn't just a 'no'. It was a very blunt:

Why have you contacted us? Two years in the fashion industry is not the basis for any kind of career with us. You've wasted your time writing this letter. You've wasted my time reading this letter.

Lauren looked at the words with dismay. She hadn't expected anyone who worked in a non-profit to be so mean.

She could feel tears threatening at the back of her eyes.

Surely just because you'd picked fashion as your very first job that didn't mean you had to work in fashion forever? How could it possibly mean that? The feeling that she was a speck of a person in a very big city grew even more vivid. And the feeling that she just wanted to go home was overwhelming.

* * *

Annie stood once again in front of the blue-grey door waiting for a response to her ring on the doorbell. She heard the footsteps coming down the corridor and felt almost a little nervous at the thought of meeting the Yamamoto woman again. Then came the sound of the lock being undone and then the door opened. Annie could see the woman's eyebrows lifting when she set eyes on her.

'Oh... hello, again,' Annie said. 'I hope you don't mind me coming round like this... but I think you dropped off two bags of clothes for the show. And I needed to first of all thank you and then, most importantly, make sure you knew how valuable those items are.'

The woman continued to look at her, eyebrows raised but no other change in her expression. 'I'm Annie Valentine, by the way. And the items are exquisite,' Annie went on. 'There are two dresses and a jacket in there which are very, very rare. Fashion gold dust to be honest. And I thought you should know that. In case... you didn't realise.' The long stare she was getting from the woman was not exactly bolstering Annie's confidence.

'I donated those things anonymously,' the woman said finally.

'Yes... and we really are very grateful,' she began. No point mentioning the fact that the show may or may not be happening right now. 'I guessed it was you from my husband's description... but he said you'd left details in the bags. And when I couldn't find the details... and I saw how lovely the items were...' she trailed off, hoping this was enough of an explanation for why she was on this doorstep once again.

The woman opened the door fully and sighed, long and sadly. Then she said, 'I'm Florence Perkins.'

'Hello, Florence,' Annie replied.

'Can't I just donate the items anonymously... that would just be so much easier.'

'Well, the problem is, with treasures like this, buyers will want provenance... proof of where these things came from and how old they are. Vintage fashion is so easy to fake, as you can imagine.'

'Hmmmmm...' was all the reply Florence made. Annie had the feeling that she wasn't really making much progress. So she decided to come out and ask the obvious question.

'Do you think those vintage pieces could be fakes?'

'Oh...' Florence looked taken aback. 'Well, no, not really. I mean I don't know much about vintage fashion, but I do know my mother was an artist, who always supported artists and she took a very dim view of fakes.'

'So... do you know anything about the items and how they might have come into her possession? Did she wear them? Are there any photographs of her in these clothes?'

'I don't know... I haven't looked... I have honestly no idea how she might have got them. They were never wealthy, my parents. Comfortable, yes. And this is a lovely house, of course, but it was bought a long, long time ago.' Florence sighed heavily again.

'I have a lot to sort out, Annie. Can't you just take the donation and be done with me?'

'Thank you so much for the donation,' Annie said again. She certainly didn't want Florence to think she wasn't grateful. 'It's incredibly generous. These are the most important items we will have in... the show.' *If it ever happens.* 'We will treasure them, look after them and make sure they are sold for what they are worth. But if there is anything else you can find out... maybe while you're clearing out the house... to let us know when and how they came into your mother's possession, that would be incredibly helpful.'

'I will see what I can do,' Florence said and looked as if she was going to close the door there and then.

'Thank you, Florence... here's my card...' Annie scrambled in her bag for a moment and managed to find what she was looking for. 'Let me know if you come across anything useful. Even a photo of your mother wearing—'

'Very well.' And with that the door was shut and once again, Annie could hear the lock turning.

* * *

It was all at a standstill. Nothing had been cancelled yet, but nothing was moving forward. Paula was calling her twice a day to ask what was going on, but so far, Annie knew precisely nothing. Svetlana had not been in touch. And Annie, even though she was slightly itching to call Svetlana and find out if anything about the situation had improved in the slightest, had told herself she was *not* calling. She was not going to crack first. She was not going to run after Svetlana and make it all better. Svetlana had created this mess; Svetlana had to solve it.

For a moment or two, Annie stared at her phone, as if Svetlana could somehow hear her and would now call with a solution. Instead, up popped a cheery little message from Owen with a photo attached.

> Making this for breakfast – bacon, eggs and
> tomatoes. Toms are a vegetable, I hope you're
> proud.

Well, she kind of was. Even though it was 11.30 a.m., was this when all students had breakfast? Didn't he have a class to go to? Should she be worried?

> Looks good. How's class going? Much on
> today?

Annie replied.

> Yeah, busy afternoon, fuelling up.

Owen fired back.

Busy with studies, she hoped. Not busy spending all his money on beer, she hoped too. Fingers crossed... she couldn't micro-manage, had to hope Owen could work it out and manage himself. She was pretty sure he would turn to them both for help if he got in a muddle – that was the main thing. Annie thought about Lauren... was *she* OK? Was she really OK? How could you ever really tell over messages and a few calls. You just had to keep taking the temperature and trust that you and your child would be in touch, connect, be there for one another if things weren't going to plan.

'I'm fretting,' she said out loud, 'because I have nothing, *nothing* to take my mind off the frets.' She would phone her own mother, she decided. Have a lovely, relaxed conversation about what was happening in her mother's garden, and what she was planning to have for dinner. They would sort out Annie's next visit. That would make her feel better and of some use this morning.

But just before she dialled that number, her thoughts turned to Svetlana again. In so many ways, they were friends. They had spent a lot of time together, they'd been through a lot together. They knew a great deal about each other and they still liked, even loved each other. *But...* there was always a but with Svetlana. She was a very wealthy woman who lived a very different kind of life. She had a full-time, live-in maid. She had staff who did her admin and ran her finances. She'd had the kind of husbands who ran business empires, multi-nationals, who employed not just one chauffeur but several, although she had finally found herself a wonderful, completely dependable man. And even if Svetlana's life was a scaled-down version of what it had once been, it was still the kind of lifestyle a Hollywood celebrity might be a little bit jealous of. The town house in Mayfair, summers in St Tropez, endless spa breaks, luxury shopping trips at the bat of an eyelid. Sometimes it was hard to even hang out with her because where did Svetlana want to go or to be that Annie could even afford?

But still... there was a connection, an admiration, a mutual respect... wasn't there? They had done so many things together. They had helped each other out. They had gone through difficult times together. There was a lot behind them... and Annie had hoped there was a lot ahead for them too. Including making this show just as incredible as it could possibly be. And now... well, look what had happened. Look where they were.

PAULA

Any news... any news at all?

came another message from Paula.
Followed by:

PAULA

Do I keep sorting through boxes? Do I stop
sorting??

ANNIE

Don't panic.

Annie knew she was already panicking.

ANNIE

Just hold tight for now. I'm sure we will know
something soon.

She looked around her kitchen wondering if it was too soon
for another coffee. Maybe she could get out the vacuum and head
for the disaster zone that was the sitting room. Max and Minnie
had spent the entire evening rushing around in there. Forts had
been built out of blankets and chairs, popcorn had been made
and probably spilled all over the place. The sofa was all crinkled
and saggy with crushed pillows and was long overdue a deep-
clean. She could take all the cushions off, vacuum out all the
crevices, strip the covers even, bung things in the wash. Yes, a
thorough tussle with the sofa, tugging off covers, vacuuming
vigorously... that would take her mind off the anxiety about the
show... or the not happening show. She might even find money
down there, in fact, almost certainly she would. She could end up
being paid for this chore!

She got the vacuum out from the small and chaotic cupboard
under the stairs and dragged it into the sitting room, which was
somehow in a worse state than she'd expected – a jumble of blankets, toys and chairs had been pulled in from the kitchen,
popcorn everywhere, sofa cushions on the floor, in piles on the
sofa, one on top of the piano... a small, exploded juice box on the
floor, its contents splattered around the carpet in a sticky puddle.

How had she not noticed all this last night? The lights had been dim, she remembered. She'd gone upstairs early for a bath, to try and take her mind off the worries about the show. The usually domesticated Ed must have been too tired to sort things out.

OK, time for the vacuum, a cloth, the tussle with the sofa and soon this would all be sorted out. She glanced up at the window, noticing in the pale sunlight that it could really do with a wash. Beyond the rose bush and the straggly shoots of green hedge in the front garden, a car seemed to be pulling up outside. Annie straightened up and took a closer look out of the window. A big, glossy, dark car had definitely pulled up right outside her house. She certainly wasn't expecting anyone, not in her current mid-vacuum state of mind. And this car didn't look as if it was delivering a pizza or a bag of groceries. She couldn't see much beyond the hedge and the low front garden wall, so she stood on her tiptoes to try and get a better view. To her utter surprise... not to mention shock, a perfectly turned-out Svetlana in heels, leather skirt, full make up, done hair, was walking, head held high, up the path towards the front door.

* * *

Annie was frozen to the spot. The vacuum still in her hand. The juice box still smooshed on the floor, the sofa cushions scattered, not to mention the blankets draped all over the place. Svetlana was at the door. If Svetlana was ever to come to Annie's house, it just could not be like this! Not on a day when there was dirt and child mess and exploded juice boxes and not to mention Annie in an outfit that could barely even be described as 'leisure wear.' She let go of the vacuum, ran her fingers through her hair and decided the sitting room was out of bounds. If Svetlana was coming in... would she come *in*? Could that happen? Maybe Svetlana was here to coldly and finally drop something off and tell Annie that this was it – the show was over, their friendship was dead and that was the end of all those good times they'd had in the past together.

Had Svetlana even seen her? Maybe there was still time to turn out any lights and hide until Svetlana went away. Then the next time she came back, Annie could be fully prepared. Her sitting room could be completely to rights like on an Instagram feed, with scented candles burning. Her kitchen could be spotless and gleaming with the aroma of fresh coffee and freshly baked cookies which she would hand out on a platter only for Svetlana, perched at the spotless island – minus its biro scribbles – to daintily refuse. Because she never let one morsel pass her lips 'between meals'. In fact, most of her sustenance was fluid-based – tiny, strong espressos, glasses of champagne and vodka martinis so strong and so cold, they left you gasping slightly for breath.

Had Svetlana ever visited her at home before? Annie scanned her memory, while still huddled at the back of the sitting room, wondering if there would be a ring at the door, or if Svetlana was merely going to deposit something and hurry back to her chauffeur. But then, if this was just a drop and dash, wouldn't she have asked the chauffeur to do it? Years back, she remembered, when she was running her makeover businesses from the basement – that's when Svetlana had been here. That's how she had Annie's address in her files. But since then, no. They met in gorgeous cafés and high-end cocktail bars, or Annie went to wherever Svetlana was staying. Annie was *summoned* more like.

Her racing thoughts were interrupted by a long and quite startling *driiiiiiing* on the doorbell. *Oh, hells bells. Doorbell of hell...* Svetlana was there, on the other side of the door wanting a showdown... wanting who-knew-what. And Annie was unready. Unprepared. *Who turns up unannounced, nowadays?* Would it have been too much to ask for a ten-minute warning text, so she could have flown about the house on a lightning tidy and changed into something much more... appropriate than school-run-Mum. As she stood rooted to the spot with anxiety, indecision and the fear of being found like this, the doorbell drilled insistently through the hallway once again. Too late... too late for anything other than opening the door, maybe protesting that she hadn't had time to tidy the house, dress up, whatever... and then listen to whatever it was that Svetlana wanted to say.

Annie trudged towards the door wondering what her fate was going to be. Maybe it had all been a little too good to be true – running a major London charity fashion show with one of the wealthiest women in Mayfair... attended by all the beautiful people. Maybe it was just never meant to be. Annie turned the lock and pulled the door back. There was Svetlana, in the kind of soft, pale grey fashion-forward power suit that she had adopted of late, along with the expensively blonde bob that had replaced her once signature up-do. To Annie's surprise, Svetlana's face broke into a delighted smile. She felt a little glimmer of hope stirring. Maybe something... somehow, could be worked out.

'Oh, *Annah,* you are home! This is good, this is so good,' Svetlana gushed, extending her arms and Annie was caught up in a hug that was a little overpowering. Gusts of perfume and hairspray enveloped her, a large diamond earring pressed against her cheek, while the firm crush of the impressive Svetlana cleavage pushed against her chest.

'I had to rush over to see you, immediately,' Svetlana told her. 'First of all, I have to say... well...' There was a pause. 'I am sorry, *Annah*... I have been ridiculous about this...' she waved her hand vaguely, 'permission. I didn't take it seriously and then it was too late and now I have caused all this trouble and the beautiful garden will not be used. I am very sad and very sorry.'

'It's OK,' Annie heard herself saying, though really, a Svetlana apology was such a rare beast that she would quite like to have dragged it out for a bit longer. 'We all make mistakes or in your case, great huge steaming disasters—'

'I have found somewhere new,' Svetlana declared, looking pleased with herself, 'and I have brought you a present and I have made it myself.'

As a small glossy bag was thrust into her hands, Annie knew it was time to invite Svetlana in. 'You're going to come in and drink coffee and tell me all about everything, aren't you? Unless you would like your driver to take us somewhere...?' Annie looked hopefully beyond the hedge at the sleek Bentley still purring gently in the street.

'No... no need to go anywhere...' Svetlana said with just the merest up and down at Annie's Mum-on-the-run getup. 'I want to come in and sit in your kitchen and talk, like friends, *Annah*. Like real friends,' and with those words, Svetlana reached out and gently squeezed Annie's arm.

Like real friends... 'Well, real friends hopefully don't mind what a state their friends' kitchens are in,' she warned, ushering Svetlana in through the front door. 'Do you need to tell your driver you're staying?'

Svetlana just waved airily and said, 'He will park. He will wait.'

'Follow me,' Annie said as she led Svetlana towards the family kitchen – a lovely, bright and spacious place which had once been lovingly and very expensively revamped in the absolutely up-to-the-moment style, but now, several years and a lot of family life later, it had a much more well-worn, even slightly scuffed air.

There were old, dog-eared paintings by the children on the once glamorous stainless-steel fridge. A pile of abandoned dishes was huddled on top of the dishwasher, Max's biro scribbles on the worktop seemed to jump out at her, but never mind because Svetlana was declaring it: 'So charming, *Annah,* so comfortable. The perfect family kitchen.' Then following her compliment up with, 'But I need to bring you some house plants... every kitchen needs some beautiful green plants.'

'No, no,' Annie warned her, 'I'm too busy, I have too much to look after. Right now, I would struggle to keep a cactus alive.'

Svetlana gave a little shrug and added, 'Maybe you need a housekeeper. Even one day a week. Why do you and your husband try to do everything yourself? This is not the way to a calm and organised life.'

'No...' Annie had to agree. But a housekeeper? Occasionally, cleaning ladies had drifted in and out of her life, but they often brought drama, did damage and put things where she could never find them. So, for the last few years, Ed and Annie had just tried to manage. But it was far from ideal. Especially since Dinah had stopped looking after the twins because Dinah always snuck some house tidying and organising of the household into her day. 'Coffee?' she suggested, directing Svetlana to a chair. 'And then tell me all about the new venue.'

'Yes, I sit, you put the coffee machine on and then you open my gift.'

'Oh... of course!' Once the machine was fired up and Annie had pulled up the chair opposite Svetlana's, she looked inside the bag. Inside the shiny gift bag was another bag made of white netting. This was tied with a ribbon and appeared to contain four substantial cookies.

'*My* baking,' Svetlana said proudly, 'not Maria's. I needed to do something special for you to apologise.'

Annie looked over at her. 'Now, that I was not expecting. You baked me cookies?'

'Yes, and one has an "A" on the front and is very special. You will eat it while we drink our coffee and I show you my videos of Gallery of Textiles.'

Coffees were made, plates set out, though of course Svetlana was not going to eat one bite of the home-made cookie herself. Then Annie took the phone and watched videos, scrolled through pictures and tried to re-imagine how this new venue was going to work for the show which was already so deep in the planning stages.

'This is the reception hall, very grand, nice columns, I can see it all filled with flowers. Then this is the grand hall. I love the art and the wood panelling and look at these chandeliers,' Svetlana enthused.

It was undoubtedly a gorgeous venue. Grand, elegant, no, more than that, it was stunning but in such a tasteful, old-fashioned kind of way. This was going to bring a grandeur to the whole event which... well, was a little terrifying. While it had been a charity show in a marquee, Annie had been able to play it down, tell herself that it was no problem, that she could pull it off... pull it together, she and Paula and Svetlana would create something amazing. But filling a space like this... it looked serious. It looked awe-inspiring. This was now turning into the kind of event that maybe she wasn't going to be able to handle on her own. Maybe they would have to bring in other professionals besides Paula, who was on mates' rates, but then professionals charged real money and wasn't this supposed to be for charity?

'Eat your cookie,' Svetlana urged.

Annie picked the biscuit up and before biting in, enthused, 'I love this place but... so many buts... how will people get there? Is it near a Tube?'

Svetlana gave a curt, 'Yes.'

'Then, how will we get enough flowers, enough models, enough audience, enough of everything to fill this place?'

The reply to this was the familiar airy hand wave Annie had come to interpret as: *'No big deal, we'll take care of it.'*

'Are they giving us use of the place for free?'

'A reduced fee that I am paying personally,' came the reply.

'We might need some more people to help us put this show on,' was Annie's next voiced thought, already thinking about who could be available and useful.

'I have faith in us,' Svetlana said. 'Now, please, eat your cookie and tell me that I should open a little bakery in Mayfair.'

This made Annie laugh. She looked at the cookie and bit in, her teeth chiming against something metal as she did so. Had Svetlana accidentally dropped something into the baking mixture and she shouldn't mention it? Or was putting lucky pennies into biscuits a Ukrainian tradition and she *definitely* should mention it? For a moment, she wasn't sure.

'Find something?' Svetlana asked and there was definitely an encouraging smile with this question.

'Maybe...?' Annie said and took a cautious nibble around the edge of the biscuit. This revealed a gold band and when she caught hold of it and pulled it out of the cookie, she was astonished to see a delicate gemstone ring with a central sparkling orange-yellow stone, propped up on each side with a small, twinkling diamond. 'Oh my goodness! What's this?!' she asked, holding it up for Svetlana.

'This is my gift for you,' came the reply. 'Not just a cookie,' Svetlana shook her head. 'I also give you a citrine stone because citrine brings energy and success. I would not joke with you,' she added gravely. 'This is my magic charm. It *vvvorks*.'

Annie's thank you after the initial, *'you really shouldn't have'* protests, was giving Svetlana a heartfelt hug before she tried the ring on. She found that it fitted her right index finger perfectly. And it looked good there. 'My bossing finger,' she said, pointing at Svetlana. 'I will bring energy and success wherever I point!'

'Come on, drink more coffee, let me open up the laptop and we need to start making plans for the show of the season at Gallery of Textiles.'

'There is going to be so much to do,' Annie warned. 'We'll have to move *everything*, re-issue all the invitations—'

'There is time,' Svetlana assured her. 'This is worth doing, no?'

For a moment, they held one another's look. 'We could pull the plug...' Svetlana mooted just as Annie couldn't help thinking how completely strange but also totally fine it was to have the Mayfair millionairess she knew best sitting sipping coffee in her kitchen.

'No!' Annie heard herself protesting. 'You know neither of us wants to do that.'

'Then we will have to work like farmers, *Annah*, from today until the day of the show.'

'Call in all the help, all the favours, all the available friends—' Annie began. But their train of thought was interrupted with the loud tooting of a car horn out in the street.

'Maybe my car is in the way?' Svetlana wondered. She shrugged and would probably have left it there if the tooting hadn't kicked off again, even louder and more insistent. 'I go and look.' Svetlana got up and to Annie's dismay headed not towards the front door, but straight into the family sitting room, so that she could look out of the window onto the street.

'But...' Annie uttered in a futile attempt to stop her. Didn't she know by now that if Svetlana had made up her mind to do something, only flames, floods, or possibly a request from her youngest son could stop her. So now Svetlana was at the window of the disastrously dishevelled room, Svetlana had had to pick her way over the juice box atrocity, while Annie hung back near the doorway, trying not to burn up with shame.

Svetlana lifted a graceful hand to shade her eyes against the glare of the midday sun. The tooting had stopped, but Svetlana's interest in the street scene didn't show any signs of waning. *What was going on out there?* Annie wondered.

Then Svetlana uttered the astonishing words: 'Is that *Lauren*? Yes, I think it is Lauren. Are you expecting her?'

Lauren?! Here? In London?! No! Annie was certainly not expecting her. She rushed over to the window, hurdling the juice box on her way, and lo and behold, there on the other side of the garden gate, a young woman was getting out of a car. A young woman with dark hair and a severe fringe, all the better to show off her heart-shaped face and high cheekbones. Even at this distance and without the prescription that her optician had recommended, Annie could see in a heartbeat that it was Lauren.

In response, there was only one word Annie could utter, a loud, shocked, 'What?!!'

17

Off-the-plane Lauren:
Beige and cream check blanket jacket
Cream sweatshirt
Baggy cream jeans
Beaten up sheepskin boots
Beige backpack
Luggage

Leaving Svetlana in the sitting room, even if this meant she would be judged forever as the shabbiest housekeeper of all time, or London-woman-most-in-need-of-a-housekeeper, Annie bolted towards the front door with all kinds of thoughts running through her mind. Lauren is back! There was a huge burst of happiness and joy to see her and be with her after all this time. But this was also mixed with – Lauren is back... Why? Is she ill? In trouble? Has something gone wrong at work, or personally? People don't make transatlantic flights and show up on doorsteps unannounced unless something major is going on.

By now, she was pulling open the front door and there she

was, Annie's beloved daughter, all grown-up and self-possessed and beautiful in so many ways and yet still, to Annie, a young girl who much more occasionally these days, just needed to be with her mum.

'Oh! Hello, my darling, hello,' Annie said as she folded Lauren into her arms and held her close.

'Muuuuuuum,' Lauren said and it sounded like a sigh of relief. For one long, lovely moment, Annie just held her tight, running a hand over the silky head just as she had done so often before over the years.

'Lauren, I have no idea what you're doing here but it's so lovely to see you,' Annie said.

'Long story,' were Lauren's words as she lifted her head from Annie's shoulder and locked eyes with her mother. Annie looked deep into the cornflower blue irises, saw purple rings under those eyes and the pale, tired face.

'Long journey,' she said, 'you must be exhausted. Ummm... important heads-up, Svetlana is here,' she added voice a little lowered. 'Is that going to be... well... any kind of problem?' Svetlana as the owner – or as she preferred to call it Founder and CEO – of Perfect Dress, was Lauren's ultimate boss, even if her day-to-day boss was Svetlana's daughter, Elena.

No sooner had Annie said this than Svetlana appeared at the sitting room door. 'Hello, Lauren,' was all she said and with a smile, but Lauren bolted for the stairs barely mumbling a reply.

'Lauren?' Annie called after her, but by the sound of the closing door, Lauren had made for the bathroom and wasn't coming back down right now. Svetlana and Annie looked at one another.

Svetlana gave a shrug and told her friend, 'I would make some more coffee if I were you. You are probably going to hear a long story.'

'I hope Elena knows she's decided to come over here,' Annie said.

'Lauren is a clever girl,' Svetlana said. 'I'm sure everything is OK, or will be OK once you have straightened her out again. Maybe boy trouble...?' Svetlana added, followed by, 'we all had so much boy trouble at this age.'

'Weren't you happily married to your first multi-millionaire?' Annie couldn't help asking.

'Exactly! Nothing but boy trouble.' Svetlana laughed. 'OK, I am going to go now and we will talk every day, meet as often as we need to, and get this new show on the road. Yes?'

'Yes...'

'And wear your ring, *Annah*,' were Svetlana's parting words before the swishing blonde hair and dove-grey cashmere suit swung out of the front door. 'It will bring energy and success!'

'I could definitely do with both,' she said cheerfully, giving Svetlana a goodbye hug. 'I'm so happy we're friends again. See you soon.'

* * *

One by one, Annie wheeled the two large suitcases that Lauren had brought into the house towards the base of the stairs.

'Shall I come up? Or are you coming down? Svetlana has gone,' she shouted up to her daughter.

And now here was Lauren coming cautiously down, somewhere between exhausted and worried. Maybe wondering what kind of reception she was going to get for turning up completely unannounced like this.

'This is a surprise,' Annie said, which was putting it lightly. 'A lovely surprise, but still a surprise. And I'm guessing people don't just bolt out of New York and turn up on their family's doorstep without a good reason. Is everything OK, babes?' she asked and when she saw her daughter's worried face in response to this question, she held out her arms and said simply, 'Come and have another hug.'

Then she and Lauren spent a long moment just hugging because hugging was everything, and much more important than words. 'It's OK to come home,' Annie said gently. 'Sometimes you just need to come home.' She could feel Lauren's chin nodding on her shoulder. 'Do you want to come and talk for a little? Or do you want to go to bed? I don't mind, there's plenty of time to talk.'

'Can I come and have tea with you? I miss tea—' this came out almost as a sob.

'Of course you can, darling. Come to the kitchen where I will make tea for you and another coffee for me.' There was a vague tinkling in the back of Annie's mind about how much she had to do. The new show venue, the fact that all the guests had to be contacted and redirected to this new venue. The knowledge that they would need so many more flowers and clothes and chairs and guests and... Owen's bank account needed topping up, apparently... and wasn't there dry cleaning to collect and a list of other chores about as long as her arm, dear God, she still hadn't picked the juice box up from the carpet but never mind right now. Lauren was here. So forget everything else for now. She would catch up with it. She would manage it all in good time.

But right now, she was going into the kitchen to make Lauren tea and listen to whatever it was that had sent her storming through the night all the way back home.

* * *

At first there was a little chit-chat and preamble: how was the flight? How are the twins liking nursery? What about Owen – is he surviving? And what about you, Mum? Are you surviving without Owen?!'

'Without you *and* without Owen, you mean?' Annie made sure to answer. 'I would like to say it's very quiet round here, but the twin noise has just expanded to fill the space. Of course, I miss you...' she insisted. 'But I'm so proud of both of you.'

Now they were settled with their drinks and the preamble was over, Lauren's eyes fixed on her mother's face. 'I was just suddenly... yeah, all of a sudden... I was just over it,' she began. 'Over New York and all its crap, over the New York dating scene times about one hundred and over being so far away from home and London and my old friends.' Annie put her hands over her daughter's but didn't say anything because the best encouragement to talk was usually for Annie to listen. 'I wanted to come home,' Lauren said, 'and I was just suddenly so desperate to come home that I went online and joined one of those budget flight club sites and bought a flight for $160 that left that evening.'

'You could have phoned,' Annie said. 'I could at least have taken the laundry rack out of your bedroom... and the exercise bike... and the rowing machine...' *Fitness trends I started but could never commit to*, Annie couldn't help telling herself off.

'The weights...' Lauren added. 'I was always stubbing my toes on those weights. And let's not forget the fact that my wardrobe is the "overflow" now,' Lauren made air quotes with her fingers, 'for your wardrobe, which means it's absolutely rammed with handbags, shoes and dresses that you will never wear again but have completely convinced yourself that you will.'

'I will,' Annie said simply, not wanting to stir up any old rants or debates. 'And what about Elena?' was Annie's careful question. 'Does she know that you're back in London.'

'Of course she knows!' came the outraged voice Annie knew oh-so-well from Lauren's erm... *volatile*... teenage years.

'And is she OK about it...? I mean, a day isn't exactly a lot of notice...'

'I've told her I've had to take a holiday, urgently. And she understands.'

'Oh... that was probably a good idea,' Annie said, relieved that Lauren hadn't handed in her notice, stormed out of the office and burned her New York bridges in one big dramatic action.

'Yes, but I've brought everything home. There's another massive suitcase arriving tomorrow... it took a different flight. Because I'm not going back, Mum. And the reason I didn't want to phone you before I came is that I just didn't have the energy to argue with you because I knew you'd try to persuade me to stay.'

'Oh...' Annie felt a little hurt by this. Hadn't she always, always tried to understand what her children were feeling and support them? 'I probably would have just sounded you out, tried to make sure you were sure, before getting on the plane. I wouldn't have argued with you to stay,' Annie told her daughter.

'Yes, you would, "it's the dream job, Lauren. Most girls your age would kill to live and work in New York, and work in fashion!" But the reality, Mum... the reality is worrying massively about tiny details which completely don't matter. Do not matter at all. What colour is this season? Next season? What cut? What print is going to wow the buyers. It's just complete and utter madness,' Lauren went on, really warming to her theme, getting the let's-bash-fashion bit right between her teeth. 'If they stopped making clothes tomorrow, we'd still have enough clothes in the world to dress the next six generations!'

'But... only if vintage makes a massive comeback,' Annie couldn't help herself.

'Muuuuum!' Lauren protested.

'I'm sorry, I'm sorry, I know what you mean. A lot of it is... trivial, detail, maybe not important compared to—'

'World politics, global hunger, pollution, climate change, you know all of those little problems...'

At this point Annie couldn't help her eyes widening. She might be unhappy with her TV gig at the moment and looking for a new opportunity, but she knew she would always and forever work in fashion. Fashion would always be Her Thing.

And this was Lauren. Lauren who had spent hundreds of hours of her life teaching herself how to cut that fringe and shape those brows so artfully. Lauren who customised clothing with her own unique sewing skills. It could just about make Annie cry. Maybe Lauren was just rebelling, underlining her uniqueness, her independence from her family and especially her mother.

'I'm working on a fashion show with Svetlana,' Annie began. 'You'll love this because it's very eco-friendly, all about recycling clothes... and some of those things are so wonderful, maybe they will last for six generations. And we're raising money for a wonderful cause. So absolute win-win. Maybe you'd like to help out on it a bit. Some really cool people are involved.' Lauren's face was stoney. 'A show... a glitzy, starry show... that might be what you need to get your fashion mojo back?'

OK, maybe it wasn't the perfect thing to say. Maybe Annie should have read the signs... Lauren was not in the mood for fashion; Lauren was obviously determined to be an eco-warrior.

But still, she didn't expect Lauren to crumple and begin sobbing. 'Fashion is killing the planet, Mum. *We* are killing the planet.'

18

Max at home:
Favourite pirate T-shirt
Denim dungarees
Slipper socks with bunny ears

'Oh my God... that was tragic. So, what did you do then?' Ed, home from school early, was delighted to find his wife at home without the twins, who had been picked up by Auntie Dinah at a loose end so she could feed them wholesome cake for an hour or two. Except Annie wasn't alone, it turned out that Lauren was at home and was still asleep upstairs, a full six hours since she'd arrived.

'I think you'd be proud of me, babes,' Annie told him. 'I took a deep, deep breath. I told her that I loved her no matter what she thought about fashion. Then I said she must be exhausted and hungry. So, I treated her very gently, just like an overwrought toddler. I made her a little bit of scrambled eggs on toast and I sent her to bed. And that's where she's been ever since.'

'Poor Lauren,' Ed sympathised. 'Major life crisis... and an

eight-hour transatlantic flight. And then having to have a big debate about fashion with you at the end of it.

'Not to mention going to sleep in a room that's full of... badly underused exercise equipment and the fallout from your fashion habit.' They laughed a little at this and exchanged a look. 'Hello, Annie.'

'Hello, babes.'

'Never, ever a dull moment around here is there.'

'No, never. And believe me I would love one. Even just one dull moment a day would be absolutely fine.'

'So, anything else happen today? You know, apart from Lauren jetting in unexpectedly from NYC?'

'Svetlana came round... which was another surprise appearance at the door, I can tell you.'

'Svetlana? She doesn't usually deign to visit mere mortals, does she? Are you not usually summoned to her palace in Mayfair?'

'Usually, but she wanted to tell me about the new venue she has found for the show and, even more out of the blue, she wanted to apologise.'

'That sounds... very unusual...'

Ed straightened up from the emptying of the kitchen dishwasher, which he was doing even though he wasn't long in from school, and probably hadn't had one moment to himself. Commuting home through busy London traffic on his bike wasn't exactly 'me time'.

'She gave me a beautiful ring and said we should have a housekeeper,' Annie told him. 'At least one day per week. And that was before she had come across the sight of both sofas disguised as forts in the sitting room... and had to hurdle over an exploded juice box.'

'Oh dear,' was Ed's smiling response. 'But I quite like the idea of a housekeeper.'

'Oh, do you now? Are you wondering if she can be young, and a little bit foxy and wear a uniform?' Annie asked cheekily.

'No!' Ed insisted. 'I'm thinking a clean, tidy house, a calmer, more relaxed wife; less stacking the dishwasher time, and more together time.'

He looked over at her and she remembered how much she liked that look on his face.

'Oh, more together time. Are you sure that's what you want?' Annie moved round the countertop and reached for him. 'That's might just mean more time listening to me complaining about one thing after the next.'

'No... less complaining, more kissing,' she said as they leaned into one another, held each other close and looked into each other's eyes in a way that they hadn't done for a while. And maybe there would have been kissing and some re-kindling, but the doorbell interrupted with a loud trill, so they broke apart reluctantly with Annie telling Ed, 'Hold that thought for later.'

'I will hold you to that.'

'I promise.' And then into the house came Max and Minette, trailing bags, jackets, crumpled paintings they had done that day, twigs, glitter paint and some post-ice-cream stickiness as she hugged them both tight. Auntie Dinah was on their heels but told Annie after a quick hello hug, 'I'm just dropping and dashing. We've had a lovely time and now I've got to get home and make sure Billie does homework and food before dance class.'

'Thank you and love you,' Annie told her sister, who was already turning to hurry down the path. So now the twins were charging around the hall, depositing shoes and things every-where, despite her instructions to 'hang that up', and 'you know where your shoes go'.

Max was practically shouting with happiness about how much fun he'd had at nursery as she herded them into the kitchen.

'And we did make pizzas and it was delicious and my one was definitely the best,' he told her, followed with, 'Hey, Daddy, can we make pizza for supper too?'

Meanwhile it was now Min who was grizzling. 'I don't like nursery. It's boring and it's not fair that Max got to stay at home all day with Mummy. I want to stay at home with Mummy too.'

'No, you don't,' Max assured her. 'Because it is so boring.'

Well, Annie couldn't help thinking, *I did what I was supposed to do, but still, not very flattering, Max.* 'All she does all day long,' he added, 'is sit on her computer looking at handbags and worrying about what to get Daddy for their...' he paused and gave a look that suggested he was concentrating, 'anni... ver... sary,' he managed carefully.

Ed looked up at her. 'I thought we weren't doing gifts, Annie. I thought we had agreed.'

'Yes, but when we said no gifts, I was lying. Were you not lying?'

'No! Agreeing no gifts means agreeing no gifts... not pretending to agree no gifts,' Ed replied, sounding a little exasperated.

'OK... understood,' she said and before she even had time to think about whether that meant they were now doing gifts or not, she had to tell her son. 'And, Max, I did not look at handbags on the computer when you were with me. Not even once! So don't say that. I am a busy lady with a busy job.' Seeing the look of surprise on his face at her slightly harsh tone, she added, much more kindly, 'I'm so happy you enjoyed nursery today,' and earned herself a dazzling Max smile and her son's little sticky paw slipping momentarily into hers.

Annie thought, above the noise in the kitchen that she could her a door opening upstairs, so she shushed the twins and told them that she had a big surprise for them.

'What, Mummy?' Minette couldn't help herself from whispering. 'What is it?'

'It's a who...' Annie hinted. And at that they could hear steps coming down the stairs.

'Is it Owen? Is he back from the 'versity?' Max wondered. But by now, they could catch a glimpse of legs in pink and white pyjamas.

And at this both the twins raced to the foot of the stairs, where they began shouting: 'It's Lauren, it's Lauren! Lauren is home!' At the top of their voices.

And Lauren charged down the stairs to meet them. Scooping them up, raining kisses on their faces and telling them how much she missed them. Annie could feel herself welling up at the sight. She immediately thought of Owen and didn't want him to be left out of this happy reunion, so she snapped some quick photos with her phone and sent them to him with the message:

> Surprise! Look who has turned up from NYC.
> She's planning to be here for a bit, so will see
> you when you're back. Mxx

* * *

It was much later in the evening, when everyone had been fed, when the twins had been finally calmed and bedded down for the night and the sitting room set to rights – including the juice box clean-up – that Ed and Annie settled into the plumped-up sofas to listen to Lauren.

'Alienated... that was how I felt,' she told them, curled into a defensive huddle in the corner. 'Like I didn't belong, like hardly anyone knew me and I didn't matter. Like a tiny dot in this giant busy world and I just had to come home.'

'Did anyone in particular make you feel small?' Ed wondered.

'I don't want to pin it all on one person, especially a boy,' Lauren said. 'I really am not the girl who's running home after a bad break-up. I am not her.' Lauren's brows pushed together daring them to challenge her.

'No, we know you're not,' Ed said gently, 'but he did something to make you change your mind about things?'

'Yeah, he did,' Lauren agreed. 'I thought...' she began carefully, 'I thought that I mattered a lot to him. But he got a new job, in another city, and that mattered a lot more than me.'

'Oh, I'm so sorry, Lauren,' Annie said.

'And his life change made what I do feel not at all important. He's moved to Cleveland to join an animal conservation society. It's important, it matters. When he gets out of bed in the morning, that's what he wants to be doing and when he stays late in the office, it's to make a difference. And that's how I want to feel about my work. I really can't care about what colour is in fashion this season and how to make another three sales before month end of a product that's probably going to get worn three times and then end up in landfill. So, if it's OK, I'm going to be here for a while, while I rethink my life.'

Annie first of all assured Lauren that of course it was OK, of course she could be at home and take the time she needed. But then, she couldn't help making something of a defence of the industry which had been so important to her for all these years.

'I do just want to say that fashion does matter more than you think. The right clothes can make people feel good about themselves, make people feel pulled together for their job interview or their divorce hearing or their child's first day at secondary school.

The comfort outfit can help women have all kinds of difficult conversations. Going to the doctor's to hear bad news, needing to find something simple to put on when you have a challenging day ahead. These things do matter. You're just looking at the trivial side, you're not thinking about how clothes are so woven into our everyday lives. Like it or not, they do matter. We are judged all the time about the wardrobe choices we've made. And we judge others too. And you know that Perfect Dress makes really good decisions about material and waste. We buy people's dresses back, Lauren. That's a little revolutionary.'

Lauren did at least acknowledge this with a nod. And then, to Annie's surprise, it seemed to be Ed's turn. 'You must remember when I first met your mum,' he began. 'I knew literally not one single thing about fashion. Nothing. I bought most of my clothes from the mountaineering shop to be practical and quite a few of the items in my wardrobe came from the school's lost property store.'

This earned him a laugh from both Lauren and her mother as they thought back to the early Ed of fraying rugby shirts and waterproof trousers that rustled as he walked. 'How did Mum ever see past those outfits?' Lauren wondered with a smile.

'I often ask myself,' Ed replied. 'And everything she says about the positive power of clothes is true. I know dressing with more care and attention worked for me – would I be married to *the* Annie Valentine, or be head of music at *the* St Vincent's if I hadn't discovered the power of moleskin jeans or a well-fitted tweed jacket.' It was Ed's turn to laugh now because he didn't want to let them think that he took anything about his outfits too seriously. 'But there's a wider social side, Lauren,' he went on, leaning forward in his seat and warming to his theme. 'Yes, fashion changes with society but sometimes it's fashion that changes society, or speeds those changes up. Think about when women first started wearing trousers, or bobbing their hair, that was an outward sign of the freedom they wanted and achieved. Women choosing to wear miniskirts represented sexual freedom, girls in Dr Marten boots, or gym clothes – it's an outward show of the strength and opportunities women demanded. You're thinking about the trivial things and you're forgetting about the revolutionary side of fashion. Fashion is always ahead of the curve. It's changing things, and it's letting us know what the world is going to look like, and where the world is going, often years ahead of time – so we can start imagining a different kind of future, or we can react and change course if we don't like it, before it's too late.'

Annie looked at her husband feeling almost tearful. She loved everything he'd said and she couldn't have put it so well herself.

'I never thought your Ted Talk would be on the power of fashion,' she teased. 'That was so impressive.'

'Thank you.' He looked genuinely pleased with the effect he'd had on his audience.

'So, what is this fashion show of yours all about?' Lauren turned to ask her mother.

'I'm working with Svetlana, and Paula from The Store – you remember her?'

Lauren nodded and said, 'Love Paula, she's like my bad auntie. Remember when she gave me gel nails when I was about thirteen and you completely lost it?' Lauren giggled.

'No...' Annie shook her head. 'I've clearly blanked that from my mind. We have some lovely real models, and some lovely volunteer models and the aim is to put on a fabulous, exciting show for hundreds of guests. Everything we show is for sale on the night. And there are going to be rails and rails of lovely things to buy too.'

'So where do all these clothes come from?' Lauren wondered.

'Not just clothes,' Annie told her, 'bags, shoes, jewellery, scarves, belts... it's a haul, a treasure trove. Basically, Svetlana cleared out her unused wardrobe and then persuaded some of her friends to do the same and it has totally snowballed. Plus, there are some very, very unique and special things I can't even talk about yet... We can't even show everything on the catwalk, so we're going to have pop-up-shops at the venue where people can browse and buy before and after the show. It's all for charity, we're raising as much money as we can for Thrive Dressing.' Annie was trying to sound as upbeat and enthusiastic as she could because she was not fully adjusted to this new venue yet. She hadn't been there. She couldn't picture or plan for it yet. Her head was still full of the magical garden in Mayfair with the fairy-lit trees and the glowing, billowing marquee and it was hard to let go of that.

'But, be honest, this is a show full of hand-me-downs from middle-aged socialites?' came Lauren's snippy question. 'Tweedy suits, knee-length skirts, stupid wedding outfits and dumb little hats?' she added to rub some quite unnecessary salt into the wound she'd just caused.

For a moment, Annie was tempted to do a little salt rubbing of her own, but she caught the expression on Ed's face, which warned her with just the smallest of smiles and eyebrow raises not to escalate. Lauren had flown across the Atlantic, was exhausted and all confused about where she was going and what she was doing next, so if she needed to do some snarling at her mother, then let it be.

'We're leaning into the retro,' Annie said breezily, 'we're leaning into looks from the noughties, nineties and even eighties. We're inviting film and TV wardrobe people along and hoping they will buy for upcoming productions.'

'Huh...' This seemed to raise a glimmer of interest on her daughter's face.

'Would you like to help with the show?' Annie asked her. 'It will be really exciting and different. It will keep you busy, so you don't fret too much about, you know, your life...' She shrugged. 'Plus, I could really do with the help.'

'Well...' Lauren gathered herself and stood up. 'I'm going to go upstairs and speak to some friends. Ermmm...' She looked at Annie and give a small, noncommittal smile. 'Yeah... maybe I could help a bit... if I have some time.'

Then she breezed airily out of the room, while Annie restrained herself from yelling or throwing something. '*Help a bit... if I have some time?*' she whisper-hissed at Ed. 'What is that all about? She has plenty of time. She has all the time in the world. She's made herself unemployed, in case she hasn't noticed!'

Ed smiled and made his favourite palms downwards calming gesture. 'It's OK,' he said gently. 'Just give her a few days. She will be in a social whirl catching up with everyone and then, when the novelty has worn off and she's starting to bore herself to tears, that's when you swoop in with your exciting fashion show to organise.'

'You think?'

'I don't want to say I *know*, but I have a suspicion.'

'Why are you better at working out our girl than I am?'

'Mothers always get it in the neck from daughters. That is the law of the universe. And can I remind you' – Ed came over to sit next to her on the sofa – 'you were supposed to be holding a thought for me? A going to bed early and making time for ourselves kind of thought.'

She put her hands on his neck and kissed him gently on the lips. 'Oh yes,' she told him, 'I'm holding it... holding the thought.'

But then a very different thought occurred. 'Oh no, Ed...' she began.

'What? What is it?'

'It's not just us and two sleeping twins in the house any more! Just when we thought we had the night-time to ourselves again, there's another kidult back in the house. You know what that's like for parental sex lives!'

'Oh yeah...' Ed nodded sadly. 'Once again, I need to resign myself to living like a monk.'

19

Jayne at the desk:
Green cord shirtdress
Multi-coloured flower necklace
Green and white trainers

Annie came out of the exit to the Tube and took a little moment to admire the street scene around her. She knew she'd been in these parts before, but she couldn't think when it had been. Years ago. On this autumn morning, there was cool sunlight slanting off the shop windows and that first rustle underfoot of dried leaves fallen from the nearby plane trees. The kind of bright autumnal day that called for your cosy woollen coat or statement faux-fur jacket – sunny but cool with little chance of rain. She turned up the collar of her jacket and made some tiny adjustments to the artfully wrapped scarf. This was fashion, after all, darlings, fashion. She had standards to maintain. It was a brisk ten-minute walk to the Gallery of Textiles and Annie did not need much persuasion to decide that fortifying herself with a takeaway coffee en route was a good idea. She was more than a little nervous. What if she didn't like the place? What if the dimensions just weren't going to work? In Annie's mind, it was never going to replace the marquee and she was finding it hard to let go of all the thoughts and plans she had made for the marquee and those precious gardens in Mayfair... fairy lights, trees rustling in the dark, the special sense that you were being let into a secret place at night. The gardens had inspired the whole show, she thought bitterly.

It was just so infuriating that Svetlana had messed up and now they were having to suffer the consequences – even if she had got a home-made Ukrainian biscuit and a citrine ring out of it. The ring was lovely, she thought as she ran the fingers of her other hand across it now. Maybe it would do as Svetlana had promised and bring them energy and success. She took a bracing gulp of Americano with a dash of milk. Ah! Well, that was at least bringing some energy to the party.

A few minutes later, and she was standing in front of the Gallery of Textiles. It was immediately lovely to look at from the outside, a beautiful stone building, well kept, with generous windows and substantial garden grounds. Maybe this building could look just as twinkly if the grounds in front were all strung with lights, what about outdoor torches, she wondered, and an enormous arch of flowers over the door? Yes... she was trying to let go of the marquee, the Mayfair residents' garden and focus instead on the possibilities that here might be able to offer. Feeling her spirits a little more lifted, she walked towards the pale green double doors and stepped inside. First impressions were very encouraging, pale honey-coloured stone floors, check, dramatic chandelier hanging from an ornate ceiling, check, showstopping staircase flowing down from the heavens into the entrance area, check. Yes, she could see a flock of fashionistas milling around here with cocktails in their hands, refusing canapés. She walked over to the reception area and asked the woman behind the desk to show her to the rooms that had been booked up for the event.

'Oh yes,' the woman pushed her reading glasses onto her head to take a closer look at Annie. 'Now that sounds very interesting, just the kind of event we should be hosting here. We're all very excited about it.'

'That's nice to hear. I'm Annie, by the way, and you...' she glanced at the woman's lapel badge, 'must be Jayne.'

'Nice to meet you,' Jayne told her.

'Likewise.'

'So, the show is in the ballroom, it's not occupied right now so feel free to go and take a look around. The four smaller rooms, two on either side, have been booked for the whole week before the event, so you can set up rails, shops, little side events... it all sounds so much fun.'

Annie could feel her shoulders relaxing a little. It was good to feel some enthusiasm and encouragement coming her way as usually, she was the one who had to generate it and radiate it out in everyone's direction. 'I'm so pleased you're all feeling so enthusiastic.'

'We are! So, straight down this corridor,' Jayne demonstrated, 'the ballroom is at the end and your other rooms are on either side. Enjoy!'

'Thank you.'

The corridor was nice, too, she noticed. Lots of potential for little tables with big vases of flowers, there was good wall lighting... maybe they could hang garlands or bunting or have something full of life and colour hanging from the ceiling.

Should she go into the little rooms first, she wondered. No, she would go straight on ahead and check out the main event first. Pushing open the door, she felt another bubble of anxiety float up again... was this going to be the right kind of place? Was she going to be able to work with it? Would it have any of the charm or magic of the marquee in the gardens? This was Svetlana, she reminded herself. The woman did have taste... and buckets and buckets of cash. Annie pushed the door aside, opened her eyes wide and let out a breath... this was... *plain* was her first thought. *Very plain*... but in a tasteful way. It was a substantial, square room with palest grey walls, elegant windows, a wooden parquet floor, four separate sets of elaborate ceiling lights, but nothing else... this room was bare.

They were going to need to create a catwalk, a full backstage area, and then seat the audience all around it. They would need lighting, it occurred to Annie for the very first time. You couldn't just dim the chandeliers in a room like this... if the chandeliers even dimmed. No, there would need to be lighting professionals, spotlights, TV lights, crew, lighting rigs... this was a whole element she hadn't even considered.

Oh God, there was a lot to do. She could feel the tension rising in her chest just at the thought of it. A lot to do. *The positives,* she thought, *focus on the positives.* This room was big enough, could definitely be made to look impressive enough, if she started right away, today. No time to lose. She took one last gulp of the coffee, gah, already lukewarm, and headed out of the room to go and check out the other spaces that Svetlana had booked.

Opening the door on the first adjacent room, she was delighted to see Paula already in place with a mountain of clothes on a table in front of her. 'Babes, I did not know you would be here already!' Annie greeted her. 'And I am so glad to see you!'

They hugged, Annie trying not to care how much of a dumpy frump this six-foot Brixton goddess could always make her feel, completely without trying because Paula was a lovely person who wore her gorgeousness totally casually.

'These clothes are not going to organise themselves now, are they?' was Paula's opener.

'So, how is it going?' Annie asked her.

'I am trying to make myself at home,' Paula said. 'I am trying not to panic that I still have about three shipping container's worth of stuff to get through and so far, the biggest category of donations is "outdated ladies who lunch outfits."'

'We will style them so irresistibly that we'll get them right back in fashion again,' Annie reassured her. 'Basically, if everyone isn't wearing a tight jacket with a matching miniskirt and coordinating hat next season, then we will not have done our jobs properly.'

Paula chuckled but didn't stop her work of sorting, folding and dispatching items into the categories of hangers, rails and bins that she'd already set up and was powering through. Annie took the hint and set her bags down carefully in the corner, then took off her coat and folded it on top of them. She didn't want finest Jigsaw tailoring to end up on a sale rail, however much she supported the cause.

'OK, explain the set-up you have going on here and I will get stuck right in.'

'You could at least have brought me a coffee,' Paul complained.

'I didn't know you were going to be here. I've already said that!' Annie retorted. 'But, sorry, I should have brought along a spare, just in case. So, tell me honestly what you think of the new venue?'

'One, I am glad I'm not working in a garage right now, there's a plus point. But, Annie, that enormous room next door is just empty space. We are going to have to work hard to fill it. Very hard. I think you need to talk to some professionals. We only have the room for the day of the show, the day before and the day afterwards, plus a few hours here and there for rehearsals. They'll have to build a catwalk and a backstage area in the morning of the pre-show day, then we'll have to do our full run-through in the afternoon and... if I know anything about models and fashion shows, it will last well into the night.'

'You're right, you're right.' Annie could feel the tension bubbling up in her chest again. 'And we'll need professional lighting,' Annie said. 'I was standing in the room, looking up at the chandeliers and thinking, we can't use these, we're going to have to have proper stage lighting and that was another thing I hadn't even thought of before.'

'And what about our compère? Are we really going with that guy?' Paula wanted to know. 'I mean, I don't know him obviously, but isn't there something hanging over him? Rumours? I always thought he was kind of too much.'

This was not helping with the feeling of *So Much To Do* building in Annie's head, throat and chest. 'He's a friend of Svetlana's. That's the problem,' she admitted. 'I think he's cheesy and old-school. He makes tasteless jokes, even dodgy jokes, and he's not the right person, but for whatever reason, Svetlana likes him and she wants to stick with him.'

Paula gave an eye roll before suggesting, 'Could we maybe pair him with someone else? Someone who will take the edge off? Tone him down, act as guardrails, laugh at him if he says something really cringe?'

This, Annie had to admit, was a good idea. A sort of compère safety net. A way of letting Svetlana have what she wanted while reining in the danger of it all going wrong. And a way of letting Annie have what she would have wanted, if she'd been allowed to choose. 'You are good,' she told Paula. 'You are very, very good. You need to help me with more of this stuff. Because Connor is in the huff that I didn't ask him to be the compère, but why don't we ask him if he'd consider sharing the limelight with Vince?'

At this, Paula finally broke into a smile, in fact, she even clapped her hands. 'Connor McCabe? Your gorgeous actor friend?'

'Of course.'

'Connor and Vince?! They will be amazing together. Connor will absolutely roast him if he misbehaves. People would come to watch that, never mind the fashion show.'

'Woah, babes, you're only allowed to have said that once,' Annie warned. 'We are all about the fashion. We are here for the fashion.'

'Yes, we are, you know we are. So come on, make the calls you need to make, and then come and help me sort through another mountain of little jackets with gold buttons that are all desperate to be taken back out to lunch.'

'They just need some up-to-the-moment handbags to zhuzh them up,' Annie replied and couldn't help thinking about the beautiful The Row handbag that someone had so generously donated. But no, no, she could not justify an astronomical price tag like that.

* * *

Several hours later, and Annie and Paula decided to buy sandwiches and eat them on a bench in the garden of the Gallery of Textiles. Because there was still warmth to the sunshine and by late September, you had to take every moment of sunny warmth that you could because it would soon be gone. Away from talk of the fashion show, they had some personal catching up to do.

Annie brought Paula up to speed on the arrival of Lauren along with the announcement that she had quit her job and was apparently never going to work in fashion ever again. Paula gave another of her impressive eye rolls. 'I hope you're not paying too much attention to the drama,' she said. 'Because boy do I remember myself at that age. Every day was a fresh drama. I had no idea what I wanted and God knows how my family put up with me.'

'I'm sure I was the same,' Annie admitted. 'I have no idea why everyone idealises being young. It's mainly complete hell. Especially when you're leaving the heart of the family that's been all around you for so long and you've not yet built up the new tribe that's going to take their place.'

'Yeah... and she went to New York, so far away from you all,' Paula pointed out. 'No wonder she got all lonely and sad and dramatic and decided she had to fly home.'

'She's in such a bad mood – with the whole world,' Annie confided because, to be honest, it was difficult dealing with this moody version of Lauren who had now moved into their home.

'I think I was in a bad mood from sixteen to twenty-six. Each and every day, the whole day. God, how did we put up with ourselves?!' Paula wondered. This made Annie laugh. 'She'll figure it out. And she has good people around her. Bring her in here to help,' was Paula's suggestion. 'She can come and hang with Paula, her old BFF.'

'You'd think she would be desperate to come in and help and, of course, hang out with you,' Annie began. 'But she's committed to giving up fashion because it's all so meaningless and she wants to do *"real things"* that *"matter"*,' Annie added giving a bit of an impersonation of Lauren's big speech.

'You know, that's nice. Good for her,' Paula said, scrunching up her sandwich bag. 'Just tell her there's not much chance of bumping into much real fashion here. It's all tweedy jackets and out of style coats and faux-fur that should have been put out of its misery years ago.'

And that was when Annie realised she hadn't told Paula or Svetlana yet about the Schiaparelli treasures that had landed on her doorstep. Was it too soon to mention the items? Of course she needed Florence to find out more. But they had been donated. And they did appear to be genuine. So, even if no more could be found out about them by Florence, maybe an expert could be called in to assess them? Maybe Annie could just mention them to Paula, while Florence was doing some more research? It would give Paula hope, the way it was giving Annie hope, that this show could still, despite its last-minute venue change, be something amazing.

'Paula, babes, we do have fashion,' Annie told her now with real excitement. 'Real fashion. Standout fashion. I haven't told you or Svetlana yet... because there are a few ends to tie up... But I think we do have the donation to end all donations.'

Paula squeezed her hands together and looked at Annie with an eager expression, then began to guess. 'We've already got Chanel bags and even two actual Hermès Birkins – even if one of them is in bright turquoise crocodile that no one is going to buy – so I'm guessing it's not a handbag...'

Annie shook her head. But now she couldn't help herself from thinking about that The Row handbag again. Every once in a while, she just couldn't help herself, she got *obsessed* with a handbag. She pictured it with all the outfits in her wardrobe; she imagined herself in scenes from her life carrying the handbag; she saw it propped up on café tables, bar stools and sitting beside her in the Tube like some kind of pet. It was ridiculous and she *knew* she already had more than enough handbags, but every so often, she could not resist the allure that somehow *this* bag was the one that was going to change her fashion life forever. It would go everywhere, it would go with everything, it would mark her out as a woman of immense taste and sophistication. She tried to shake it out of her head. But like a teenager with a massive crush, it was irrational and she could not stop thinking about it. And the crush bags, she knew from past experience with a fuchsia-pink YSL and a teal-blue Mulberry, she had worn them until they had almost fallen apart. So, occasionally, for a love affair like this, it was worth it. But at £2,400... no, no, no.

'We've got Chanel suits...' Paula began with her process of elimination, 'and God knows how many Chanel-alike suits, so it can't be Chanel. We've got one Yves Saint Laurent le smoking suit... so can't be that.'

'No, keep guessing,' Annie encouraged her. 'Fashion gold dust... Fashion nirvana...'

'We've got one very crumpled Westwood ballgown, with a stain on the front, but I would be happy to see more...'

Annie shook her head as Paula insisted. 'No, no, don't tell me, yet, I'm still guessing! Is it vintage? Like truly vintage, like... one of the greats?'

Annie nodded her head. 'Oh my God... original Christian Dior New Look?' was Paula's next guess as she started to look properly excited.

'That is a good guess,' Annie had to admit, 'but think even older, we're talking pre-World War II... museum-worthy.' Annie went on, 'I can't believe that someone has handed these things over to us.'

'Oh my God... Oh My God... pre-World War II, but not vintage Chanel...'

'Think French,' Annie hinted. 'Not Chanel but another woman.'

'Vionnet?' Paula gasped. 'The inventor of the bias cut?!'

'Even better, my darling,' Annie decided to put Paula out of her pain. 'I have been given three items of genuine Schiaparelli... including a lobster dress.'

Paula was now wearing the same look of astonishment that Annie had worn when she had pulled the dress out of the bag and then seen the original label.

'No!! You can't be serious! Not Schiaparelli...' Paula whispered. It was incredible that so many decades after the death of this designer, two women on a bench in west London, still holding a sandwich each, were going into complete raptures about a white silk dress with several lobsters on the skirt. It was quite some testament to the power of this designer's creations. 'Schiaparelli...' Paula repeated, completely in awe. 'You're right. This is museum-worthy. We can't let some random millionaire buy that dress or any of the other things. We have to tell the V&A, the Met in New York, we have to make sure it goes to a fabulous home where fashionistas like us can come and pay homage. These aren't just clothes these are pieces of fashion history... fashion art.'

'Yes, and I completely agree,' Annie told her, 'it is beyond amazing that we have these things, but—'

Paula began to look concerned. 'Uh-oh,' she said. 'But...? I do not like the sound of this.'

'The items, in fact, let's call them the priceless fashion treasures, were donated by a lady who wants to remain anonymous, and she inherited them from her mother.'

'And? She doesn't like fashion? She doesn't like money? She

had no idea what she was giving you? And you now feel guilty?' Paula asked.

Annie shook her head slowly. 'No more complicated than that,' she had to admit. 'You see, Florence, who donated the clothes. She has no idea how her mother got these clothes. She wasn't a wealthy woman. And if there's going to be a public sale, that will be investigated. I think Florence is anxious about what might come out.'

20

Fern at home:
Soft pink cords
White lace collared blouse
Pink Shetland wool cardigan
Pearl earrings
Dainty gold watch

It was never an easy journey for Annie to get out of the snarl of late-in-the-day traffic and onto the motorway east to go and visit her mother. But twice a week, she made it. And twice a week her sister Dinah made it too. So their mum, who had live-in care, felt as loved and well taken care of in her old age as Annie and Dinah had been in their childhood. Annie loved, loved, loved her mother, a fiercely proud, independent, encouraging, interfering, infuriating, constant in her life. She couldn't think when Fern (she and Dinah sometimes called her by her first name amongst themselves) had ever let her down. Their dad had left – or more likely been booted out – when they were small and Fern, their stalwart, their bread-winning chiropodist mum had recovered remarkably quickly. She had taken charge of everything and worked tirelessly. With the help of a no-nonsense childminder, she brought Annie and Dinah up and even wangled scholarships for them to one of London's smartest girls' schools.

As adults, Annie and Dinah had found that Fern interfered in the best kind of ways in their lives. She gave sensible and honest advice. She was a lovely grandma, who gave thoughtful, well-chosen gifts and had been such a reliable presence in their lives. There at parties and gatherings, endlessly trying to matchmake Annie with a new man, when her first husband had died suddenly. Yes, Fern had never, ever let them down. But the thing that had happened quite slowly over the past few years was that's Fern clever, hard-working brain – the one that had provided all that sensible advice, all those clever income-boosting schemes and unconditional love – that brain was now letting her down. She wasn't 'gone' but she wasn't her full, vibrant, no-nonsense vital self. She was fading.

Sometimes she forgot small things and got very upset, some-times she forgot big important things but hardly seemed to notice at all. The erosion of her memory and her thought processes was just endlessly sad, especially to her daughters, who would have given anything to have her around, the way she once was. And Annie often wondered if she'd really appreciated her mother to the full, ten years ago, even five years ago, when she was still vital and fully in charge of her life. She wished she'd spent more time with her and that they'd done more things together that she could look back on and remember. But she'd been caught up in the swirl of busy family life and trying to build her career. And she reminded herself, even in retirement, her mother had been busy, too, filling her days with friends, day trips, gardening, redecorating, and trips abroad with her two besties. She'd always seemed content, never lonely. So, maybe Annie didn't need to feel so guilty, but still there was this feeling that the time left was limited and was she making enough of it. Once people were fading, or once they were gone – that was always the regret you were left with: if only we'd had more time together. *She's still here!* she told herself firmly, *she's not dead yet!* There were still long chatty cups of tea to be drunk together, and trips to the garden centre to be had. Annie would take Fern out Christmas shopping in the months ahead, maybe even a trip into London together... to The Store even... or Liberty. Her mother had always loved Liberty. And Fern would come to theirs for one weekend every month and for three or four days over Christmas. There were still many happy times ahead she reminded herself. The traffic stopped and Annie found her lipstick in her handbag. As she applied it carefully and patted the skin under her eyes dry, she let the music from the car radio lift her heart. She pulled her shoulders back and smiled at her reflection in the mirror. Her mum was still here. There was every reason to be happy and to make the most of today.

* * *

'Hello, my darling, so what are we going to do today?' were Annie's words of greeting as she hugged her mum tightly and followed her into the kitchen, where her carer, Rosalia, was setting teacups and a plate of biscuits onto a tray.

'We're having tea in the sitting room, aren't we, Rosalia?' Fern replied. Rosalia smiled and confirmed. Then Fern added, 'Then we'll talk about the big show, Annie, and how you will have some clothes from me.'

'Tea sounds lovely and I am loving the look of those biscuits! Absolutely famished. Been about five hours since anything passed my lips.' Rosalia immediately offered to make her a sandwich, but Annie refused this saying the biscuits would keep her going until she and Fern had dinner together later in the evening.

'What do you mean we're going to get clothes from you?' Annie asked her mum as she ushered her out of the kitchen and into the sitting room while Rosalia followed with the tea tray.

'Yes... for your show,' Fern said, settling down into her favourite armchair, a comfortable upright covered in a cream and pink rose strewn chintz. *Laura Ashley,* Annie thought, her mum had bought it not long after she and then Dinah had left home. *She must have enjoyed having more money to herself, wanted to buy herself a comfortable little treat.*

Annie ran her observant eyes all over the beloved lady, approaching the eighty mark, in front of her. Fern, who used to be a stocky, bustling figure, had lost weight over the past two years and had begun to look much more like the little old lady that she was. She was neatly dressed, as always, in a pair of soft pink cord trousers, a pretty blouse and a pink cardigan. She coordinated with her chair, Annie thought with a smile. Fern's hair was a white bob, shorter and thinner than it had been in the past. In fact, around her face it looked a little wispy. The weight... gone. The hair... thinning. Fern's eyesight... dimming along with her memory.

It felt as if she was leaving Annie quietly, in stages, as if she didn't want the exit to be sudden, or dramatic, she was going to just very quietly fade away, bit by bit. Annie blinked away the tears that were threatening, took a fortifying gulp of tea and smiled a little harder. 'I love the idea of your own fashion show, Annie. You are so talented, you deserve every success,' Fern said.

'Oh, it's not really my show,' Annie jumped in, 'Svetlana is the brainchild, the main event. She's set it all in motion. I'm just her glorified helper, really.'

Fern fixed her daughter with a kind look. 'I love the idea of the show. A charity show, to help women move on in their lives. You will be wonderful, my darling. And I'm going to give you some clothes. Come on, help me up and I'll show you what Rosalia and I have laid out upstairs.'

So, holding her mother's arm, Annie guided her up the stairs into her neat little bedroom where a selection of clothes and accessories were laid out over the bed. 'You and Rosalia sorted this out for me?' Annie asked, feeling very touched. Fern nodded and sat herself down on the edge of the bed. 'That was lovely of you.'

'I hardly wear anything in my wardrobe any more,' Fern confided. 'You and Dinah and...' now came the momentary pause that suggested the wheels were turning, 'the girls,' she settled on, 'come and take what you want. Leave me with my gardening clothes and practical things.'

'Mum!' Annie protested. 'There are so many parties and Christmases and ladies who lunch events ahead. You'll need more than just your gardening clothes.' Fern held out her hand to show that she wanted Annie to take hold of it.

'Yes,' she said gently, 'parties and Christmases. Best to leave a few nice things in the wardrobe. But these...' she gestured to the pile on the bed. 'These can go now. To your fashion charity... charity fashion... you know,' she said with a sigh of effort.

'I know,' Annie said and kissed her gently on the top of her head. Annie cast her eye over the items that had been carefully laid out. She picked up a lovely camel coat that she remembered helping her mother to buy years ago in John Lewis... a friend's daughter's wedding, she remembered. Yes, there had been a time... fifteen, twenty years ago when Fern seemed to go to at least one wedding a month as all her friend's children got married. The last five years had been much more sombre, as Fern attended one funeral a month as those friends, who'd been planning weddings and partying, just a few short decades ago, all began to pass away. *'Charcoal grey,'* Annie remembered her mother instructing on a shopping trip a few years ago, *'I'd like a soft charcoal grey coat for funerals. Black is so draining on the complexion, even if you're a bottle blonde like me.'* *'With a soft lilac scarf,'* Annie remembered advising, *'everyone needs a little soft comfort and a soothing colour close to hand at a funeral.'*

'This is a gorgeous coat, Mum,' she told Fern now. 'I don't think I can let you give this away. I remember us buying it together... for a wedding...'

Fern glanced over but just gave a little dismissive wave of her hand. 'Oh... too heavy,' she said. 'I like my little quilt... quilted... one.'

There was a thing Annie hadn't considered, little old ladies finding their clothes too heavy as they grew smaller and frailer. Underneath the coat was a wonderful lizard skin clutch that her mum had owned for decades. The clutch that had accompanied her on every kind of fancy, dressed up event. There was absolutely no way that that was going to be sold off, Annie decided. Far too many memories. If she opened it up, Annie was sure she would find a packet of her mum's trusty paper tissues and a whiff of her special 'going out' perfume Chanel's fabulous No 5. No, no that couldn't go. She sorted expertly through the other things on the bed and it felt easy to make decisions. Anything that was associated with direct and warm memories would have to stay, either in her mum's wardrobe or in Annie's own. Anything that was neutral – wedding outfits she didn't help her mum to choose, or couldn't remember her mum wearing, hand-bags with no associations, hats... well, she couldn't get sentimental about hats somehow – this kind of thing could all be boxed up and added to the giveaway collection. Annie was surprised at how emotional she felt at the thought of her mother donating old and treasured clothes. Just the sight of those old, woven Jaeger labels brought a rush of nostalgia for her much younger mother coming home after a shopping trip, eager to show off the lovely skirt or gorgeous jumper she'd bought for herself. Yes, she and Dinah needed to keep many of their mother's items, even if Fern didn't want to keep them, for all the memories they brought.

As she chatted to her mother and divided the items up into donate and keep, Annie thought about Florence and that entire, jam-packed house that she was patiently working her way through, all by herself it seemed. Annie felt a deep wave of sympathy for the woman. What a sad and completely draining task. And the house was vast, she would have all the kitchen contents and packed bookcases, art works, and clutter to sort through, let alone packed wardrobes of clothes. Weeks and weeks of time. And always the worry about *'should I have given this away or kept it?'*

And now this decision to anonymously donate such priceless and important items... and Annie burdening her with having to find out where the items had come from. She should offer to help Florence, she decided. She was the one with the fashion contacts, so why not put Florence in touch with the people who could help?

* * *

'The funny one...' Fern had a look of confusion and anxiety across her face as she looked at Annie across the dinner table. 'Who is the funny one?' She couldn't remember who she was trying to ask her daughter about but Annie smiled and set her fork down.

'The funny one, that has to be Owen, doesn't it, my boy, your grandson?'

'Owen?' for a moment Fern didn't look convinced. But then she decided maybe it was Owen.

'Let's send him a message and see if he's around,' Annie suggested. 'On my phone... remember he's gone to university in Scotland.'

'Scotland?' Fern sounded vaguely horrified.

'I know, so far away... I do miss him.' She wasn't quite sure if Fern was following. It was coming up to 7 p.m. and her mother was getting tired and that was when the fading and confusion seemed much worse. She typed out a quick:

> Hello, O, I'm at Grandma's. How is your day going and do you want to send her a little message?

Ping...

She waited. Then felt quite ridiculously happy to see the little dots appearing to indicate that Owen was alive and well and reading messages on his phone.

> Hey, Mum

Owen began in that stream of tiny messages which he and every other kidult seemed to have to do.

> All good.

> Fun times.

> How is Grandma? Big hug from me.

Wait… I'll send her a crazy cat dance, she'll like that.

Annie wasn't convinced that Fern would, but she sent Owen a smiley face and some thumbs-up emojis anyway. And after a moment or two, some video or maybe animation or maybe something created in an AI bot's fever dream popped up onto her screen involving a blurry cat serving tea out of a teapot. But Annie didn't think Fern needed that kind of confusion in her life.

'Owen sent a message to give you a big hug,' she told her mother. And got a smile in return. 'Are you getting tired?'

'Oh no. But I don't like this fish,' Fern said in a tone that sounded almost like Minette's. 'I think I'd like to eat my trifle.'

'Maybe one more mouthful of fish?' Annie wondered, looking down at the plate. But Fern's face was set. 'Trifle,' she said.

'Shall I look in the fridge?'

Fern nodded.

When Annie opened the door of the fridge in her mother's kitchen, she was surprised to see that the top shelf was packed with individual M&S trifles. She took one out to take a closer look at the contents – thick custard, fruit chunks, sponge and a generous dollop of cream on top. Not exactly health food. And she couldn't remember much trifle ever being served by her mum. So, she wondered if this was a comfort food, a nostalgia food from her mother's childhood even. Maybe once you reached a certain age, you were grateful for every day and you weren't going to care about whether you should be eating one or even two trifles a day.

By the time Annie had finished up in the kitchen and had a goodnight call with the twins, Lauren and then Ed in turn, Fern was dozing in front of the TV. So, she helped her get ready for bed. And it was lovely to gently brush her hair, hold her hand and kiss her goodnight before she got into bed.

'You are spoiling me, Annie,' Fern told her.

'Yes, I am and there's nothing wrong with that. You spoiled us all – in a good way,' she added.

'Your fashion show...' Fern added dreamily. 'I don't think I can come. I'm a little busy.' Annie wondered if her mum meant that the show would be a little too busy for her, as she couldn't imagine there was a packed schedule ahead for her mum these days, especially as her two close friends had passed away in the last year.

'No problem, Mum,' Annie said gently. 'Lauren will be there and she'll make a little video for you to watch.'

'On the TV?'

'Something like that, yes.'

'Yes... the show... where you help the women who want to move on in their lives. Show them dressing for success. It's a lovely thing, Annie. A lovely thing.' *Show them dressing for success...* oh for goodness' sake! That was of course the perfect, perfect idea. As well as the professional models and the dance school girls, they had to talk to the charity and see if there were some women they were helping who would like to be involved. And now Annie's mind was racing on ahead imagining glamorous makeovers, getting the women to pick the music they wanted to strut down the catwalk to – and if they were a little shy or scared, they would go in pairs, holding hands if needed, supporting each other and doing all the good things that the charity was all about. And wouldn't Lauren love to help with this too? Because it would be worthy and purposeful.

'Mum, you are a genius,' she said, which made Fern giggle. 'Goodnight, sleep tight and I will see you in the morning.'

* * *

Once her mum was tucked up in bed, Annie settled into the sofa with her laptop and phone and fired off a volley of messages. Svetlana updates, Paula updates – and asking them both what they thought of the idea of doing a Thrive Dressing section in the show. She thought it best to get their approval before she went to the charity to ask.

Time is tight to arrange it all,

she typed,

But the more I think about it, the more I think it is a genius idea and we should do what we can to make it happen!

When it was finally bedtime, she turned off the sidelight and lay in the guest bed in the guest room looking, eyes wide open, at the dark ceiling. Honestly, she had thought she was tired, but now that the light was out, now that it was late and she had a packed day tomorrow and really should be sleeping, now her mind was brightly awake, clear as day, absolutely no chance of sleep whatsoever. All kinds of half-baked plans, suggestions, ideas and to-do lists were whirling around her head. She thought of the section of her wardrobe at home filled with all the gadgets and potential cures she'd bought in the past year to help her sleep. Valerian teabags, an acupressure mat and matching pillow, cashmere bed socks, lavender infused eye masks, a weighted blanket... pillow spray, magnesium cream, so many different vitamins and pills... nothing seemed to have worked for her.

The acupressure mat... she found herself giggling at the

memory. This 'modern equivalent of an Indian bed of nails' had proved to be so spiky that as soon as her skin had made contact with it, she'd had to try and get up, but somehow she'd fallen back down on the thing and it had dug in even worse. Until she'd had to shout for Ed to get out of bed and help her. 'For God's sake, Annie, what next?' he'd protested. 'How is stabbing yourself before bed going to help? Here's an idea for you... have you thought about giving up coffee? Or maybe not drinking it after say 2 p.m.? I think you'll find your entire sleep issue will just disappear.'

They'd gone to bed in a huff. Annie angry that he didn't understand how coffee was the only thing that got her through the day. Ed annoyed that she couldn't take this simple and obvious piece of advice. And to make things worse, one of the twins had called out in the night and when Ed had got up to go and check on them, he'd trod hard on the acupressure mat in his bare feet. So confined to the depths of the cupboard it was. Ed deserved a lovely wedding anniversary gift was her next thought. Even if he'd told her not to get one for him.

She switched on the light, picked up her phone and turned, inevitably, even though her eyes were burning with tiredness, to Google.

Perfect wedding anniversary gifts for men

she typed in. When a profusion of perfume bottles, rings and handbags appeared, she was confused, until she realised she had typed in:

Perfect wedding anniversary gifts for me

Men

Annie corrected her mistake. She looked at the suggestions that had been provided. Personalised golf clubs?! Oh, for heaven's sake. 'Siri?' she asked wearily. 'What do I get Ed as an anniversary gift?' There was a pause. That weird moment when you realise the computer is always listening. Siri wasn't thinking though, Siri was obeying the task to collect the most appropriate data. It took only moments for Siri to reply and this reply startled Annie. The answer was so good, clever, perfect! Why hadn't she thought of that?

21

Lauren with jet lag:
Baggy, light blue jeans
Black T-shirt
Big red wool cardigan (Mum's)
Pale blue trainers

Lauren lifted her head from the sofa cushion and looked around the familiar sitting room of her family home. She may have recovered from the jet lag, but she hadn't yet recovered from her big decision. She had thought quitting her job, leaving New York, and deciding to do something more worthwhile with her life would give her a great big rush of energy and optimism but instead, she was sprawled across the sofa at 11 in the morning. Ed was at school, the twins were at nursery, her mum was prepping for the show, no doubt rushing about in a crazed frenzy of trying to get everything done in time, even Owen was away at university. Lauren groaned with sheer pain at the thought of her goofy brother currently having his life more together than she did. And it wasn't as if she wasn't trying... she was scouring job ads and sending out CVs on spec. Even back in New York, she'd sent about fifty query letters out to companies, charities, organisations... all kinds of bodies that sounded as if they were doing interesting and worthwhile work. Her approach had been: *'I've learned a huge amount about marketing, communication, and social media being part of a small team in a creative business that could be so useful in helping your company/charity/organisation to become more visible and grow... then something about what interesting work they were doing... followed by... would you be interested in discussing possible openings?'*

She didn't do the CV attached thing because she did not want people at worthy, serious organisation she was approaching to look at the words 'Perfect Dress' and 'fashion company' and immediately dismiss her as frothy and never even reply. No, better to keep the mention of fashion till the last possible moment now that she was bent on changing careers. But as yet, there had either been no reply from the organisations in London that she was the most interested in, or just those awful *'Thank you for your interest, we have no openings at present'* that killed hope and made you feel that it was all utterly impossible and you were never going to find anything and would be condemned to a life on the sofa forever. She had forced herself not to look at her messages or her email more than once an hour. Because sitting waiting for replies was going to kill her. No one was getting back. No one had an opening. No one wanted her...

Oh! She gave herself a shake. Lying on the sofa sending herself into a downward spiral was not going to help. She would go into the kitchen and make a drink, nice and slowly. Then she would drink it, maybe with a light snack. And when she came back, then she would look through the messages/email/socials once again for any sign of life. Something Ed would say about 'watched pots don't boil' came into her head and she smiled at the cute, old-fashionedness of that. Not to mention the smart-alecky answer she always used to give: 'But that's against the laws of physics. The pot will boil whether I'm watching it or not!'

* * *

Her drink was drunk and her snack was eaten when she came sloping back into the sitting room and decided it was a respectable enough gap to allow herself to check messages once again. Ohmigod, there was one WhatsApp... from a name she did not recognise! She opened it up quickly.

> Do you have any experience with organising live events?

Was the question and from Preeta from Clean Up Fashion!

From Clean Up Fashion!! This was definitely interesting... this was a charity that did very worthwhile things and might actually find it useful that she had worked in fashion.

Right... live events... live events... yes, there had been fashion shows in New York for Perfect Dress, but generally, these had been small-scale and she couldn't really claim to have had a huge amount to do with them. Mainly, she'd just run errands for Svetlana and Elena. Anything else she could mention...? School things...? But that was so long ago.

> Particularly the publicity/marketing side?

dropped the new WhatsApp message. *Publicity!? Marketing?!* Yes, she had done loads of that for Perfect Dress, tonnes, never stopped... but for a live event... she had to work for these people. She had to think of something... she could feel her palm start to sweat underneath the phone. Think... think... live event, market-ing, publicity. Something you could ideally be doing right now...

Mum...!

This was of course the thought that came into her head now. She could help her mother with the charity fashion show, sticking closely to the marketing and publicity side – not running around London on one million little errands. And wouldn't Clean Up Fashion love a charity show that was all about sustain-ably recycling fashion and putting unwanted clothes into the hands of new owners? Yes, she should definitely help with the show and tell Preeta all about it.

Just one major problem though... hadn't she made complete fun of the show? Hadn't she told her mother no, she really didn't want to help because it wasn't 'her thing' any more. Lauren did feel slightly stupid about that now. It was going to be quite embarrassing having to ask her mum if she could help, after all... but if anyone would forgive her, it was her mum. She picked up her phone and read the messages again very carefully. She gave a few moments thought to her reply. Then began to type, feeling as if her whole life, her entire future depended on these words.

> Hi, Preeta, thanks so much for getting in touch. Right now, I'm helping to promote a charitable/sustainable fashion event happening in London on October 1st. I have done lots of other marketing/publicity work. Is that the kind of experience you're looking for? I'd love to...

Talk? was that too forward. *Chat?* Too casual...

> tell you more.

she decided on. For a moment, she considered asking for a call. In fact, she even thought about hitting the call button. That would be the best, bravest thing to do. Her mum would totally cheer that on. But... Lauren quailed at the thought of ringing. What would she do if Preeta actually answered? Or what if, even worse, she had to leave a message? No, no, no that was too complicated. She would have to go with her message. Put it all into the message. Create Message Gold.

> I'm Lauren btw. I would love to find out about any opportunities at Clean Up Fashion. Thanks so much.

OK, she read the whole thing over again, palms almost slippery with stress-sweat. OK, she hadn't made any typos. She didn't sound too desperate. She didn't sound too formal, or too casual. In fact, she sounded like a dynamic, busy girl doing all the right kind of things. Definitely the kind of person Preeta would surely want to meet. Lauren took a breath and hit send. Then couldn't resist giving a little scream to express both the excitement and the terror of what she'd just done. And now, of course, she needed to talk to her mother. She needed to get signed up to working on this fashion show just as soon as humanly possible.

She dialled Annie's number. 'Hello, darling, how are you doing?' came the caring but slightly breathless voice that suggested her mother was on-the-go, on her way, en route to something urgently important.

'Can I come and work for the show?' Lauren asked, deciding she might as well just come out with it.

'Of course! Of course you can! Fantastic! We need all hands on deck!' was Annie's first reaction. Followed by the almost suspicious, 'And... can I ask, what's caused this sudden change of heart?'

'Oh... so bored,' Lauren told her, making her voice sound all lifeless and fed up. 'I do not want to sit around waiting for people to not get back to me.'

'They will, darling,' Annie assured her. 'Honestly, who wouldn't want the amazingly talented Lauren working for them?'

Lauren found herself smiling, even though this was praise from her mum, so it didn't really count. 'Do you want me to come over to the venue?' Lauren asked.

'No... we're not at the venue today. So, I want you to stay at home, get on your computer and think of some clever ideas.'

'Such as?'

'Well... we've emailed people to tell them about the change of venue and...' Annie sighed, 'suddenly we have a lot of "sorry, no thanks" replies coming in. A lot,' she emphasised. 'In fact, if I see one more, I'm probably going to start crying. We can't put this whole, elaborate shebang on just for an audience of friends and family. That isn't going to work. That isn't going to get donations rolling in for us.'

'Oh dear, Mum,' Lauren sympathised. 'What is the problem? Do you think people liked the idea of the Mayfair garden more than the Gallery of Textiles?'

'But this is such a cool place!' Annie protested. 'I don't know... it's just fashion people. One person decides something is a bit "old" or "uncool" or who-knows-what and then they flock to make the same decision together.'

'So, we need the "cool" tide to turn,' Lauren said.

'Exactly! That is exactly what we need. Any ideas?'

'Hmmmmm... between you, Svetlana and me... we must have a few social media followers...' Lauren speculated.

'More than a few, babes. I'm nearly at 10,000 and Svetlana, she has tens of thousands. She was born for social media but she doesn't even realise and only posts about twice a year. But whenever she does – viral.'

'So, we need to do posts, not the boring stuff about where and when the show is, but lovely pictures of the best things coming up for sale. Get people very excited.'

'Great idea,' Annie had to agree. 'Why didn't I think of that?'

'Guess you need the comms skills and the marketing brains,' Lauren joked.

'Very good thing you have them both and you are around.'

'And can we get Svetlana to post? Sounds like she has the knack.'

Annie hesitated. 'You're not going back to Perfect Dress are you?'

'Ermmm... I don't think so...' Lauren agreed.

'Well, there is a conversation you need to have with Elena before you can fully jump into the show. Otherwise, it could cause a lot of upset.'

'Yeah...' Lauren agreed, heart sinking slightly because she wasn't looking forward to that.

22

Model Gwen:
Slim grey jeans
Tight cropped grey vest top
Black leather bomber jacket
Black pointed ankle boots

'OK, my darlings, thank you all hugely for turning up on a boring old Tuesday evening all the way out West for rehearsals. We want to make this the best time for you, so we have some nibbles and soft drinks over there,' Annie swept her hand in the general direction of the hasty buffet she and Paula had set out twenty minutes ago, curtesy of the Tesco Metro beside the Tube station. The rehearsal was two full weeks ahead of the show, because this is how difficult it had proved to fit it into the ballet girls packed schedule. Quite frankly, the ballet girls were about ten times busier during the day and evening than the two professional models who were also here tonight to show the ballet girls the ropes. And the amazing thing that was going to happen, on the actual day of the show, was that Anoush, the French model that

Annie had 'discovered' in Paris, way back when she was helping to launch Perfect Dress with an imperfect, cobbled-together fashion show in some random church, Anoush – who now had bookings with Chloe and Stella and Acne and all those mega-names, not to mention 1.2 million followers on Instagram, she was coming over to London *for free* (!) to be the star attraction on the night. However, tonight was about Paula and Annie finding the right outfits for each of the girls, working out the running order and practising the catwalk strut.

The two professional models, both friends of Paula's, were Gwen – five foot ten, intricate black and tan braids twisted up into a high ponytail before they fell down to the middle of her back. She was a gorgeous mahogany tan and lean, muscled like an athlete. The second model was Phyllis, a golden limbed, honey-haired beach girl, who looked like she'd just swerved in on a surfboard. These two girls knew each other well, so they were in a huddle of two, chatting animatedly and sipping water from monster metal Stanley cups. Meanwhile the three ballet girls – Bria, Shivani and Chloe – were in a huddle of their own a safe four or five metres away from the models. No sippy cups, instead, they had little juice bottles with straws. Maybe that was a dance school thing. Shivani was the petite, gymnast bodied of the three, her black-brown hair tied up in a strict dance-school bun. Bria, who had that Celtic look of pale, freckled skin and dark, wavy hair, was the kind of athletic size 10 who would probably be ideal for about eighty per cent of the clothes. Then came Chloe, the tall, spindly, crinkled-haired blonde who Annie already knew was going to make a fabulous bride for the show ending. But why have just one bride? They had racks of wedding dresses. Let's have six brides... maybe they could even rustle up a seventh. Seven brides had a ring to it.

'Girls, it is so lovely to see you all,' Annie began. 'Thank you so much for coming! Paula and I have set out rails and rails of all the very best clothes, so we want you to look through the racks and tell us what you like the look of. I think it's always better when the models can get a feel for things, see what catches their eye, what they might like to try on. We don't want to put you into anything that's going to make you feel uncomfortable. So, go, look through things. Then we've set up a little changing area over there, so you can get experimenting. Paula and I are here with safety pins, needles and threads and seaming tape to make sure that we can make everything fit and look as gorgeous on you as possible,' she added with her friendliest smile. This earned her a few little whoops from the seasoned models, while the dance girls gave her an anxious look. She realised she would have to look after them a little more tenderly. They were seventeen and eighteen, still a vulnerable and body-conscious age. 'You follow me, my darlings,' she instructed. 'Let's go look at the racks and see what we can come up with for you.'

So off they went to sift through the wonders carefully curated by Annie and Paula, after hours of sifting through cardboard boxes. While the grown-up models seemed to get stuck in pretty quickly, pulling out candy-pink, slithery gowns and bright velvet trouser suits and oooohing over ballgowns and tea dresses, the dance girls were shy and unsure. They flicked past one or two things and giggled a little. They blushed and seemed to make each other increasingly nervous and embarrassed. Annie and Paula found themselves exchanging slightly worried looks. The girls weren't happy. They were looking at these 'mum clothes' and beginning to worry that they would look stupid up there on stage. They were beginning to wonder what they had let themselves in for... and maybe how they could get out of it. Annie knew she had to nip this in the bud.

'You girls must be so used to dressing up and glamming up to go on stage,' she began. 'Tell me about your favourite TV shows. I bet you like *Gossip Girl? Emily in Paris?*' There were some nods and smiles in response to this. 'We are definitely going to find some Emily looks here...' she flicked deftly through the rails. 'This white dress with the big roses, pure Emily. Let's put that one out for us... now this one, all greens and blues, that's going to be amazing for our two dark-haired girls... what else? What other inspo do we want to call on? *The Summer I Turned Pretty?*' She suggested, pulling out a floaty floral dress.

This got a burst of enthusiasm too. 'And we have wedding dresses to try on too,' she pointed to the bridal rail. She'd thought this would be for later, but why not get the big guns out and really bowl them over. The dance girls looked at one another, eyebrows raised.

Bria was the first to break with a little shriek. 'Wedding dresses!!' she cried. 'C'mon, we have to try those! Shivani, Chloe, I have to see you in wedding dresses. Let's all get into wedding dresses and take photos. *Scream!*'

'Here's the rail,' Annie pointed. 'Knock yourselves out. Just go gently on the zips and seams. These are delicate fabrics with lots of silk and tulle.'

'OK,' they assured her. Almost an hour of dressing room buzz followed. As the seasoned models got louder and more excited about things, changing in and out of garments at speed, the dance girls followed their lead.

'Look at this, I love it,' Chloe said, admiring herself in a sea of bluebell-themed ballgown in the mirror.

'Then you will wear it,' Paula said, pinning a label to the back of the dress with:

Chloe/evening

Gwen and Phyllis were having a slight tussle over a slinky fuchsia-pink halterneck evening dress.

'I so need that!' Phyllis was insisting.

'Maybe you do, but I look one hundred per cent dope in this,' Gwen insisted as she scrutinised her lithe physique under the rippling pink silk in the mirror. 'Brown skin and fuchsia is the match made in heaven. I look like Grace Jones in her nightclub era. So, bad luck, white girl,' she teased her friend. 'Go and find something pastel!'

Meanwhile, Annie could sense that Bria, although she'd been in and out of a few nice things, hadn't yet found the wow item. 'Bria... we have this idea for a whole eighties section. We have a bit of an explosion of eighties clothes, especially skirt suits. We have TV and film wardrobe people coming, because they buy a lot of vintage, so we need to show all this power dressing off to its best advantage... and I'm thinking you, lovely shapely legs, great for skirts, nice broad shoulders perfect for the power jackets. You could lead the eighties for us. We'll curl your hair, give you some bold lipstick... any favourite eighties songs we could blast down the catwalk while you strut?'

She knew from her own children's taste in music that many a 'vintage' eighties song was popular again.

'Oh...' there was some life to Bria's face now. 'Well... I like Madonna.'

'Perfect!' was Annie's verdict. 'We all love Madonna. In fact, Paula, why have we got no music on while we're doing this?'

'Good question!' Paula took out her phone, found a glass to put it into and instructed: 'Siri, play Madonna's greatest hits, please.' And within moments, Madonna's 'Vogue' was livening everything up and Annie was guiding Bria into a silky blouse, a bright checked skirt suit, then bouffing up her hair a little.

'Wait, wait,' Annie was searching the shoe rack, 'what size are you?'

'Six,' Bria replied.

'Oooooh, these,' Annie suggested, holding a pair of kitten-heeled pumps. 'Oh, and leave your ankle socks on. That is perfect!' And for the first time that evening, Bria saw herself in the mirror and gave a huge grin of approval.

'Oh yes!' she declared. 'And I bet there's eighties jewellery in your boxes somewhere. Clip on earrings, chunky necklaces.'

'Of course!' Annie assured her. 'Paula and I are going to get all that together once you've picked your outfits. We will be styling you from head to toe.'

'This is so exciting!' Bria said and turned to admire her friends again, one in a wedding dress and one in the *Emily in Paris* cream with big roses tea dress. This was starting to give Annie a feeling of... excitement, nostalgia, and even purpose. She had so missed the makeovers she used to do at The Store. The real life, down and dirty makeovers, where women came in looking sad and uncertain and overwhelmed, and left renewed, reignited, remembering just who they were supposed to be. She caught Paula's eye.

'I miss The Store,' she whispered.

This just made Paula smile before she instructed the girls loudly. 'Time to learn how to strut your stuff. To the catwalk!'

* * *

There wasn't really a catwalk. Not tonight, not for rehearsal. That would have required engineers, roadies, rigging, insurance waivers, clipboard wielding men in hi-vis jackets – and a much bigger budget. What they did have was a runway of 'approximate length and width' marked out with whatever Paula and Annie had been able to find – several brochures, two high-heeled shoes, an empty Pret sandwich box, three coffee cups, half-full, and, for symmetry, a pair of tatty evening bags that had seen better nights. Still, they had discovered a proper speaker, so Paula connected her phone and instructed Siri to: 'Play fashion show, chapter one,' and all at once, the venue was pulsing with music that made everyone feel as if they had just upgraded to Milan.

'Right, Gwen and Phyllis, you are on!' Annie instructed. 'Show us all your best moves, so our beautiful dance girls can see what they need to be doing.' Gwen and Phyllis did not disappoint. Gwen in the slinky fuchsia and Phyllis in a classic black evening gown both strutted with lethal precision, hip bones jutting and swaying from side to side, in classic catwalk style. The walk always looked slow and slinky but it was surprisingly pacy, designed to march the dresses out there and sell, sell, sell. The dance girls were clapping them on and it was impossible not to be caught up in the buzz of the moment.

'OK, my lovely dancers,' Annie called, 'jump in and just follow Gwen and Phyllis up and down. Copy the walk, the twirl at the end of the catwalk, and slouch, babes! Give it all the moody slouching that you can. Hand on hip, hand on hip, smoulder, smoulder and *turn!*' Naturally, the dancers nailed it. So used to moving in new and interesting ways, they had the slouch, the walk and the turn down within moments.

'This is brilliant!' Annie beamed. 'You look so professional!'

* * *

When the rehearsal was over and the girls had departed, Annie and Paula were left to label up all the outfits with names and running order and carefully box them up for the real event. And that was when Paula asked what the update was on the Schiaparelli items and the other special treasures.

'Are we going to be allowed to show them? Will that be a special final round at the end... after the bridal party?'

'Oh...' Annie began. She had no news yet, and had to find the time to visit Florence, see how she was getting on and offer to help. 'Trying to find out more, urgently,' Annie told Paula. 'And if we are able to show them... we'll probably need security guards. I mean those dresses could be worth hundreds of thousands of pounds.'

'Ha... remember when the new jewellery came into The Store? And there would be guards with helmets and vests and those suitcases that were handcuffed to their wrists?'

'Oh yes! I do remember that. It was so exciting! God, I miss The Store,' Annie declared.

'You do not,' Paula declared. 'It was drudgery, those hours, that crummy pay! Even with our staff discounts, we could barely afford a pair of tights from that place!'

'But we were such a good team and it was lovely being there, surrounded by staff and all the clients, even the difficult ones. It felt like a community, a family even.'

'I think you're remembering the very nice things and forgetting a lot of issues.'

And maybe this was true. The pay had been poor and sometimes the work had been stressful or utterly boring. But there had also been so many nice things about it. 'The seasons...' she went on, 'remember how much love went into Christmas... the pre-Christmas windows, the décor, all the excited women coming in to buy presents and outfits, and all the hopeless husbands on December 24th needing us to choose everything for them.'

'And the total and utter carnage of the sales...' Paula

reminded her, 'let's not forget about that. Annie, you work in TV now, you are living the dream!'

'It's not the same,' Annie confessed. 'Not the same team feeling at all. We only see each other for part of the year. There's different crew every time. It feels insecure and as every season closes, I'm convinced they won't hire me again. They'll bring in a younger number.'

'Don't be silly,' Paula protested. 'You have a fan base.'

'I'm not being silly. It happens in TV all the time.'

The trials of freelance TV life were huge, Annie couldn't help thinking to herself. It always looked so much more glamorous from the outside. And, to be honest, she had loved the freelance freedom and the long breaks between filming seasons when the children were small. But lately, maybe because she was older and life was more serious, she was beginning to long for something more stable and solid, something that didn't rely on being popular with strangers, where she was in danger of being upgraded to a cooler model; something that felt like a real career with promotions and career goals and sick pay and all the things that hadn't mattered so much when she was younger. But no need to dump all that on Paula right now, especially as she was in the early days of running her own company. Annie pulled her phone out to check it and was a little surprised to see she'd missed four calls from Lauren... now what for goodness' sake?

23

Lauren at home:
Grey jogging bottoms
White sports socks
Huge black and white T-shirt
Neon pink hoop earrings

'I need to call Lauren,' she told Paula, who immediately scowled.

'Will you at least help me finish packing up here before you get involved in your next family drama,' Paula insisted. Reluctantly, Annie put her phone down. Of course she should help Paula and they should pack up for the night before she got back to Lauren and listened to whatever mini-drama she had no doubt blown up into monumental proportions in her mind. Paula was holding up her own phone and taking some pictures. 'For the 'Gram,' she said, 'got to get the feed about the show buzzing.'

Annie smiled and posed beside the box of clothes they were packing up. 'Hang on,' she suggested, 'let's just drape a sleeve or two over the edge artfully, as a little teaser.' Paula took the photo, checked Annie was happy with it, then with some rapid-fire tapping, she'd edited and enhanced it, captioned and uploaded it to the Instagram page. For a moment or two, Paula seemed to be staring at her screen with a strange expression on her face.

'What's wrong?' Annie asked. 'Has Svetlana posted something strange?'

'No... errrrrm... the last post on this account has had 10,560 likes and over 2,000 shares and it was only posted twenty-five minutes ago.'

'That sounds like a lot... I thought we only had a few hundred followers on this account.'

'Correct,' Paula said.

'What's the post of?'

Paula turned her phone around and there was a photo of the beautiful lobster dress lying spread out on the clean white duvet of Annie's very own bed.

'But—!' Annie protested. 'We don't know if we can sell it yet! We don't know enough about it! What if it turns out to be a fake... or stolen... or who knows what? Oh God! I have a horrible feeling Lauren did this and now she is having a panic. Good grief! I'm having a panic! We're not supposed to be saying anything about those items yet. We have to wait and see what Florence can discover first. But now she's gone and announced it to the whole bloody world. Oh my God, the likes have gone up past 13,000 just while I've been looking. This is crazy!'

'I need to phone her, she has to take it down,' Annie added, scrambling for her own phone.

'Comments are flying in,' Paula added.

* * *

'Lauren, it's me. What's going on?' Annie asked her daughter, as she tried to keep calm. 'You have to take down the dress post. I had no idea you were doing that. That is not cleared for sale yet. So nice and quickly now, please, take it down!'

'What?!' Not surprisingly, Lauren sounded very taken aback at this instruction. 'Not cleared for sale?! But why didn't you tell me?'

'Well... I had no idea you were going to do this, did I?' Annie spluttered. 'Why would you do this? Why would you go through stuff without asking me, then post it online? What even made you think of doing this? I asked you for some ideas!'

'Well, I looked in those bags for nice things to photograph for the show's feed. I wanted to create some buzz. You didn't say that I couldn't,' Lauren protested. 'I can't take it down now,' she pointed out. 'It's going to be at 20,000 likes in a minute or two. There are nearly 1,000 comments. It's been shared, reposted... This is insane. I've never seen anything like it.'

'Lauren! Oh my God! What have you done?' The full realisation that the Schiaparelli dress was out there on the internet before there had been any information from Florence was only beginning to dawn on Annie.

'There were so many refusals coming through,' Lauren protested. 'So, I thought I better try and do something to get people excited again. So, I went to the bag and chose the nicest things. I didn't know!' she repeated.

'It's all gone mad,' Annie said. 'It's been shared over 6,000 times now. Does that mean it's definitely too late to take it down?'

'So what's the problem exactly?' Lauren asked.

'The problem is... well, the dress has been donated, but we don't have enough information about it to be selling it... we don't know if it's genuine for a start. And Florence, who donated it, doesn't know either. What wording did you use in your post?'

Paula was the one who read aloud: 'Vintage treasures/Fashion Gala Charity Sale, London, Oct 1st.'

'That sounds OK... no over-promising,' Annie added.

Then Paula squeaked. 'Look!! The latest comment is from the New York Museum of Costume... they want to talk to us about buying the dress, pre-sale.'

'OMG, there's a comment from PaigeP...' Annie said, scrolling down the list. She could hardly believe it. A comment from PaigeP! Annie's very own fashion guru.

'What does she say?' Lauren asked from the other end of the line. Annie read out: '"Can't wait to come to this show and see what other astonishing treasures are for sale. This looks like the event of the season..." Oh my good bloody grief. This is unbelievable.'

After a deep breath, Annie told Lauren, 'OK, sit still, don't post anything else. Don't reply to anything... I'm going to try and work out what to do next. Oh, now I've got Svetlana on the other line. See you soon, babes.'

Annie ended one call and accepted the next. '*Annah!* Have you seen the socials? We have arrived!' Svetlana gushed. There was so much enthusiasm in these words that Annie didn't think now was the time to talk about permissions not being in place and those sort of... ermmm... minor details. 'I have all these messages and emails coming in,' Svetlana was telling her, 'asking for more information, asking for interview... did I even know about this famous dress, *Annah?* Did you tell me and I forget? There is so much going on, I can't remember what you have told me about this or not.'

Annie decided to slightly fudge it. 'Same, my darling, same...' she said vaguely. 'Look, we've had a wonderful rehearsal here. Let me get home and I will speak to you tomorrow about all the vintage treasures we have. So, don't do any interviews until we've spoken. Well, of course, you can be interviewed, if you want. But can you please keep it a bit vague until I get you all the details? Is that OK?' She wondered if that was going to be enough. She knew the fashion pack, vintage Schiaparelli had been dangled before them and they probably wouldn't stop until they got their hands on it.

'I've had an idea,' Svetlana said, 'I think we should have some gold VIP tickets, selling for... £500.'

'What! That's a lot... people will expect a lot of attention for £500.'

'*Tscha*... but we will give it to them, no?'

Five hundred pounds... gold tickets... Annie had the feeling, yet again, that things were getting out of her control. Just when she thought she was back at the reins, another problem or plan seemed to appear. It was exhausting.

'Leave it to me,' Svetlana said, 'I will make the tickets, I will pick the guest list... some very interesting people are about to get an upgrade.'

I need to remain calm... Annie was telling herself. I need to go home and get through the evening, then I need to go and see Florence first thing tomorrow. She'll be in the house... she'll talk to me... she'll help me to sort all this out before the full fashion pack descends. Even as she had these thoughts, likes and comments were still pouring in.

Schiaparelli original!!
This is incredible!!
What's the provenance of this dress?
Can you prove it's authentic?
Does the V&A know this dress is going up for sale?
Surely the Louvre should be informed?

She decided it might be best to close the phone for now and focus on getting home. 'So, what exactly is going on?' Paula had to ask as Annie put her phone in her bag and turned her attention to getting the last boxes packed up. 'Is there a problem with selling those amazing clothes?'

'I don't know yet,' was Annie's honest answer. 'Look, hopefully I can get this all completely sorted out tomorrow. That's the best-case scenario. So, let's not worry about it until we need to. Why don't we try to get excited about all this amazing hype and attention we're getting.'

'If you get everything all cleared for sale, then you are a hero, Annie. If you don't get it cleared and we have to completely backtrack... that could be a big, noisy fashion scandal, Annie. And it will be a long time before you hear the end of it.'

'Got it, Paula... got it,' Annie said, feeling her heart begin to race. The words 'a big, noisy fashion scandal' ringing in her ears. Fashion scandal... career suicide... *let's not worry about it until we need to?* Had she just said that? Well that was going to be impossible.

24

Annie at the door:
Navy blue wool princess coat
Navy blue cardigan
White vest top
Layered pearl necklaces in multi-shades
Pink, blue and black pleated midi-skirt
Black, heeled boots

Ed had left for school, the twins were both at nursery, Lauren was at home making social media posts according to exact instruction, the internet was still blowing up about vintage Schiaparelli dresses coming up for sale in London soon... and Annie was once again standing quietly, hesitantly, in front of the blue-grey door where this story had all begun. She tugged a little at the lapels of her coat, smoothed a hand over her hair and admitted to herself that she was feeling nervous. Florence was grieving the death of her mother and preparing for the sale of a beloved family home. She'd wanted to donate the items anonymously and probably had not wanted to be involved in any kind of digging up of the past. And now, here was Annie on her doorstep, telling her that the digging up of the past would have to be done. Because the dress had been made public. Florence couldn't turn back now. Everyone wanted to know if that dress was real and where exactly it had come from.

Annie put her hand up to the doorbell and wondered exactly what to say and how to say it... she would have to hope that her words would turn out right. She pushed on the bell, not too short, so that Florence wouldn't hear if she was tucked somewhere at the back of the house, not too long. She waited and listened for any sign that Florence was in the house. There was the sound of footsteps now, coming down the corridor. Then a series of unlocking and unchaining noises and finally the blue-grey door was opened. Florence looked startled to see her on the threshold.

'Oh... hello, Annie. I didn't expect to see you... Aren't you busy putting on a huge fashion show?' There was always something a little too brusque about Florence. She was all closed and buttoned up. She never seemed very pleased to see you and she certainly didn't give the impression that she wanted to make a new friend. She was in her familiar dark, complicated clothes, her neat, silvered bob looking smoothly washed, brushed and sharply cut.

'Very busy, Florence... busy as the proverbial bee,' Annie told her cheerfully.

There was a pause between the two as Florence waited for Annie to explain why she was on her doorstep at 9.30 a.m. 'Florence, would it be OK if I came in? I wanted to talk to you privately, if that's OK. I won't take up too much of your time.'

'You look very serious...'

'Do I? Oh... it's not that bad!' Annie smiled and tried to act a bit more relaxed. 'I'm sure we'll get to the bottom of it.'

'Oh... hmmm...'

Something of a frown seemed to cross Florence's face, so now Annie was wondering if maybe Florence knew, or suspected, what she was here to talk about. Florence turned from the door and began to walk down the hallway. She didn't exactly invite Annie to follow her, but Annie did anyway, closing the front door gently behind her. Florence turned right with Annie following into what had once been a beautiful sitting room but had grown faded over the years. The chintz curtains looked worn and the fabric was threadbare and torn in places. The thick pink carpet had a matted look to it and the furniture was saggy and tired. There was no denying the beauty of the paintings though. They had not faded over the years. Big, bold landscapes, portraits and abstracts full of bright sunshine colours and deep, cobalt blues. 'Those are so beautiful,' she told Florence.

'Not painted by my father,' Florence explained, 'but chosen by my mother. She loved everything to be bright and bold and vivid.'

'The minimal home I'm imagining you live in is going to look quite different with all these hanging on the walls.'

'Oh no,' Florence shook her head. 'I couldn't live with these. They would be screaming at me. I have a friend who might like them.'

'Oh, I see...' Annie said, but she wasn't sure if she did. It just seemed harsh to give your mother's things away because they didn't match up to your stringent taste standards. Hadn't she just agreed to house a lot of twenty-five-year-old Jaeger items because she couldn't bear for her own mother to give them and all the memories they contained away?

'Have a seat,' Florence suggested. Annie sat in one of the large, flowery armchairs, but Florence didn't take a seat. Instead, she went over to a bookcase and located a carved wooden box, which she opened up. Then she approached Annie holding what looked like two folded letters in her hand. 'I'm guessing you want to talk to me about the Schiaparelli dresses. Am I right?'

Annie nodded but didn't say anything about the publicity yet.

'I have discovered some background information as I've been sorting through the house. But I don't have the full story yet.' She handed the letters to Annie, who unfolded both pages and could see that both were from the Fondacion Dubois-Lafayette in Paris and sent many years apart. They were addressed to Florence's mother, Emily Perkins, and had been sent directly to the house. Both referred to 'items' from 'a private collection' that had been designated for the Gallery but had not arrived there. The gallery said that it had 'reason to believe that these items are in your possession'. The Gallery urged Mrs Perkins to contact them and in the second letter there was talk of legal action if she refused to make contact or offer any explanation as to how the items came to be in her possession.

'And do you think this is reference to the Schiaparelli pieces?' Annie asked Florence. 'There isn't anything else in the house that this could refer to?'

Florence's lips seemed to draw into a line at these words. 'Are you suggesting that my mother went around purloining all kinds of items without permission?' she asked frostily.

'No... no, of course not. I'm sorry if that's how it sounded,' Annie was quick to reply.

'My mother was artistic, creative, she could be vague and a little careless of the details, but I'm certain she was honest. She was always scrupulous about filing her accounts, her taxes, returning borrowed items to friends, from valuable books to pieces of Tupperware. That doesn't sound like the behaviour of someone who would steal things she knew to be valuable.'

'No... of course it doesn't... I just meant, how to be sure it refers to the clothes. Not a misunderstanding over something else?'

'Well, this Fondacion in Paris has a huge costume and textile section with all kinds of historical couture items. I looked it up; it even has some Schiaparelli items on the website. A wonderful pink cape with a fabulous gold embroidered sun... the same design as the sun on the black evening jacket.' A thought seemed to occur to Florence.

'On the website, it gives the name of the benefactor. Do you think I should try to find out more about them? Try to contact them... maybe they would know something? I mean, it is extraordinary to think that these wonderful things, which could have been on display in museums across the world, have been hanging in my mother's wardrobe for years... maybe even decades. And I don't know the first thing about how they came into her possession. It's just so very strange, Annie... a genuine mystery. I expected to come across all kinds of things as I emptied this house. I expected to come across all kinds of feelings and memories and difficulties and I worried so much about all the decisions I will have to make... what to keep, what to sell... donate... throw away, absolutely none of it is easy...'

'No.' Annie agreed gently.

'But I didn't expect anything like this. For a story, a mystery, perhaps some unknown dimension of my mother I didn't even know about to be discovered.'

'She lived for ninety-four years – that's a long and interesting life. There might be quite a lot of things you find out about her and your father while you're packing up. A house can hold a lot of secrets,' Annie added – especially one so large and packed full, she thought.

'So, the Schiaparelli pieces and the other lovely vintage items... I suppose I thought I could drop them off with you anonymously, see them go to good homes and keep it all completely hush hush from my mother's side. I completely underestimated how valuable and famous they were.'

'Well, you're right there,' Annie agreed. 'There was no way we were going to sneak these dresses up onto stage and just quietly sell them off to a museum or a very wealthy collector. They are world-famous... which is why what's happened is a bit of a problem...'

Yes, it was time for Annie to admit that there was a problem. The photo had been posted online, the fashion world had paid attention and now, Florence was rapidly going to have to solve the mystery of how her mother came to own a world-famous dress before the entire fashion show went down in a flaming ball of reputation-damaging scandal. Even thinking those words was giving Annie a sickly jittery feeling.

'The truth is, Florence,' Annie decided it would be best to just get this over with, 'an image of the lobster dress has been shared on social media, in connection with the show, and—'

'It's all blown up,' Florence said, understanding straight away.

'Yes... we've been asked for more information, for interviews. Famous museums want to talk to us about a pre-sale purchase. So, it's a lot to deal with.'

'And what have you said?'

'Barely anything, Florence, that's why I was at your door first thing. I need to ask you what I do now. Maybe we need to consider together what's best.'

Annie couldn't help being impressed with how calm and fearless Florence appeared, as she listened intently, with one hand on her hip.

'Florence, you look like a woman who has an important job, you must have managed a crisis or two.'

'Well, that's a whole other issue,' Florence said as she finally took a seat. 'I'm a judge,' she said finally. 'Retired.'

'Oh! I didn't expect that,' Annie admitted, managing to sound a little less surprised than she felt. 'Explains all the black outfits though,' she risked with a smile.

Florence caught her eye and smiled back. 'You'd think I'd want a change out of the office.'

'Maybe you love colourful underwear.'

At this, Florence looked momentarily taken aback, but then she gave a burst of laughter. 'Very funny,' she said.

'And are the big sunglasses for disguise purposes?'

'Something like that,' Florence said.

While Annie wondered about two artistic parents producing a daughter who had become a judge, she asked, 'So this is why everything needs to be done anonymously and keep you and your mother well out of the limelight. And certainly, free from any kind of ownership doubts.'

'Yes and, ideally, I need to establish how these items got to my mother, so they can be sold with an entirely clean conscience.'

'Yes,' Annie agreed.

'How long have we got till the show now?'

'I don't even know if I want to think about that. I just have no idea how we're going to get ready in time and that's not a lie... your Honour,' Annie joked.

Again, she was treated to another burst of Florence's laughter. 'A judge...' Annie mused. 'For serious crimes?'

Florence gave just the slightest nod to confirm and added, 'Retired now though,' to remind Annie.

'No wonder you're a private person. I mean, do you have security... a bodyguard? Do people ever want to...?'

Florence shook her head. 'No, no, it's not Sicily. I think there's a code of honour among criminals that the judge is only doing their job. But, yes, my circle of friends is small and I live in a top-floor flat with a video entry phone. That's enough security for my liking.'

'It's funny you live in a flat, when your parents were such obvious gardeners,' Annie said and this was based on her observation of the front garden alone. Behind the house, she expected there was a wonderful town garden with a café table, parasol and profusion of flowers.

'I have a lot of pot plants,' Florence told her. 'And a lovely terrace. So, back to the problem of the dresses and their origins... how long do I have? How long can you hold the fashion pack at bay?'

'This is a big ask, Florence, the fashion pack is very determined. You've not really got more than a day or so to at least give me something to work with... something I can tell them. At the moment, we are saying nothing, just "coming soon" and "all will be revealed".'

'Right.' Florence leaned back in her chair and frowned. 'I will start with the Fondacion that had contacted my mother... and track down the donor of the other items. If that gets me nowhere, I will be in touch and we can brainstorm other ideas.'

'Let me take your number, if that's OK,' Annie suggested. 'So I don't have to turn up at your door like a fashion stalker.' Annie's phone had been pinging steadily throughout their conversation and as she got it out to take Florence's number, she couldn't help just taking a scroll through her notifications.

Svetlana's gold VIP passes were going down a storm.

Paula was pointing out that with 500 extra guests, more chairs, more speakers were needed. Plus, she added frantically:

> And btw who is doing the music? Have we def
> booked DJ? And what about lights? We talked
> about needing lights, has that been actioned?

Message from Anoush saying she was thrilled to be flying in for this.

Message from Owen… thank God! He was alive and finally in touch!

> Mum, I have no money left… like zero. What's
> happened? Have I been robbed?

Casual Connor:
Chunky petrol-blue merino roll-neck
Soft black cords
Cashmere socks
Grey suede Birkenstocks

'Owen! It's me, Mum, I just got your message,' she barked into the phone as she left Florence's and began to walk towards the Tube station. By some miracle, he had actually picked up. At least having zero money meant he couldn't afford to be anywhere but in his room eating whatever morsels might happen to be left in his fridge. She pictured him looking dubiously at the pot of cottage cheese she had bought him but she was completely certain he'd never touched.

'How are you?' she asked, a little bowled over with happiness at the sound of his voice. It had been over a week since they'd spoken.

'I'm good apart from this,' he told her. 'Going to class, study-ing, practising, making friends, doing my laundry, remembering to eat...' He reeled off the list. 'It's a lot,' he added. 'Sometimes the laundry takes the hit. My T-shirt is getting a bit stiff with all the deodorant I've had to spray on it,' he joked.

'Yes, it's a lot,' she agreed, 'learning how to look after yourself. It's a pretty good life skill though. So... have you spoken to the bank? Have they noticed anything? Have they frozen your cards?'

'Spoken to the bank?' Owen protested. 'This isn't the 1990s! You can't speak to your bank. Turns out you can send the chat bot a message, which it says will be answered in two working days or you can be in a queue for about three hours to talk to some poor exhausted person in the Philippines.'

'Yeah...' Annie sighed. There was a lot about the trials of adulthood that Owen was about to learn. 'Have you looked through your statement online?' was her next question. 'Can you see anything odd? Names you don't recognise? And there's *no* money left... from the monthly money we've given you and your monthly loan money?'

It was not lost on Annie that this was the 12th. Not even mid-month.

Owen was clearing his throat awkwardly. 'Well, the payment for my halls went out... that was a biggie.'

'Yeah...'

'And I've looked through everything else and... well, food is expensive...'

'Yeah...'

'And going out and buying drinks is expensive...'

'Yeah...' she agreed, getting the feeling where this was headed. 'And I thought I had more money in my account when I looked, so I bought a very cheap second-hand guitar off someone, which was a brilliant deal, but now... well, some payments have gone through from last week and...'

'Basically, are you the one who has emptied the bank account? Not some mysterious AI bot scammer.'

Now it was Owen's turn to mutter, 'Yeah,' in a downhearted way.

Annie was keen not to rush in and offer to fill the money crater Owen had created. The first month of adulting was always going to be hard. 'Have you already paid the guitar guy?' she asked.

'Yeah.'

'Do you think there's any chance you could say you've changed your mind? Or could you get half your guitar money back and tell him you'll pay the rest and pick up the guitar next month?' Annie suggested.

'Mum!' Owen complained.

'Well... you've got three choices here: return the guitar, go into overdraft, beg parents for money now and you'll have a lot less next month. Or there's find some work up there, I suppose. Maybe guitar lessons,' she ventured.

'Not a terrible idea.'

'Busking?' was her next suggestion. 'Now that you've got a nice new-to-you guitar. I don't think that's particularly lucrative though.'

'If I get some money back for the guitar... for now... will you and Dad advance me £200 on next month?'

'A hundred and fifty,' she countered. 'And you'll have to discover the joys of beans on toast and quiet nights in playing... dominoes,' she joked.

'Very funny, but everyone else is broke too now, so maybe we'll all stay in and watch TV together.'

'Sounds like a plan.'

'Did Lauren ever run out of money in New York?' was Owen's next question. This made Annie laugh.

'New York!! Of course she ran out of money in New York. She was in New York! In fact, she still owes me money, thanks for the reminder!'

'OK, gotta go. Speak soon. I'm off to speak to a guy about a guitar.'

'Love you, Owen, take care. You don't have to talk to me every day, but you have to message. At least every second day. OK?' She wasn't about to tell him that her new way of checking he was alive was opening Instagram to see if there was a recent update on when he had last been on. She wondered how many other mothers all over the world took a little peek on social media once a day just to see the little green dots and know that their loved ones, even if they weren't messaging or replying to messages, were safe and well.

* * *

'Connor McCaby... it's your best friend Annie calling,' Annie began in her nicest possible voice as she came out of the Tube and began to walk briskly towards the Gallery of Textiles. 'How are you doing? And how much cashmere do you need before winter kicks in? I may be able to source N Peal, direct from the manufacturer, maybe even some last-season Missoni.'

'Oooooh, Missoni, I think I could rock a multi-coloured crocheted cardigan. I've lost the holiday weight and my trainer thinks my shoulders are almost perfect. Almost, Annie, because we need something to aim for. Now, what hideously insulting and demeaning thing is it you need me to do in order to earn my crocheted cashmere?'

'Well... I don't know if you're going to like this.'

'No, I already know I'm not.'

'You know about our fashion show, and by the way, everyone is talking about it and everyone is coming.'

'Funny you should say that,' he interrupted... 'I heard two people, and they were important and stylish people talking about it in the gym sauna this morning.'

'Oh... really? Is that good?'

'That is very, very good. So... hit me up, what's the request?'

'Svetlana has hired Vince Hastie to be the compère—'

'WHAT? You can't go with him,' Connor protested. 'He's so outdated. Honestly, he's not even last decade. Some of those jokes are from the 1990s.'

'I know...'

'And there are rumours...'

'I know...' Annie said.

'And some of them might be true...'

'Yup... most likely...'

'And honestly, Annie,' Connor sounded serious, 'he could be a liability to put on stage these days, because some really odd and inappropriate stuff could come out of that man's mouth.'

Annie sighed. 'Svetlana knows him and she's booked him and I'm terrified.'

'You should be. The whole thing could be a PR disaster if he's involved.'

'So, my friend Paula, you remember her...?'

'Love Paula, she learned everything from you.'

'No, she has her own sassy style too,' Annie wanted to make that clear. 'Anyway, we had a very, very good idea. Paula's idea really—'

'Sack Vince and use me instead?'

'We can't sack Vince...'

'Oh no...' Connor paused. 'I don't think I like where this is headed.'

'We think if you compère with Vince, you'll be amazing. You can just completely roast him if he does anything cheesy, call him out if one inappropriate syllable comes out of his mouth and best of all, you'll be able to bring joy, sparkle, laughter and charm to the evening, where Vince would have brought... just cringe.'

There was a longer pause. She respected it and gave Connor time to think.

'This is for charity right? I'm going to be paid in cashmere and goodwill.'

'Maybe even a vintage Mulberry messenger bag if you play your cards right...'

'Any Burberry?' Connor decided to up the offer.

'I can get my hands on Burberry for you... does this mean you are thinking about it?'

'Too soon, Annie, too soon... more bribery and flattery are required.'

Gallery of Textiles was in view, Annie had lights to find, a DJ to interview, so, so many clothes to sort out – a tsunami of clothes – and all the other things on her list. But still, she sat down on one of the benches set out in front of the gallery and gave Connor fifteen minutes of her undivided attention. Because, she decided, it was totally worth it.

Everything she told him was true. He would be wonderful; he could totally work a double act with Vince and make it very funny. An audience of important and interesting people would be there and it might lead to interesting opportunities. Plus, he would be doing her a huge, huge favour and she always knew she could count on him and he could count on her. At the end of her long, persuasive talk, he was basking in her flattery. She could hear it in the warm and sunny tones in his voice. But then out he came with the proviso: 'I think it's a good idea, but I'll have to talk to my agent.'

'What?!' she protested. 'No! I want you to say you're a yes now!'

'New agent, baby, I can't do anything without checking in with him first. He's very protective, very mission focused. I can't go wandering about doing things that are "off brand" any more.'

'Well, when can you check with him, Connor? Can you give me an answer later today? Tomorrow?' Annie was aware that her voice was rising and she sounded a little panicked.

'Ermmmm... not till the end of the week. He's on his wellness retreat – Bikram yoga and a detox. He "steps away" from his phone during this time and gives himself a "mental reset."' Annie took a breath. She tried to imagine herself on a wellness retreat, doing Bikram yoga, eating only healing, detoxing food, stepping away from her phone and her giant mental checklist of obligations. A mental reset... how would she feel, how would she think, how would she be after a total mental reset?

It sounded wonderful. Sounded like exactly what she should book herself in for after this show was finished. 'Well, babes, that sounds completely incredible. But you send him a telegram if you have to and tell him that helping out his oldest friend for charity is totally, 100 per cent on McCabe brand. And you will be knee-deep in cashmere, babes. Knee-deep.'

'For you, Annie, I will try. And that's a promise.'

26

Action Paula:
Fuchsia pink blouse
Lashings of gold chains
Turquoise blue wide-legged trousers
Gold trainers
Interesting glass, Perspex and semi-precious stoned rings

So, then it was time to say goodbye to Connor, shoulder her bags, brace herself and get into the gallery and get on with the many tasks of the day: clothes, sort lights, perk up Paula, soothe Svetlana, rein in fashion pack, make no comment and cross fingers, music... scour websites and reviews, ring round to check on availability, chairs, order more, find more, bring in all the chairs in the surrounding area, VIP guests, talk at length to Svetlana about what else could be done to make the VIP guests feel as VIP as possible... without making all the other guests feel second-class, of course. Then there were those very persistent Instagram messages and now emails from the New York museum curator. Carina Delroy was very, very interested in the lobster dress. She was very insistent about having a call, exploring options, getting a consortium together to make an offer that would take the dress off the table and sweep it to New York.

ANNIE

We're not ready to talk about the dress yet.

Annie messaged her once again:

ANNIE

As soon as we are, you will be the first person to get my call.

CARINA

Make it so.

I've already bought my ticket to the show and I'm about to book my flight.

Oh my good grief... this woman was keen.

* * *

It was a long day at the fashion show coalface. As soon as Annie had dealt with one problem, another would crop up. There wasn't enough coffee in the building to deal with all the headaches and there wasn't enough time to go out and get more. When she looked at the time, somehow the day had galloped away and it was approaching 7 p.m.!! For a moment, she suffered the terrible thought that she'd completely forgotten to collect the twins. But then she got her bearings, remembered that it was Ed's early finish and the twins would no doubt be home now, full of nice food and fun and hoping to get some time with her before bed.

'Go, go, Paula, you've been here even longer than me,' Annie urged her friend. 'Yes, I'll get this last lot down to the basement.'

See, that's how lovely the Gallery of Textiles people were, they had given the show its own little section of basement storage space, so Annie and Paula could wrangle all their boxes and rails into order. Annie loaded up with the two boxes and one large carrier bag that she could manage and headed for the lift. The Gallery of Textiles had closed its doors hours ago, so it was all locked up and the main lights were off. But there was a fire door at the back of the building that they were allowed to leave by when working late and there were several security guards in a little back office, who kept an eye on the building overnight. Some of the room must be alarmed, she guessed, but there hadn't been any issues with walking along corridors or going up and down to the basement after hours. So, she cheerfully shouldered her load and took the lift down to the basement.

Once she was there, it was a right turn down the corridor to their storage room. Annie set down her boxes and bags and took out her key. She slipped the Yale key into the lock, opened the door and carefully pushed in the timer light button all the way to give her as long a blast of light as possible. These old-fashioned timer lights were a pain, always popping out and leaving you rushing back out to push them in again. But, in a building of this size, she could understand why they didn't want to risk lights being left on in a basement storage room for hours on end.

* * *

Annie moved the cardboard boxes into the basement storeroom and wedged her tote bag in the doorway. Then she lifted the boxes one by one onto their places on the shelf and, now that she was down here, decided to look for the box labelled:

Handbag stall, Box 7

Just a little peek in there wouldn't hurt anyone, she reasoned. She just wanted to check, she told herself, that all was well. Spotting the box, she took it down and opened the flaps – and there it was. The immaculate *Devon* bag, so impeccably made by The Row. Tan, shiny as a conker, with a heavy gold zip that screamed quality. She ran her hands over the satiny calf-skin surface. She knew she had fallen in handbag love. It was too late – she was already mentally pairing the bag with her camel coat and her brown boots.

New, the *Devon* would cost four thousand pounds. Four. Thousand. Pounds. She stroked the flawless leather. 'You'd be wasted on anyone else,' she said, fully aware she was now talking to a handbag.

She'd been so virtuous earlier, pricing the bag at £2,400 and putting it into this box, instead of sticking through a much smaller personal donation and rushing the bag home with her. Maybe just one tiny try-on... before saying a mental goodbye and trying to forget about it forever.

So, the bag was out, over her shoulder, and –

Click.

Darkness.

The light was off. Then the door sort of sighed with the pressure of an internal draft and pushing her tote bag out of the room, shut with the definite click of a Yale lock. *Oh, for crying out loud!*

She was in pitch blackness, without the slightest glimpse of light, complete blackness with boxes on the floor, bags on the floor, quite the obstacle course between her and the door. She held the handbag to her chest. 'They're going to find me like this,' she whispered, 'in the dark, hugging a £2,400 handbag – from a charity sale!'

She had to calm the heck down and get out of this room

before anyone appeared and jumped to any wrong conclusions. The light was just on the other side of the door, she reasoned. Yes, the door was locked, but the lock's release knob was on her side. She just had to find the door. She turned and slowly, gingerly, stepped forward, trying not to trip. There were boxes everywhere and something metal scraped underfoot.

'Completely fine,' she told herself. 'Just logically following the shelving to the door.' Except she had lost her bearings and was already picturing that scene from *Silence of the Lambs*.

If Paula hadn't gone home, Annie would probably already have been rescued instead of being down here auditioning for a true-crime re-enactment.

Annie!!

She put her hand out and touched a shelf. 'OK, I can follow the shelf and get out of here... eventually. I can,' she told herself, mentally promising that she was never, ever falling for another handbag again.

27

Mrs K. Lawson:
Blue tweed skirt
Blue silk blouse
Blue wool cardigan
40 denier tights
Suede pumps
Sapphire and diamond earrings

Florence sat in front of her computer and saw that the email she had been hoping for all day had landed. But now she felt somewhat nervous about opening it. Already, the time spent finding out more about how priceless items of couture had ended up at the back of her mother's second wardrobe had revealed some fascinating secrets. Her mother might not have wanted Florence to know these things at the time, but finding out now, when her mother had passed away at the fine old age of ninety-four had turned out to be strangely inspiring.

Her mother had had an affair...! At the age of fifty-eight. Only a few years younger than Florence was now. Florence had followed a strange chain of events to arrive at this discovery. First of all, posing as a student working on a dissertation, she had contacted the Fondacion Dubois-Lafayette to ask who all the registered donors of Schiaparelli clothing were. It turned out that there was only one donor of four items – a Mrs Robert Fielding, who had made the donations thirty years ago in the 1990s.

The curator was happy to give her a 'care of' address for Mrs Fielding with a lawyer's office in London. Well, as soon as Florence had obtained this information, she'd been 'off to the races', using her own legal investigation skills to contact this office, have a conversation with the legal team who had looked after the Fielding family affairs and establish that Mrs 'Robert', in fact, Margaret Fielding was no longer alive, nor were her sons, Terence and Leo, but Mrs Fielding had a daughter, Kate, who was in her eighties but might be happy to have a conversation with someone trying to establish the provenance of some vintage couture.

'What did you say the designer was called?' the young lawyer at the end of the line had asked her.

'Schiaparelli, Elsa Schiaparelli.'

'Sorry, you'll need to spell that for me. I've never heard of her.'

'No? She invented the bias cut, the wrap dress, shocking pink, culottes for women and visible zippers.'

'Well... where would we be without visible zippers?' he asked, sounding a little sceptical.

'Or shocking pink?' was her reply.

* * *

The lawyer contacted Mrs Kate Lawson, née Kate Fielding, and later that day, Mrs Lawson phoned Florence and they had a long and revealing conversation.

'The first thing I need to tell you is that I'm not a student,' Florence had confessed. 'I'm finding out about these items for family reasons.'

'Ooooh, how intriguing,' Mrs Lawson had replied with a chuckle. 'Well, why don't you start at the beginning and let's see what we can unravel together.'

So, Florence decided to tell Mrs Lawson the whole story. She was in the process of gradually clearing out her mother's house. She'd come across clothes that she'd recognised as being rather special vintage clothes, and she'd decided to donate them to a large charity fashion show. Well, no sooner had she done that, than she'd found letters from the Fondacion asking her mother to hand in items that belonged to them. And one of the fashion show organisers had tracked her down and turned up at her door to ask if she knew that the clothes she'd dropped off were price-less fashion artefacts, possibly worth hundreds of thousands of pounds and was she sure she wanted to donate them.

'Goodness me, I bet that was a surprise!' Mrs Lawson sounded thoroughly entertained by it all. 'So, what happened next?'

'Oh, you will laugh, but the organiser's daughter posted a photo of a dress online and now the entire fashion world is beating a path to this fashion show and a museum in New York is trying to make a pre-emptive bid. So, as you can see, I rather desperately need to sort out if these things belong to me or not.'

'Indeed... And what about the museum in Paris, the Fonda-cion? Aren't they interested in the dresses too?'

'You know, I don't think they've seen the post, for whatever reason, because when I phoned up to make Schiaparelli dona-tion enquiries, no one mentioned it,' Florence said, which to be honest, had been something of a relief. 'But word is bound to get out.'

'This is all very exciting,' Mrs Lawson told her. 'I'm thrilled to be part of it. And you know how it is; secrets are made to be told. So... I suspect we are going to unearth a secret between us here.'

'Really?'

'Oh yes,' Mrs Lawson said, her voice much bubblier and more enthusiastic than expected for a woman of her age. 'Now, tell me what your mother was called.'

'Emily Perkins...'

'Oh my goodness... Emily Perkins, and did she spend some time in Rome during the 1990s?'

'Yes, she did. She got some special scholarship to go and be the artist in residence somewhere... I think it might have been the British School in Rome.'

'Well, my older brother Terence had a wonderful job in Rome between 1994 and '96, something to do with the Diplomatic Service, and we all suspected that he had a girlfriend. In fact, my mother was very concerned. Terence was married, unhappily, and my mother was very worried about his reputation. Imagined him being kicked out of the service. But in Rome, certainly in those days, I think it was quite the thing for men and women to have strings of lovers. I hope this isn't shocking news,' Mrs Lawson added quickly.

'Well... I certainly didn't know about this,' Florence admitted. 'My parents always seemed happy. They were married for a very long time and were good friends to one another.'

'Yes, but something happens at the end of middle age, doesn't it? We often want to seize that last chance at life.'

Florence paused, as she let everything that had been said so far sink in. Her mother had still seemed young in her fifties and her father... he'd enjoyed getting older, staying home, staying in, being absorbed in his work. And Florence in her thirties at the time, climbing her career ladder hadn't thought too much about what was going on in her parents' lives. She'd been happy for her mother to get the Rome opportunity: '*A year of art in Rome!*'

'So, you think your brother and my mother spent time in Rome together? Possibly having a very glamorous time, going to parties and enjoying the artistic and diplomatic life... by the sounds of it.'

'Something like that,' Mrs Lawson confirmed. 'Sounds lovely, wish I could be doing something like that instead of hobbling about my house on a stick.'

'So... how do the clothes get involved?'

'Oh yes, of course, so... our mother, who must have been my age back then, suddenly decided to pack up the family house and move to a flat. I think the heating bills, the upkeep, and rattling round a big place was completely getting to her. So, helpers were drafted in to sort through her things and... I think it's called "downsizing" nowadays and it is fairly normal. But back then, we all thought she'd completely lost her marbles – I mean, moving?! At eighty-four! And all sorts of treasures from her glamorous life as the daughter of a diplomat in Paris, and then the wife of a diplomat, not to mention the mother of a diplomat, were gathered up and sorted. Some things were sold and some very special things were to be sent to various museums – the V&A in London and then this special fashion museum in Paris.'

'The Fondacion Dubois-Lafayette?'

'If you say so,' was Mrs Lawson's reply. 'And guess who was responsible for taking the items over to Paris on his way back to Rome?'

'Terence,' Florence guessed. And felt a flutter of excitement as she understood what must have happened. Terence must have looked through the items and decided that some were just too lovely to hang unworn in a museum, so instead, he'd packed up two dresses and a velvet jacket and taken them on to Rome to his beautiful and illicit girlfriend. This did mean that the clothes were her mother's. They'd certainly not been taken from the Fondacion. The fact that Mrs Fielding had meant for them to go to the Fondacion surely didn't matter. The legal part of Florence's brain was informing her that possession was, famously, nine-tenths of the law. Terence had had the dresses and he'd given them to Florence's mother.

'Do you think all these years later, we could find any kind of proof that this is what happened?' Florence asked Mrs Lawson.

'I haven't looked through all her old letters, by any means... maybe there would be something there. Hmmmmm...' Mrs Lawson was obviously thinking. 'When exactly was your mother in Rome?'

'September 1993 to July 1994, the academic year. I remember because I was doing bar exams in 1994 and we joked about being students again.'

'My mother kept a diary all her life. And she also organised her photos very meticulously in dated boxes. So, I will see what I can unearth for you. And meanwhile, I don't think you should worry too much. It sounds to me as if you have inherited some beautiful clothes and you should be allowed to do with them as you choose.'

'It's been fascinating talking to you,' Florence told her. 'Thank you so much.'

Mrs Lawson promised to be in touch soon and both women agreed that it would be lovely to meet in person, so the next time Florence was anywhere near Sussex, she would arrange to visit.

* * *

And now only a few hours after the phone call, the email from 'K. Lawson' had landed with the intriguing title:

Surprising evidence!

Realising that her fingers were shaking slightly, Florence hit the open button.

28

Evening Florence:
Black flared stretchy trousers
Black and grey chunky cardigan
Black T-shirt
Fluffy black sheepskin slippers

Annie had escaped from the dungeon and now she was back home. She came into the hallway and set down her bags feeling almost tearfully grateful to be here.

'You're so late!' Ed called out from the sitting room. 'Babies are in bed. Lauren and I have already watched twenty-five episodes of *The Summer I Turned Pretty*!'

Good grief... it had taken Annie almost forty minutes of fumbling around in the dark to finally get to the door of the storeroom. Forty minutes! Forty minutes of wondering if she was ever going to get out, if she was going to have to pee in a corner of the room, try to eat a lesser handbag to survive... surely leather had some protein or basic nutritional elements... if she wasn't going to be found until four days later when Paula realised she was going to need to check a box or two... and quite hallucinatory thoughts about a murderer with night-vision goggles... Anyway, she had eventually reached the door, turned the knob, unlocked herself, pushed the light button in and everything had been put to rights. The bag had gone back into box no.7. In fact, she felt as if she'd finally seen some cold, calm sense about that bag. It was just a bag. It was just a piece of crafted leather to hold things in. A bag was not going to change her life, get her out of this dark room, find her a new career... or any of the other things she was hoping it could do. She was going to have to do all of those things. For herself. Without the £2,400 bag. In fact, being locked up in the dark had put things into perspective and she could now think of about fifty things she would be better spending £2,400 on. So, once the lights were back on, the bag had gone in its box, everything else had been neatly filed away and then she'd picked up her own bags and hurried up the lift, out of the fire door, down the street to the Tube and home.

'I'm very tired,' Annie told Ed. 'I got locked in the storeroom for nearly an hour.'

She expected some tender love, care and sympathy in response to these words, but instead she heard Lauren issue a 'What?!' followed by a burst of vigorous laughter, followed by Ed, trying hard to keep a straight face, telling her that there was some dinner left in a pot on the hob.

She slunk into the kitchen and gratefully helped herself to some of the ratatouille Ed had made earlier. She sat down at the island with the plate of food, knife, fork and a much-needed glass of wine. Checked her phone, no reply from Owen to the message she'd sent earlier. *That bloody boy,* she couldn't help saying under her breath. Honestly, he was going to cause her to worry herself to death.

* * *

At almost the same time the following evening, just as she was about to check for the reassuring green dot beside Owen's name, as she still hadn't heard back from him, her phone began to ring. And it was Florence.

'Hello, my darling, how are you?' Annie began.

'I have very exciting news!' Florence began. 'Tell me your email address and I'm going to send you two very important pictures.' Annie told her and then put her laptop up on the counter so she could see these pictures in full.

'OK, coming through,' Florence told her. Annie waited for a few moments and then here it was, Florence's email. A forward of an email from a K. Lawson, named:

Surprising evidence!

'This sounds intriguing—' Annie said.

'Open it,' Florence encouraged her.

'OK,' Annie said, hitting the button. It was a colour photograph of a man and woman, who looked to be in their late fifties, early sixties. It was a formal portrait, standing side by side, the man holding out a box with a medal before him. Both were very smartly dressed in a three-piece grey for the man and a navy skirt suit and hat for the woman. If Annie had to guess when it was taken, she would say late eighties, early nineties, judging by the woman's hair, shoes and shoulder width.

'Who am I looking at?' she asked Florence.

'You are looking at Mr and Mrs Fielding. Mr Fielding has just been presented with some sort of Italian service medal that they dish out to diplomats.'

'Oh...'

'Now look carefully behind them...' Florence went on. Annie made the photo larger on her screen.

'Oh my goodness... is that the claw of a lobster on a white dress that I can see behind them?'

'Yes, and above it the head of my very youthful-looking fifty-eight-year-old mother. Terence was her lover in Rome. And he gave her the items. His mother had entrusted them to him to take to the museum in Paris, but not all of them made it there.'

'Oh my word!! How exciting and intriguing. Surely somewhere there must be a better photo of her in that dress. I bet she looked wonderful in it!'

'She was such a glamorous woman, wasn't she? But scroll on down.'

Annie did as she was told and now saw another photograph of a diary entry. It was rather spidery handwriting in black ink. She scanned through the words until she saw the relevant lines.

I gave Terence the items I wanted to donate to the museum in Paris. He was supposed to drop them off when he passed through en route to Rome. Well, the museum phoned me today. They have only received four pieces. That bloody son of mine has taken two dresses and the black velvet jacket to Rome. He must have! And they won't be for his wife. Certainly not. They will be for this woman he has told me about. Emily P whoever she is. He says he wants to get a divorce and marry her. But she won't hear of it. She wants to return to her husband in London, apparently. Quite right. Terence needs to give it up and return to the side of his wife, before he blows up his entire career. Gave her my Schiaparelli! The insolence of the boy. Still, if she can wear those clothes, she must be a very lithe and graceful woman. I haven't been able to step into them since I exited my thirties.

'Provenance!' Florence declared.

'That's incredible...' Annie exclaimed. 'And such a fascinating tale. I hope you're not too upset about your mother...'

'No, no... my father was very preoccupied with his work. I think it's understandable that she had to... take a year out perhaps.'

'Those items belong to you,' Annie told her. 'And they are worth a lot of money, Florence. I think you should take some time to carefully consider what you want to do with them.'

'Isn't your show in only a few days' time now?'

'It doesn't matter. We can say we made it all up, we created the photo with AI for the publicity...' This thought had only just occurred to Annie, and she would use it if she had to protect Florence. 'If we tell them there's not a dress, everyone will forget in a few days. There are still many amazing things to sell. Your clothes are safely at home with me. I can bring them back to you if you want. Just say the word.'

'Will you give me tonight, Annie?' was Florence's request. 'I'll call you in the morning to let you know what I've decided. And thank you... you've been so helpful. So kind. Really. It's made everything about my task in this house better.'

'Thank *you*,' Annie said and felt herself breaking into a smile. 'Goodnight, Florence. Call me when you know what you want to do.'

* * *

'Ed? I haven't heard from Owen all day today, or all day yesterday and he hasn't been on Instagram for twenty-four hours, which is a bit weird.'

It was bedtime, Ed was brushing his teeth and Annie was making a final check of all her social media feeds, and her messaging apps and taking a last look for Owen and his green dot on Instagram. 'You know, I'm just going to call him...' she said, as she dialled and Ed did a round of rinsing and gargling. She found 'Owen' in her contacts and pressed call, but as expected, the number rang and rang with no reply. He never answered. That was normal. Every young person in the entire world had their phone on silent at all times, so why was she even bothering?

'Annie, please stop worrying about Owen,' Ed said as he stepped out of the en suite and into the bedroom. 'Have you tracked him? On "where's my son right now.com"?'

'Yes,' she admitted grudgingly. 'It's registering at his halls of residence.'

Ed rolled his eyes.

'So why are you worrying?'

'Because I don't think it's moved from there in two days.'

'But how do you know?' Ed protested. 'You can't have been tracking him every minute of the day! You've been insanely busy.'

This was true. There was no getting away from the fact that Ed had a point here.

'So, he could have gone out, done things and gone back home again... and I've just not noticed?'

'Yes.'

'But why not reply to my messages, even with a smiley face?'

'I don't know!' Ed shrugged. 'He's a student in his very first term. He might be spending hours trying to work out how to use the washing machine, or how to drink beer upside down... I don't know, but I am certain you would know if there was any kind of problem at all.'

'But we don't even have a number for anyone else who lives in his flat. Why didn't we think of that?'

'Yes... we should have thought of that. Then you could have your anxious phone calls ignored by not just one boy but a whole group of them.' He smiled. 'Owen would die if you started phoning other people to check up on him. And rightly so!'

'Suppose...' Annie admitted grudgingly.

'So big, big day tomorrow... the Day Before The Show...'

'You have got us a lovely babysitter from your school, haven't you, for the day of the show? Because you, Lauren and Dinah are all coming, remember. I am going to be away all day tomorrow. From dawn until very well after dusk. Ideally, I'm going to get Lauren to come to Gallery of Textiles with me too. All day. There is so much to set up! So, Dinah is doing nursery pick up and will be with the twins until you get home. OK?'

'Yes, I have the head girl, no less, she is coming to babysit our precious twins on Show Day.'

'Impressive.'

'OK... OK, busy lady, get into bed. It's snuggle up and sleep time.'

Ed turned the cover down and began to get comfortable. 'Come and join me,' he encouraged with his most encouraging smile. 'How about a pre-sleep shoulder massage?'

'You are too good to be true,' she told him and smiled back.

'I'll be very glad when the show is over. You've not been able to think about much else and all the stress,' he added. 'You've been talking in your sleep.'

'I have not!'

'You have... about Owen, and about Devon? From The Row? Honestly, those words, clear as a bell and over and over, last night... when I admit you were a bit traumatised from being locked in the storeroom...'

Annie could tell from the completely strained look on Ed's face that he was trying very hard not to laugh, once again, about her being locked in the storeroom. No, that wasn't fair, there had been some sympathetic noises from Ed last night as he'd listened to her storeroom drama but hearing that she'd been talking about a handbag out loud in her sleep was a touch mortifying.

'So *who* is Devon?' Ed wondered. 'And does he row? Has he got ridiculously big biceps? Is he "hench"?'

Now, it was Annie's turn to giggle. 'Oh yes,' she said. 'Wait till you meet Devon... our backstage bodybuilder. No! Not really!'

'So who is he? She? They?'

'She is a handbag.'

Ed groaned and put his hands over his eyes. 'No, Annie, no! Not a handbag. You can't be talking out loud in your sleep about a handbag!'

'Honestly, I am not buying another handbag. We know that. We know I have enough handbags, all the handbags. No need for even one more bag.'

'Correct.'

'So don't worry about it.'

'Are you sure? I don't need to walk you to the handbag cupboard and make you count your handbags before bed?'

'No... no, thank you.'

'So, come to bed,' he urged her.

'Yes, of course, let me just go take my face off, brush my teeth. I'll be right there.'

But once she was in the bathroom, she was looking at her phone, scrolling through messages, looking at her to-do lists, and spotting a reminder to herself put in the calendar months ago about their wedding anniversary. She did *have* to get Ed a present.

She really did. He was too good not to deserve a lovely anniversary present. And she did have the most amazing idea, but she hadn't done anything to make it a reality. And unless she did something very soon, it wasn't going to happen.

'Siri?' she whispered into her phone. 'You've got to help me with some internet shopping...'

29

ONE DAY TO GO

Model Anoush:
Shaggy, cream faux-fur coat
Tight pale jeans
Cream knee-high platform boots
Orange and burgundy knit
Huge gold-hooped earrings
Neon pink trolley bag

There was literally too much to do, Annie thought as she buzzed up and down in the lift for about the seventeenth time this hour, arms full of boxes and bags. The rooms seemed to be full of everyone – from complaining Svetlana, to stressed-out Paula, to Connor and Vince arguing about lines, to Lauren taking photos, posting and rolling her eyes every time Annie looked at her, to the dance girls worrying about 'But do I look good in this?'

They had scheduled a full dress rehearsal for 4 p.m. and by 3.30 p.m., Paula and Annie were just about ready to go lie down in darkened rooms as the arguing about outfits and shoes and belts and who was wearing what reached fever pitch. It was at that moment that a smartly trouser-suited woman walked into the main event room, pushing a wheeled suitcase and issuing a brisk and decidedly American: 'Good afternoon, everyone. I believe I need to speak with Annie Valentine or Svetlana Wisneski-Roscoff.'

Annie stepped forward and found herself being introduced to Carina Delroy of the museum in New York. 'I've arrived in London. I've come straight over because we're going to buy the Schiaparelli items, there's just no question of us not doing that. We have a donor who is going to make it happen for us. So, let's get talking.'

She might be dainty, petite and looking just a little tired from her transatlantic flight. But there was no question that Carina was on a mission and she was going to succeed. 'Hi, Carina, so lovely you could make it. We are so, so busy right now,' Annie told her. 'We're just about to start the dress rehearsal. Your interest in the items is amazing though, honestly.'

'Is anyone else as interested as us?' was Carina's first question.

'I think it would be fair to say, you're the only person here in the room pushing your suitcase directly from the airport.'

This at least made Carina smile. 'Good,' she said.

'Look absolutely no one is negotiating right now. So don't you want to go to your hotel... freshen up... and Svetlana and I can talk to you in... an hour or so?'

'No... I'm not going to my hotel before we talk,' Carina insisted. 'I'll probably fall onto the bed and not surface for six hours. But I could go and get some coffee. Then come back in... forty minutes. Does that sound OK?'

Forty minutes... forty minutes...! Annie looked at the catwalk, the models, the frazzled Paula. Florence still hadn't called to say what she'd decided and Annie didn't want to push or rush her at all. And where was Svetlana anyway? Off in another room, complaining about something else, no doubt!

'Yes, come back then... and we'll see where we are. I'll make sure Svetlana is around to talk then.'

'Great. See you very soon.' Carina went out, but as soon as she'd left, the door burst open and in came their star model, Anoush. A totally pared-down, dressed down version of the beautiful model whose face had graced catwalks, billboards, ad campaigns – but it was definitely her.

Everyone in the room couldn't help staring and smiling as she ran over and flung her arms around Annie.

'Hello! How is the woman who discovered me?!' she gushed generously.

'Anoush!! Very funny, you were a mega-star who could never have gone undiscovered, babes.'

'I hope I'm not late, it took so long to get off the flight. What is there a shortage of? Steps? Buses?' She gave that hands in the air, French-style shrug. Then set down her bags, her jacket, and headed for the backstage area, telling Annie: 'This is all coming together brilliantly. I'm so excited to be doing this. Now where are my model family for the show and what am I going to wear?!' Her starry, but still down-to-earth presence was utterly galvanising as she introduced herself to the other girls and began to compliment them on their hair, their eyes, their outfits.

Annie sidled up to Paula to tell her, 'I'm going to have to go off for a bit and sort things with Florence, Svetlana and our new friend, Carina... are you going to be OK for dress rehearsal?'

Paula looked at Annie and told her, 'Don't worry, looks like me and Anoush have got this. You come back to us when you're ready.'

* * *

First came calling Florence. She really had wanted to wait until Florence was ready, but Carina was going to be back very soon wanting news, action and deals. So Annie rang Florence's number. 'I'm sorry to call for news. I don't want to rush you...' Annie began.

'It's fine,' Florence assured her. 'I think I've made up my mind. I just wanted to dwell on it a little more... to make sure.'

'Shall I call back later?' Annie added, trying to sound as if there was all the time in the world.

'No, it's OK, Annie. Here's my decision. The lobster dress and the orange dress...' Annie could feel her breath tightening in her chest. She even closed her eyes as she waited for this decision to land. 'I'm going to let you sell them both for charity.'

'Oh my God...' Annie heard herself squeak. 'That is so exciting, so amazingly generous of you. It's incredible.'

Wow! she couldn't help thinking. This was going to mean so much for the charity and the level of donations. This was going to boost the coffers by tens of thousands... and it would put the show on the map. This was now a major charity fashion event, selling very important items. She was finally beginning to feel proud and excited that her name was on the invitation.

'Well, my mother didn't buy the items, she was loaned them on their way to a museum, so I think that's totally fitting, but I am going to be selfish and keep that beautiful velvet and gold jacket for myself. I just love it. It's so soft and gorgeous and fits me very well.'

'Good for you, Florence,' Annie said.

'Yes, I'm planning to wear it every once in a while. Maybe I'll attract a handsome diplomat who wants to show me a good time,' she said with a warm giggle in her voice.

'Oh, you will!' Annie assured her. 'And this is amazing, amazing news! Thank you so much. I can't wait to tell Svetlana. I can't wait to tell the very important woman who has flown in from New York.'

'Really?'

'She wants to make a pre-show deal. She has a donor with very deep pockets. She is buying those dresses.'

'Absolutely no pre-show deal, Annie,' Florence warned her. 'We have to have on-the-night bidding and raise the roof.'

'Oh, I agree and that is totally what Svetlana will say too. Speak soon, speak very, very soon,' Annie said, knowing she had to ring off and get back to the rehearsal. But this was so exciting, she felt almost breathless with the thought of the buzz this show would now create.

There was a brand-new round to plan now – the Schiaparelli round. What music? She wondered. That was a detail to be decided. But she could already picture Anoush in the lobster dress closing the show.

That was going to both bring the house down and raise the roof.

30

Bed Ed:
White cotton T-shirt
Tartan pyjama bottoms
Battered vintage sheepskin moccasins
Leather bracelet from 'the M&Ms'

Caught up with the dress rehearsal, she hadn't looked at her phone for over two hours, so surely, surely this was going to be the moment when she took it out of her bag, glanced at the screen and at last saw some sign of life from her son. This was going to be it, surely? Owen knew it was October 1st tomorrow. Surely he could remember how important this day was for her? Even if he didn't, he must know he'd been out of touch for three days. He wasn't going to keep her waiting and worrying any longer, was he? Even if the complete idiot had lost/sold/given his phone away to someone more deserving, *surely* he could find some way by now of letting her know that he was OK? An email even. She was easy enough to reach by email. Even Owen could remember helloAnnie@annievalentine.com, couldn't he? Annie reached into the folds of her bag. She flipped the phone over and looked at the screen. There were about fifteen notifications all demanding her immediate attention but, scanning quickly, she could see that not one of them was from Owen, or offered any glimpse of news about Owen.

Never mind, she had to just put her head down for now and get on with the one million things which still had to be done.

* * *

'Annie... for the fifteenth time tonight, will you please stop worrying? Owen's phone is registering at his flat,' Ed told her with a sigh of exasperation as they prepared to get under the covers. 'If it was signalling from a deserted woodland or a boat to Bermuda, then you could be worried. But he's at home.'

'But he's been at home for three days solid. And I've had nothing, not one word of a message, not even a wink emoji, not even a thumbs-up. And he hasn't been on Insta for two days either and Ed, this is just not like him.' She really was becoming properly worried and she wanted to make Ed see this.

'Annie, he's a fresher! He's going out, making new friends, forming a rock band, trying to keep up with his lectures and his reading list, trying to make himself dinner, or at least buy himself dinner... he's busy. He's even too busy – and I know this is hard – but he's too busy to talk to you. Or even message you. He probably hasn't even opened your messages.'

'No,' she agreed. Because they were registering as unopened.

'And I know that must be difficult for you, but he's going to be fine. I promise. Please, please stop worrying. You have enough to worry about. Tomorrow is a very big day.' She really hoped Ed meant the show. He was fine with the agreement to postpone their wedding anniversary celebrations until it was all over, wasn't he?

'Come here,' he said, moving towards her in the bed so he could put a heavy, comforting arm around her and hold her tight. 'Try to relax. It's going to be fine,' he soothed. 'Tomorrow is going to be fabulous, a triumph, and Owen is doing amazingly well and will phone you in a great burst of news and apologies when he's realised how long it's been since he spoke to you.'

Annie closed her eyes and held on to Ed. Usually, this soothing voice, this heavy arm and warm body could bring her all the comfort and reassurance that she needed. Yes, she could feel herself start to relax a little. He was right, wasn't he? She was stressed about the show and driving herself into a frenzy about her son. He was fine, of course, he was fine. She took some deep breaths in, out, and tried to think about relaxing more. She needed some sleep. If she could just have a good night's sleep, then she would be ready to take on everything that tomorrow was going to bring.

'Night night, my darling,' Ed said gently and kissed her on the cheek.

'Goodnight, boyfriend,' she replied. But twenty-five minutes of lying listening to Ed falling into a deeper and deeper sleep, Annie realised it was absolutely no good. Night-time made everything worse. The quiet, the darkness... it felt as if it was crowding in around her and with every moment, she grew more awake and more worried.

This was Owen. This was her darling number one son. And even if everyone now knew him as fun and funny and fun-loving and always busy, surrounded by friends and music and a non-stop party atmosphere, she knew all the sides of him. The very thoughtful, very quiet side, the sensitive little soul inside who had once been so lost that he'd barely spoken for a whole year.

She was connected to all the Owens, and it just didn't feel at all right to her that she'd heard no word from him for so long. Yes, three days, everyone kept saying 'just three days', but he always sent her something. Wherever they'd been in the world, they'd always exchanged some little message or joke or line about something. And then the abandoned Insta... it wasn't right. Something wasn't right.

Like all those other mothers who had told the newspapers they'd woken up in the middle of the night convinced that something wasn't right – she was now one of them. She had to act on this or she would never forgive herself. No one up there even knew him very well. What if they all thought he'd gone home and he'd actually gone missing? What if...? What blinking iffing wasn't going to do her any good at all. She had to do something or she was going to go crazy. No, she thought, getting out of bed as quietly as she could. She was already completely crazy and now, in a moment of absolute clear, level-headed sense, she really did have to do something.

Determined not to wake Ed, she scooped up the big pile of clothes on the chair beside her dressing table, sure that she would find an outfit in there. Because the crazy, frenzy of worry was clearing and in its place was the simple thought: *I need to see Owen.*

And the only way she was going to see Owen was by getting into the car and driving to Scotland. OK, so... she was going to get dressed and get into the car and drive to Scotland.

* * *

The journey had begun in relief, enthusiasm, excitement even. *It's just seven hours,* she'd told herself. *It's only 11.15 p.m.... I'll be there by 6 a.m. and then I'll see Owen, make sure he's OK and drive*

*home and I'll be back, ready to do the show by 2... 3 p.m. It'll be fine. I'll
be so much more relaxed, happier, I'll calm right the heck down and
enjoy it all.*

For the first hour, she'd felt amazing – bright-eyed and wide
awake, enjoying every single song playing on the late-night radio
channel, wishing she'd thought of doing this yesterday, foot flat
down, whizzing along quiet motorway lanes a shade over 80
mph, convinced this was going to be fun, an adventure. By hours
two and three, it was a very different story. Her eyes were blurring
with tiredness and strain. There were lorries everywhere. It had
started to rain. She realised she'd completely forgotten to factor
in getting some sleep between now and the fashion show. What if
Owen wasn't there? Wouldn't that be even worse? Then she'd
have to stay in Glasgow and panic and, well obviously she'd miss
the show, but if Owen wasn't there, missing the show would be
the last of her worries. Maybe he'd gone on one of those crazy
student challenges... they'd dropped him naked on a hillside
with a pound coin and he had to find his way back... or something completely bananas.

'OWEN!' she shouted out loud to herself to somehow express
the frustration... to shock herself into staying awake and driving
for another... oh good grief... four and three quarter hours.

One hour later, there was only garbage on the radio and she
was shouting at it to stop. Then shouting at Siri and commanding
he played her favourite playlist. She passed a sign for the Lake
District that read 186 miles and that was a low moment; she
thought she might cry. *Maybe I should turn back now?* She asked
herself as Cher wondered how to turn back time from the loud-
speakers.

Must have coffee... was the next coherent thought, so several
miles later she pulled off into a service station that, well, if Cher
had found herself standing in this entrance foyer, she may well

think she'd succeeded in her time-travelling mission. The next two hours were a blur... there was the caffeine buzz and that did definitely help.

Then there was just sinking into a deep, calm state of tired but alert concentration. She got Siri to play her country and western songs, especially on a trucking theme. She tucked in behind a great, shiny white lorry and followed it steadily for mile after mile, pretending she was a lorry driver on the nightshift, carrying an urgent delivery of up-to-the-moment fuzzy jackets, this season's winter must-have to the fashion-hungry Glasgow hoards.

'Beep, beep, beep, we've got to get the chocolate-brown fleece and sequinned party dresses through,' she said out loud. 'Oh my God, I'm delirious,' she added, also out loud. 'Owen, I can't believe I'm doing this.'

But she had to stop talking to herself because it was driving Siri crazy. 'Sorry, I do not know that song,' his calm and unruffled tones assured her. Hour six was a low hour, she sank down into her chair, felt the dark gloom of hills and darkness all around her and knew that her blinks were getting dangerously long. She had to stay awake. If she even hit the rumble strip once, she knew she would have to stop and have a nap, because dying after crashing off the motorway in an exhausted heap was not an option. No, not an option! She told herself out loud again.

She pressed the button for the window to open and got a gust of cold, damp air in her face. She opened the window some more until it was fairly blasting at her. Scottish air! How had she missed the sign. She was in Scotland! Surely there couldn't be too much further to go. Just the faintest glimmer of paler blue seemed to be breaking over in the east and could that be dawn? Then she must be getting near... at so many points in this long, exhausting, possibly ridiculous journey, she'd been so close to giving up, so close to turning back home, or pulling up for a sleep that seeing the approach of dawn, seeing the sign that said:

Glasgow 55 miles

was just such a little overwhelming. She felt her dry, tired, blurring eyes sending out a dribble of tears. 'I'm nearly there, Siri. We've made it—'

'Playing "We Made It" by Circa Waves.'

'No, Siri, nooo.' She glanced at the dashboard where the digital clock told her it was 6.45 a.m. Back at home in Highgate, her alarm would be going off.

* * *

Soothing angelic harp tones began to fill the bedroom and Ed, usually a sprightly, spring-out-of-bed kind of morning person felt tired enough to hiss, 'Turn it off, Annie... turn it off,' because the clock was on her side. He put out his hand to give her a little nudge and was very surprised to find empty space. She wasn't in bed. *What!* This never happened. She hated to get up, insisted it was the worst fifteen minutes of her day.

'*Ermmm... thirty minutes more like,*' he always corrected her.

'Annie... are you all right?' he asked out loud, as if she might be over by the wardrobe, or somewhere within shouting distance. 'Annie?' He sat up and clicked on his bedside light. No sign of her. And her side of the bed was cold, as if she'd been up for ages. And that pile of stuff on her chair was gone. And her phone wasn't lying on top of her bedside table... *And happy anniversary to us*, he thought a little bitterly. *Has she already headed off to the scene of the show, this early?*

He swung out of bed and groped about with his feet for his battered old sheepskin slippers. Then he went to the bedroom door, opened it and listened. There was no sound at all. It didn't sound as if she was in the bathroom, the kitchen or anywhere else in the house. It was very quiet, as if he was the first one up. He padded downstairs to the kitchen, where his phone was out on the island countertop, as if Annie had put it there especially for him to see, because he wasn't as glued to his device as she was. Beside the phone was a Post-it note which had an arrow drawn in thick felt tip. The arrow pointed to the phone and under the arrow were the words:

I can explain

He picked up the phone and saw a notification for one of her dreaded voice notes. *Now what*, he wondered, as he pressed play. Whatever he'd expected, nothing had prepared him for the words: *'Babes, I know you're going to think this is mad, but I'm driving to Glasgow...'*
WHAT?!!!!!

Annie's phone began to ring. As it was 6.52 a.m., she knew exactly who that was going to be and quite frankly having to listen to a stream of *what did she think she was doing/was she out of her mind/of course Owen was going to be perfectly fine/did she realise today was the day of the show* etc., etc., was too much. She was driving to Glasgow, so surely it would be OK to just let the call ring out and pretend she was out of signal? She would phone Ed back just as soon as she had some real news about Owen. And just thinking about what the real news would be sent a fresh blast of nerves round her system and she pushed her foot down on the pedal a little further.

Half an hour later, she was approaching the edge of the city. The orange glow of the streetlights mixed with the first signs of pale blue light from the heavy brooding sky. She sat up in her seat, knowing she would have to pay close attention to Siri's directions. There were motorway changes, underpasses, slip roads and roundabouts to negotiate before she could get to the place where she and Ed had dropped Owen and all his most important possessions just two weeks ago.

Of course, more than anything, she hoped she was wrong and Owen was completely fine and had just forgotten about her in the busy whirl of his new life. If that was the case, she was going to be furious with the trouble he'd caused her. Absolutely furious! And right now, as she negotiated a turnoff from one motorway, so she could join another, she tried to keep thoughts of everything being fine and her being furious right at the front of her mind. Because the alternative was too frightening and soon enough she would know, so for now, she had to keep her ears on Siri's instructions and her eyes and her thoughts firmly on the road. The constant little tings coming from her phone told her that the world was waking up, and everyone involved in tonight's big event was coming to life with questions, instructions and last-minute panics. She would deal with it. There was time. It would be sorted. But right now, Owen had to come first.

She was on a town dual-carriageway now, with a 30 mph speed limit and she knew she didn't have far to go. Another turn-off, three more roundabouts... past the Lidl, where she'd bought Owen that last farewell bag of groceries, putting all the things in the basket that she knew he liked. Along with plenty of other things that were probably turning into mush in the bottom of the shared fridge. She wasn't surprised to feel tears slipping from her eyes at the thought of this. *Oh God, Owen, please be OK, please, please, let everything be OK with you. I won't be annoyed if everything is OK. Honestly, I'll be bloody freaking delighted.* And she knew it was crazy to be here, but it was also the right thing. How could she possibly have her whole mind on the show tonight if she didn't know what was going on with her precious son?

She turned right as Siri instructed and now nudged the car slowly along the street where Owen's accommodation building was.

'You have reached your destination,' Siri chirped cheerfully as Annie drew up, her eyes scanned the front of the building for the window on the second floor that she remembered was Owen's room. The windows were wide open and it was immediately obvious, to her horror, that the black scorch marks on the brick-work at the top of the frame meant there had very recently been a fire. Her heart stood still.

31

Trev on duty:
Red and green tartan shirt
Navy blue chinos
Hand-tooled leather belt with western buckle
Chunky leather slip-on boots
Multi-coloured friendship bracelets

Stumbling to open the car door in a panic, Annie got out onto the pavement and bolted for the entrance of the building. She pulled open the heavy glass door and rushed towards the reception. There was no one there, so she didn't even pause, just ran straight to the flight of stairs and went up them as fast as her weary legs could carry her. Floor one, then floor two, then out into the corridor and down towards flat number 22. She tried the door but it was locked. She hammered on it loudly and for long enough to establish that no one was coming to answer. Oh no, oh no, oh God, now what?! She turned around and hammered on the next available door. Finally, a very sleepy looking boy, hair on end, in a grubby T-shirt and pyjama bottoms opened up.

'Has there been a fire?' she asked urgently, following up before he could even reply. 'Is everyone OK?'

'Yeah,' the boy replied in what felt to Annie like slow motion. 'Some legend tried to dry his T-shirt in the air fryer.'

'His T-shirt? In the air fryer?' Her mind tried to make sense of the words. Could that have been Owen? 'Is he OK?' she demanded. 'Where is he? Where's everyone from the flat?'

'Ermmmmmm...'

Annie wanted to shake him, she really did.

'I think everyone got moved to another flat. It really did smell terrible. And I think the air fryer guy might be in hospital.'

'What?! Where?! Who?' Annie squawked. But all she got in reply was a shrug. 'Maybe speak to Trev on reception. He'll know.'

'There's no one there!' she just about screamed, all this terror not to mention extreme sleeplessness catching up with her now.

'Ermmmmmmm...' The boy rumpled his hair, just the way Owen sometimes did and for a moment, Annie thought she was going to have to sit down, right here in the hallway, and sob.

'There's a bell on reception,' the boy added. 'Give it a ring and Trev'll come out.' Annie didn't need to be told twice, she broke into a trot and headed back towards the stairs. Trev was back on reception when she got there and didn't even seem too fazed at this stressed-out, hyped-up, quite frankly mad woman blurting about fires and hospitals and Owen and where on earth was he and was he all right? Trev had manned the reception desk at various halls of residence for a long time now and he had seen it all before. He knew that the best policy always was to remain calm and calming.

'OK, are we talking about the "incident" in flat 22 on the second floor?'

'Yes! Is everyone OK? Did anyone get hurt?'

'OK, and do you mind telling me who you are?'

'I'm Annie Valentine, I'm Owen Leon's Mum. That's the flat he shares with five others. And I haven't heard from him for three days.' If she didn't find out within seconds what was going on, how exactly Owen was and where exactly he was, she was going to lose it, honestly she was going to have the hissiest of diva meltdowns. The supermodels would have nothing on her.

'OK, Mrs Valentine,' Trev began, still checking the screen in front of him, 'I can tell you that there were no serious injuries, apart from to the décor of the kitchen. Everyone got out fine. They put the fire out themselves but the fire brigade came round to make sure everything was safe. Now... according to the incident log... everyone has been temporarily rehoused in a flat in the east end of the city...'

'Where?' she asked immediately.

'Wait... except for Owen Leon – that's your son, isn't it – who was taken to the QE Hospital in the south side.'

'Owen's in hospital?!' she gasped, thinking really dramatically terrible thoughts now – imagining Owen's face burned off, or Owen's lungs ravaged by inhaling terrible plastic-fumed smoke.

'It does look as if he's spent the night there, but we're not amazing at updating logs on this desk, I will admit.'

'Any details?' she asked, her voice sounding all wobbly and uncertain, exactly reflecting how wobbly and uncertain she felt herself. In fact, she was going to hold on to this nice solid reception counter to steady herself.

'OK there, Mrs Valentine?' Trev asked and suddenly he was by her side, proffering a plastic chair for her to sit on. 'Let's take a wee seat,' he urged. 'OK there?'

Yes, it was definitely better to be sitting. The spinning had stopped and she was feeling a lot less tingly. 'Right, I'm going to pop into my office for a glass of water, then I'll call the hospital for you and we'll get an update. OK?'

As she gulped the glass of water down, Trev was making the call and noting down the details. 'Right OK, ward 14, expecting to be discharged today. That's great, thanks very much. His mum is here and I think she'll want to go down and get him. That sound OK? Right you are then. Thanks.'

Trev turned to face her with the update.

'He's still at the hospital, they're happy to let him go today and you are fine to go down there now and see him. How does that sound?' Trev treated her to another big smile. Honestly, he was a saint, this man. An absolute saint. 'I take it he's no phoned you with all this news?'

She shook her head. He shook his too sympathetically. 'They are absolute numbnuts at this age. That's all I can say. Believe me, he's not the only one.'

'Thank you, Trev. Is it far from here?'

'Are you in the car?'

When she nodded, he assured her. 'Ten minutes' drive. It's after seven though, so be warned, the parking is an absolute killer.'

* * *

Siri guided her to the hospital where she managed to find a parking space. Then she hauled her weary self to the hospital lobby, where another friendly person on reception pointed her in the direction of the right ward and she trotted along corridors that were already busy as it approached 8 a.m. Somewhere, in some compartment of her mind, she realised that this day was very quickly going to unravel completely out of control... she had a major London event to get back to... even now, she could hear all the urgent bleeps and dings her phone was making as people desperately needed her input on all kinds of unforeseen questions, hitches, last-minute glitches. But right now, laser focus was carrying her onwards towards ward 14. Here it was... she pushed open the door and found herself in that world of blue lino, busy people in scrubs, a confusion of doors and corridors. But there was the nurses' station, they would be able to help her.

'Owen Leon?' she blurted. 'Where would I find him. I'm his mum...' dangerous voice wobble on that word.

'Oh hello, yes, of course... you just follow me,' said a friendly nurse with strikingly pretty lipstick.

'Is he OK? Apparently he's going to be allowed out today...'

'Yes, he's doing well. I'm not sure he'll be doing much cooking for a while though,' the nurse joked. She knocked on the door loudly before pushing it open for Annie with the words, 'Hey, Owen, your Mum's here.'

Annie stepped in and there, at last, was Owen. He was sitting up in bed awake – very unusual to see him awake at 8 a.m. And his face was split into a big grin and it looked fine, perfect, just like it should.

'Owen!' she gasped, still astonished that all this had happened. Still not exactly sure what emotions she was feeling apart from massive, overwhelming relief. He looked fine, absolutely totally fine. Why was he here? What was wrong with him?

'Hello, Mum...' he waved both his hands at her slowly and as she registered that they were covered in big thick bandages, making them look like huge paws, he couldn't resist joking, 'Tinky Winky says hello.'

32

Sleepless Annie:
White sweatshirt with burgundy designs
Pink flouncy skirt
Long tan winter boots
Dark pink woollen coat
Cream, pink and tan mohair scarf

'Owen!!' She absolutely rushed at him, just could not wait to be hugging him. 'Owen!' she repeated, holding him tight and running her hand over his rough and tumble hair. 'For goodness' sake,' she added. 'I've been so worried! And no wonder, you set your flat on fire! And didn't even think about letting us know!'

'Hardly,' he protested. 'I set my Clash T-shirt on fire and the air fryer got a bit melted and there was lots of smoke, but I put it all out, smothered the flames with a tea towel like a good boy scout. Honestly, they've made a total drama out of it.'

She was sitting on the edge of the bed, looking him over carefully. It took her a moment to work out what was slightly different. 'You haven't got any eyebrows!'

Owen gave a fairly casual shrug in response to this. 'Oh yeah,' he shrugged. 'But they'll grow back, won't they?'

'Hope so. And what about your hands? What's the story?'

'Yeah... they're a bit burnt. Molten bits of plastic stuck to the skin apparently. Some pretty impressive blister action. That's why they've kept me in. Well, A), I can't do anything for myself and, B), they need to make sure when the skin grows back, it's nice and stretchy or I could lose some mobility, which would obviously not be good. I told them I was a concert violinist, just to wind them up. The doctor went a bit pale at that.'

'Owen!'

'Well, I wanted to make sure they'd look after me properly and they have. It's a very nice hospital,' he said approvingly. 'And Glasgow nurses are super nice. In fact, Glasgow people are super nice.' He gave a 'How're ye doin' pal?' in his best imitation of a Glaswegian accent.

'Nice of you to tell me you'd had a fire and landed in here. I've been worried sick. Couldn't you have phoned?' She looked at his hand bandages. 'Or asked someone to phone me?'

'I forgot to bring my phone... I think it's back at the flat. I hope it's back at the flat. Couldn't remember any numbers, not even our home phone.'

'You could have got the uni or your halls to phone us. They have all the numbers,' Annie told him.

'You know, I just thought of that this morning,' he replied. 'So I was going to ask one of the nurses to help me do that. There was a lot going on yesterday,' he said in his defence.

'I've not heard anything from you for three days!' she protested.

'Well... I was locked in my room for two days doing an essay, then this happened... and they did give me some pretty strong painkillers. But sorry, didn't mean to worry you.' He put his hand on hers and gave his 'please forgive me' smile.

There was a comfortable pause as Annie smiled back, and neither of them needed to say any more. Annie couldn't help noticing how soft the bed was and how cosily warm this room was. Now that she knew he was OK, all the adrenaline that had been coursing through her system, keeping her awake, powering her on through her long drive and the drama of arriving at his halls, seemed to have left her. And here felt like a snug little cocoon away from the world, away from all the messages on her phone, the questions to answer, the one million things that had to be done, sorted and organised. Couldn't she just close her eyes for a moment and have a tiny little rest here, away from it all?

'Mum... are you OK?' Owen asked.

'I'm very tired,' she admitted. 'I left London at 11 p.m. and I've been on the go ever since.'

'An all-nighter?' Owen asked, sounding almost impressed. 'How did your show go? The big fashion thing?'

'Nice of you to ask,' she gave a big, wide yawn, 'but it hasn't happened yet. It's tonight.'

'*Tonight*?!' there was no hiding the surprise in his voice. Even a daft eighteen-year-old who'd tried to dry his T-shirt in an air fryer could tell that being in Glasgow on the morning of the event you'd been planning for months was not exactly ideal.

'I have to go back to London, but I don't know if I can – I've had no sleep, Owen. I might drive the car off the road. And you're not going to be able to do any driving for me with the Teletubby hands. You'll have to come home,' she realised. 'At least until you can use a phone, not to mention wipe your—'

'OK, Mum, but we'll have to think of a workaround for that. I'm not having you or Ed—'

'No! Definitely not!' she agreed.

For a moment, she wondered how quickly a bidet could be installed. But would he be able to turn on the tap…?

'There are trains to London,' was her next thought. 'We looked them up, to make sure you could come and visit us whenever you wanted.'

'Yeah… all day long. But what will you do with the car?' he asked.

She honestly felt too tired to even think. Owen was here and he needed help. The show was there, all the way back in London, seven hours' drive away… four and a half hours on the train away and she had to sleep. She had to or she was going to just collapse under the effort of it all.

No, wait a minute. First of all, she had to go and speak to the nurse. She of the striking lipstick. Annie felt she could count on a woman with such good taste. When she was out of the room and spotted her target in the corridor hurrying to her next assignment, Annie went up to her. 'Do you have just a second for a few questions, if that's OK?' she asked.

'No problem, come over to the station then we can look up Owen's notes on the system.' Once the computer had been consulted, it was clear that Own could leave today, if he was going somewhere where he could be looked after. He would need to be seen again in five days' time. 'And he has to do his exercises, keep stretching out the fingers, make sure that skin isn't growing back tight,' were the instructions.

'OK… OK… we will go back to London on the train and then we'll bring him back here on the train for his follow-up appointment. So, when do the bandages come off?'

'Keep them on for the train, but they can come off at home and we'll give you something lighter.'

'And one more question, sorry…' Annie could see that she was busy and needed to head off to the next thing on her list. 'Parking here is free?'

The nurse nodded.

'And can you leave your car in the car park overnight?'

She nodded again.

OK, Annie thought to herself, *a plan is forming.*

'Just keep him exercising his fingers, make sure he understands he's in for it if he doesn't,' the nurse added.

'Yes, of course. Your lipstick, by the way, completely perfect on you.'

'Charlotte Tilbury,' they both said together.

'It's a dream,' Annie added.

'Wait... I know you,' the nurse exclaimed. 'You're Annie Valentine from the TV show! You made me buy this lipstick!'

* * *

Annie and Owen took a taxi to the station. They had to dash across the enormous concourse under a Victorian glass ceiling to get onto the 10 a.m. to Euston before it departed. Once they were in their seats, she answered all the messages that could be settled with a text or a note and called to answer all the questions that couldn't. The news that she wouldn't be at the venue until 3 p.m. at the earliest was greeted with disbelief. But she tried to reassure Paula and Lauren that she would be right there at the end of the phone, fully tuned in and able to answer any question whenever.

'We've made great plans, we are organised,' she assured them in turn. 'If you need anything from me, I am here and I will sort it. I will be right there, in the twinkling of an eye. I'm flying along on a very fast train. Had something to deal with. I will be there, honest, I promise. Sit tight, I'm on my way.' But she did have to urge them, 'Please no one tell Svetlana, just say I'm off doing something urgent for the show.'

Then finally, it was time to phone Ed and explain everything. He was in class, of course, so she left a voice note, a bit long, a bit rambling, but she had now been up forever and hopefully he would understand. 'Owen is fine... apart from a pair of burned hands, which are going to heal up perfectly, but otherwise, he is totally fine. He put his T-shirt in the air fryer... I can't imagine... Anyway, we are rushing back to London on the train – don't worry, I have it all figured out, babes. Speak very soon. Call me right back when you can. Love you.' But it wouldn't have been any use if he had, because as soon as Annie had switched off her phone and tucked it into her bag, her head fell against the head-rest, and despite her promises that she would be available for every call and every query, she sank deeply into the comfy plush of the velour and was asleep almost instantly.

33

SHOWTIME

PaigeP:
Skinny black leather trousers
Charcoal grey silk cowl neck vest
Silver and diamond sculptural earrings
Designer sunglasses
Black finest cashmere shrug jacket
Highest platform black patent pumps
Up-to-the-nanosecond clutch bag

Like all wonderful, milestone events in her life, the fashion show passed in an intense blur of moments that even as they were happening, Annie felt she needed to imprint onto her mind so that she could remember them. She kept finding herself thinking: *This is extraordinary, I need to remember this... as well as the eleventy-hundred things that are all happening at exactly the same time.*

As soon as she arrived at Gallery of Textiles, all underslept and rumpled from the Glasgow adventures and the train – and with Saint Dinah drafted in at the last moment to take Owen and his hands from the train back to home – there was a flurry of last-minute hitches, crises, and downright tantrums to sort out immediately. There weren't enough chairs! Then Svetlana was in the main hall complaining that the flowers were awful. Paula was stacking rails and the sales stalls all around the edge of the room and in several other smaller rooms in a wordless fury about Annie being so late to set-up day.

'Paula, I am so sorry,' Annie said, as soon as she found her. 'Another family bloody crisis, as is normal, but don't worry, I have dealt with it. All is fine, Owen is fine, he's just burned all the skin off his hands... and he has no eyebrows or eyelashes... but, hey. He's going to be fine... fine... fine.'

Trying to put the entire Glasgow adventure out of her mind, Annie listened to Svetlana's complaints first.

'We have nearly 800 guests and 500 chairs!! The flowers... I hate all these white funeral flowers. They make the place look like some government official has died and we are holding a wake not a fashion show!'

'OK...' Annie looked at the floral arrangements set out in the enormous room... they were very white and stately; she could see Svetlana's point. 'We need more helpers.'

Annie decided this was the first problem to solve. There was her, Paula, two members of Paula's events staff and several more coming later, but this was going to need a lot more bodies to fetch, carry, command for last-minute tasks. A day like this needed extra people just hanging about ready to help at the slightest moment's notice. 'Lauren needs to bring in literally everyone she can find from her friend group. I'll tell Ed to send every responsible sixth former round to us from 4 p.m. onwards. We need willing bodies in every corner of the room to help fix things. Now, calm, my darling. This doesn't kick off until 7 p.m., and it is only...' Annie glanced at her phone, '3.30. So we have hours to sort *everything*. Honestly, all the best shows come together on the last day.'

'The chairs? The flowers?' Svetlana reminded her.

'Let's speak to the staff at the front desk. We've hired all these chairs in, but I bet this building has loads and loads of chairs of its own,' was Annie's suggestion. 'They won't be as lovely, but that won't matter once the beautiful behinds are perched on them.'

'The flowers?' Svetlana didn't budge. She wanted an answer on this. And she wasn't going anywhere until she got it.

'Let me go and speak to Paula and see what she needs from me, then I am personally going to sort the flower problem. OK, just trust me.'

* * *

Paula needed help, she told Annie. 'All the help you've got. All the help you can give.' So for the next hour solid, until all the young helpers arrived, they hauled boxes from the basement room, decked out rails, stacked tables, made sure every item for sale had a ticket. They worked out how many bodies would need to be at each stall and each rail to make sure that every fashionista would be able to buy all the fashion they wanted to.

'How are people going to pay?' Annie asked her friend, hoping this was something Paula had thought of.

Paula rolled her eyes. 'What kind of amateur do you take me for? They can either pay cash and we have a lockbox in every room, or they can scan these little rented handsets with their cards and all will be transferred direct to the charity.'

'Sounds perfect. Well done.'

'Same with the items that are bid for on the runway. Someone with a handset will just run over to the winning bidder, cards will be swiped and... all done. Items over £10,000 will have a different process, and the buyers will expect that.'

'And you're going to organise the army of helpers, as soon as they start arriving?' Annie asked.

'Yeah, I'll organise... because you are going to have your hands full with the compères, the models and the runway show.'

'Oh yes... I am. And can I just say, Paula, you are a genius event organiser. This show will put you on the map.'

'Thanks, babe... we all want it to go so well,' Paula replied. 'I'm frightened just thinking about how well I want it to go.'

'Going to be *fabulous,* babes,' Annie said, hoping and hoping this was true.

* * *

By 5 p.m., the tension, the feeling of out-of-control chaos was ramping to danger levels. Yes, Annie might have solved the flower problem – she'd gone to the nearest three supermarkets and bought them out of everything colourful she could lay her hands on. Then she'd flower-bombed the stately white displays, sticking sunflowers, roses, dahlias and bright blue ornamental thistles everywhere that she could find space. But everywhere else, problems were cropping up. The construction of the catwalk was taking longer than expected. The DJ wasn't happy about the space he'd been allocated. Connor and Vince were meeting for the first time and going over their routine together. Only for Connor to sidle up to her and complain. 'How can I work with this guy? He's a complete buffoon!'

'You will just have to, Connor, please,' was all she could say, as she tried to carry an enormous heap of clothing into the makeshift backstage area and get all the right things set up for all the right models, before they went to pieces... what with Gwen and Phyllis still arguing over who was going to wear the fuchsia and the ballet girls all huddled up and anxious with nerves.

'I don't know if we can do this...' one of them blurted as Annie and her armful of clothes came into sight. Annie knew a few moments of her offering calm and reassurance was needed to nip these feelings in the bud.

'Of course you can,' she began with her kindest smile. 'You girls are performers. You've got some pre-show adrenaline flowing through your systems and it's making you feel jumpy, but I promise you, when the lights are on and the music is pumping, you are going to love it and totally rock it.'

'But Bria heard that PaigeP is coming,' Shivani worried. 'I mean... PaigeP! She goes to all the best fashion shows in the world. We're going to look like complete amateurs to her. I really don't think I can do this.'

'Or me...' Chloe worried.

The argument about the fuchsia dress was still going on in the background. And for a moment, absolutely frazzled, Annie just wasn't sure if she could do this herself. *PaigeP was coming...* she really was coming to their hastily cobbled together show that might go well or might teeter off the rails and into disaster at any moment.

By the end of this evening, they were going to have pulled off a fashion show that put their name on the fashion map in London, or they were going to have been in charge of a potentially career-ending disaster. She could hardly even think about how high the stakes were. It was at moments like this, that Annie felt she had to lean on a higher power... and that higher power was currently striding around in front of the catwalk shouting at minions to re-position chairs.

'I'm going to get Svetlana, right now, and she's going to come in here, talk to all of us and remind us why we are doing this show, why it's such a great idea and why we all have to pull together.'

Connor, Vince, all the models, Paula, Annie, the DJ, Lauren, plus some of the Lauren friends, school pupils and other helpers all assembled beside the catwalk and Svetlana, in pink Chanel, because this was definitely a day for the fashion greats, stepped up onto the raised catwalk and delivered her speech like the motivating army general she was.

'All of these clothes, they were just hanging in wardrobes all around London, wasted,' Svetlana began, looking deep into the eyes of her helper audience. 'The money was spent, they had been *vorn*, their owners had forgotten all about them. And I wanted to take all of these things that were once wonderful, expensive and loved, and make them useful again. They are coming out to dance, to play, to find new homes. And all the money that is raised tonight, money from nothing, from items gathering dust and attracting moths...' she pulled a face, 'this money is going to a wonderful cause. People who want to go to their job interviews and their big events and the important moments in life looking together, looking wonderful, they are going to have that chance, because of you.' She paused to let these words take effect.

'And it's not just the outfits. This charity gives training, coun-selling, guidance, and gives everyone who wants it the help they need in those times when things haven't worked out and they are feeling down and feeling lost.

'We have all had those times. Every single one of us,' she said looking at each face in turn, meeting eyes, bonding with her troops. 'And if someone is there to help you get back on your feet, choose a nice outfit, style your hair, lend you a lipstick, tell you you can get back out there and do this – it makes all the difference.

'Darlings,' she went on, 'I could not do this show without every single person in this room. Every one of you is going to make this an amazing evening that people will talk about for a long time.'

Rising to the kind of crescendo that was going to galvanise them all, Svetlana ended with the words, 'I know we are going to raise £1 million tonight. One million pounds to help people! And next year, we are going to come back and do it all again – even bigger, even better! So, please, go out there, play your part, and with the whole of my Ukrainian heart, I thank you.'

There was an electrifying round of whooping, cheering and grinning in response to this. And the DJ captured the mood perfectly with a loud blast of Daft Punk reminding everyone that they'd all *come too far to give up who they are*. Finally, Annie could feel her heart lift and her belief begin to grow that They Could Do This.

* * *

Finally, it was 7.35 p.m., the audience was seated, the lights were low, and backstage, there was fever-pitch anxiety. Annie, Paula, superstar Anoush and all the other models were gathered, dressed, made up, all ready for take-off, sweating so much with heat, with fear, Annie wasn't even sure how she and the models could still be wearing make up. Anoush had already promised the dance girls that she would walk down the catwalk arm-in-arm with them all on that opening number. It was going to be Madonna's 'Vogue' because they all loved it. Arm-in-arm march, release arms, twirl at the bottom and march back. 'You will love it, the audience will love it and from then on, you'll be fine,' she had promised. And it was hard not to believe a kind and beautiful superstar in towering heels, with another six inches of height from her wild and untamed mane.

Annie kept peeking out into the audience, scanning for faces... there was Svetlana, surrounded by all her grandest friends, then a smattering of fashion journalists and influencers; Ed – God bless him, dressed exactly as instructed – beside Dinah, who'd been freed by the arrival of the head girl to babysit. Lauren, Annie knew, was not in a seat, because she and her friends were tearing around sorting one million last minute things, manning stalls, rails, guiding late arrivals into back-row seats... Annie's TV crowd was there and so many other guests, hundreds and hundreds of people. She scanned once more for PaigeP. Could she—? Would she come? There didn't seem to be any sign of her yet.

'Break a leg, Annie.' It was Connor whispering against her ear. 'We've had the signal. It's showtime.'

And then the blur of intense images, feelings, excitement all began. Connor and Vince, striding out onto the catwalk to open with jokes, some cheesy lines from Vince followed by an imme-diate mauling from Connor. *Omg, did he really say that? Did Connor just say he would offer Vince's toupee a saucer of milk if it started miaowing?* No matter, everyone was laughing... including Vince. Another peek into the audience and Annie spotted Florence! Oh, and she was wearing the Schiaparelli jacket, of course she was... how fabulous. Not only that, but underneath there seemed to be a gold blouse, not black. And beside her was a very beautiful old lady, white hair, silver dress, stunning diamond chandelier earrings, which Annie could see even at this distance. Could that be Mrs K. Lawson? Annie wondered. Maybe she had decided she wanted to come up to London and sit with Florence to see these precious items, once worn by both of their mothers come back to life and hopefully go off to exciting new homes for a huge, charitable sum. Looking at Florence in gold and Schia-parelli, Annie couldn't help thinking that perhaps the dresses had brought an exciting new chapter to Florence's life just when she needed it.

And now Connor and Vince were ending their turn, the music was ramping up and the girls were holding tight to Anoush, about to come on... that's when there was a small flurry of activity in the front row. There was a shuffling, standing, making room and there, taking her front row seat at exactly the last moment, was PaigeP.

'Ohmigod!!' Annie gasped and when the dance girls looked at her with panicked expressions, she decided not to tell them about the latest guest. It was too much pressure. Instead, she broke into a grin and told Anoush, Bria, Shivani and Chloe: 'You are all fabulous and it's showtime!'

So out they went. And then it was far too fast and too busy for Annie to do anything other than concentrate on the girls and together with the small backstage army, focus on undressing and re-dressing them, fluffing their hair, adjusting their lipstick, helping to push up zips and find missing shoes and tuck in bra straps and tape loose hems and do whatever was required to keep the show on the road. Round after round of fabulous items went out there. There was music, applause and the sound of the bidding mounting higher and higher.

'Come on, this is gorgeous stuff... this skirt, I think we can do one better than £850,' Connor was urging the crowd. 'Think of the good this will do... and £950 and... done!'

So very dizzyingly quickly, it was the 1980s round... then it was the ladies who lunch round... and already there were just two more rounds to go before the wedding round.

And then wedding music was playing and the girls all in their wonderful bridal finery were heading down the aisle. There was

Chloe with her halo of wild, frizzy curls and a bouquet of the palest pink roses, just as Annie had imagined from when she'd set eyes on her. After the brides came the special moment when four women who had been helped by the charity and beautifully styled in auction-item clothing by Annie and Paula came out and didn't just twirl up and down the catwalk, they spoke in their own words about what the charity had meant to them and urged everyone to dig deep for the headline items of the evening.

'And now, ladies, gentlemen and everyone in between, here we are...' Connor was back on stage, sounding excited but serious and every eye in the room was on him. 'It's the moment you have all been waiting for, your chance to see the most wonderful treasures of the night on the runway. We're going to start the bidding for these items at £30,000, so do not wave your bidding number at me unless you are serious and ready to pony up the cash.'

A hush descended and then sophisticated jazz, from the height of the cocktail lounge era, struck up and every one of the girls came onto the stage in turn in the best vintage items the show could offer. First the dance girls in glorious Christian Dior and Yves Saint Laurent. Followed by Phyllis in a ball dress that Madame Chanel had touched with her very own hands. Then it was time for Gwen to emerge in the orange and pink Schiaparelli that caused cheers and even tears from some of the most dedicated fashionistas in the audience. And as the other girls stayed out on the runway, forming a guard of honour, out stepped Anoush looking completely sensational in the lobster dress.

At that point, the atmosphere turned electric. More cheers, even screams... something a little close to Beatlemania was going on. Something even of a surge towards the runway. So much so, that both Connor, Vince and now Svetlana felt they had to come onto the catwalk and help to calm the situation down.

'It's wonderful, wonderful stuff... and let's all remember why we're here,' Connor reminded them. And as he began to talk about the work of the charity, Annie didn't think she'd ever been so proud of her friend. Oh, so professionally, he brought calm and togetherness and real warmth to the mood. And that was when the bidding began.

The dresses all sold for magical numbers. Magical! Annie and Svetlana were holding onto each other's arms backstage and trying to stem tears as the tens of thousands flew upwards. 'I have someone on a computer backstage totting everything up, we were already close to a million before these dresses went out,' Svetlana whispered.

'That's amazing! Amazing,' Annie told her.

'We do it again next year. Promise me!' Svetlana said.

'Ermmmm... maybe ask me in a week... or a month, babes... it's been a lot!' was Annie's honest response. And then everything was sold and the compères were back telling the audience they must go and enjoy the stalls and buy more for this wonderful cause. But not before Svetlana, Annie and Paula were all whisked onto the stage and Svetlana was holding the microphone and delivering a thank you speech worth of Oscars night. Svetlana was truly magnificent, Annie couldn't help thinking. She had given so much of her time, of her money and of her own fabulous wardrobe to make this show happen and to reel in the very big bucks for the charity.

'Thank you so much to every single person who has made this show possible...' Svetlana began her long list of thank yous. She had thought it through carefully and everyone was fully appreciated, from her 'right-hand women' Annie and Paula, to the compères, models, music maestro, all the helpers, the audience, her husband, everyone, even the florist who'd provided the 'funereal' flowers got a mention, proving how happy Svetlana must be feeling.

'We're already planning to do this all again next year, even bigger, even better...' Svetlana told the audience. Annie felt Paula's arm around her waist and the two looked at each other with raised eyebrows...

'Could we?' Annie asked.

'Never say never,' Paula replied with a smile.

'So, if you have any treasures hiding in your wardrobe, you know who to come and speak to,' Svetlana told the crowd, earning herself another round of applause. 'Our Schiaparelli donor wishes to remain anonymous. But I would like to thank her, really, truly from my heart.'

Annie caught Florence and Mrs K. Lawson smiling and clapping enthusiastically, diamonds and gold sparkling in the lights. Once the unrestrained response from the audience to this had calmed down, Svetlana promised to give them an update of the running total of donations in around twenty minutes and issued her last instructions to the crowd: 'So please wait for that, but meanwhile, chose a drink and a canapé from our army of helpers, and head to the rails, to the beautiful stalls we've set out in the adjoining rooms, and buy a bargain, *buy, baby, buy!*'

* * *

Annie helped as much as she could at the stalls and the rails, where it felt like Boxing Day at The Store before the era of internet shopping. People were grabbing at things and tapping their cards before they'd even looked at the price tags. A scan of the handbag stall told her that the handbag she'd bonded with in her storeroom lockdown had gone. In fact, almost everything they'd set out so carefully and tastefully had gone. But there was no time to be sad about the loss of The Row's rare calf-skin treasure because as Annie, in her gold caped dress, headed out of one room and made for the next, she almost walked straight into the path of PaigeP. Maybe it was the adrenaline, or the champagne she'd just swallowed, or the sheer success of the night, but Annie felt bold enough to blurt out to her fashion heroine: 'I'm so delighted you could make it, PaigeP... Honestly, it has made our night. Your attendance and the lobster dress, these were the absolute highlights for me.'

Through her rose-gold tinted glasses, PaigeP seemed to give Annie a haughty up and down. 'Do I know you?' she asked.

'I'm Annie Valentine. I was one of Svetlana's right-hand women on this. I do fashion on TV... and funnily enough, you helped me choose this dress...' she gestured to her gold cape-dress, 'in Ralph Lauren,' Annie added in the hope of jogging a memory. PaigeP gave absolutely no sign of recognition. Never mind, this was Annie's moment and she decided she better try and take it. 'I love your work on *Stylesetter,*' she went on. 'I'd love to talk to you about anything I could do for the publication... in any way at all. I have so much TV and fashion experience...' She heard herself tail off, the confidence ebbing from her voice.

PaigeP did that mean up and down appraisal of Annie once again. Honestly, it was cold and calculating and even Annie, in her forties, with so many years of experience behind her, felt small and humiliated.

'Annie Valentine... oh no, you're too mainstream for us,' PaigeP said. The final nail in the coffin. PaigeP turned and stalked off. It was crushing. Even as Annie told herself it didn't matter, and it had been a long shot and that PaigeP was much nastier than she'd thought, Annie could still feel tears of humiliation at the back of her eyes.

But then, from the main room, came Svetlana's voice loud and clear on the microphone. 'Listen up, everyone, I have such exciting news. Our running total so far for the show... you just won't believe this... we wanted to raise £1 million and we're already at £1,430,000 and counting. This is incredible, people, incredible! So, two things, first of all, keep on buying, let's see if we can make it £1.5 million...'

These words were hardly sinking in for Annie, £1.5 million worth of wonderful things would now be happening and helping because of this show. This really did make every moment of pain worthwhile and yes, she would sign up for next year. And maybe PaigeP would not be invited. Ha!

'And as we are doing so well,' Svetlana went on, 'we are going to donate everything over the £1.3 million mark to another amazing charity that I have been learning about called Clean Up Fashion because I believe this is another wonderful cause for us fashion people to be involved with.'

As Annie listened to the enthusiastic applause, she knew at once who had planted this idea into Svetlana's mind. Lauren, of course – clever, generous, 'I want to do something useful with my life', Lauren.

This was amazing. She needed to go and find Lauren and congratulate her. Never mind hoity-toity PaigeP, this was £1.5 million pounds, something to really be proud of! Just as Annie was straightening her shoulders and breaking out into a smile right across her face because £1.5 *million*... two women approached her with big smiles and seemed incredibly keen to meet her.

'Oh, hello, Annie Valentine,' the first one began, 'we're so happy to meet you! I'm Jasmine and this is my colleague, Fliss.' Annie took them in, two unusually stylish women, one around the forty-ish mark, the other a little younger, she guessed. Both wearing beautiful outfits, standout jewellery, hair and make up all wonderfully considered. 'We so want to talk to you, if you have a minute...?' Jasmine began and she looked quite excited about what she was going to say.

'Yes, of course I have a minute for two ladies with such awesome accessories,' Annie said with a smile. This made them both laugh.

'So...' Jasmine said, 'we want to set up a meeting... we want to talk to you about luring you away—'

'From what?' Annie wondered, no idea what they were referring to.

'From TV...' Fliss was the next to speak. 'Well, for most of the time... But you can still do some TV, in fact, that would be great.'

'Yes, it would be very helpful,' Jasmine confirmed. 'But mainly, we'd want you to come and work for us. On a proper employed, full-time basis.'

'We need you. We've all decided we need *you*,' Fliss confirmed.

'What for?' Annie asked, her head spinning a little. *What on earth was this about?*

'To bring real style, oomph, pizazz, what women, in particular, real women, want...' Jasmine went on excitedly. 'So yes, we want you to call us. We'll set up a meeting. Come in, meet the whole team. We want to explain to you why we would be perfect for you.'

'Yes, seriously,' Fliss added. 'We know all about you. Your TV show, your social media, this event tonight. We are basically your fan girls and we want to talk it all through with you. And, hopefully, make you an offer you can't refuse.'

Both smiled at her again in the same excited, expectant way.

'But who are you?' was Annie's next question.

'Oh God... I'm so sorry, did we not say?' Jasmine asked. 'We're so excited about tonight, this amazing show, and about having this chat with you, that we've fluffed our intro. We're Jasmine and Fliss and we're the joint Heads of Fashion at M&S.'

'*M&S*??!!' Annie couldn't help herself... it came out a little more shocked than she had meant it to. But *M&S*... yes, of course there were some nice items in M&S, didn't she have some in her own wardrobe? But... M&S?! Home of pants, prawn cocktail sandwiches, sensible handbags made of pleather and truly unspeakable shoes.

'Yes, M&S,' Fliss said quickly. 'And I know, I know what you're thinking. I bet you're thinking pants, prawn cocktail sandwiches and extra comfy, wide-fit shoes. I know, I know. And those things are very important. The necessities of life. But there's so much happening that is very exciting. We have brands in store now. And I bet you know that we have Jaeger, which both our mums adored.'

'Mine too,' Annie agreed.

'We also have some of the people who put Topshop on the map back in the day...'

'Oh... Topshop... absolutely loved Topshop.' Annie was listening intently, she was trying to get her head around it. The joint Heads of Fashion wanted her to come and work for them? With them? Full-time, employed... but she could still do some TV...

'We're aiming to be John Lewis meets Topshop with a sprinkle of both your old haunt, The Store, and your TV show, *How To Be Fabulous,* because everyone deserves to have style in their lives. Don't they?'

They knew her.

They knew all about her. And they wanted her! Annie had to check this opportunity out, didn't she?

34

Night-time Minette:
Pink and white pyjama onesie with cloud pattern
Bear dressing gown with ears on the hood
Knitted pink bootie slippers
Hair in four plaits 'to make it princess-y'

It was unbelievably late by the time the taxi approached the Valentine-Leon home. Annie might have expected to be completely exhausted by now, but all the drama, success and sheer excitement of tonight had pumped litres of adrenaline into her system and in fact, she felt *ah-mazing*. Like an athlete, who'd just won gold, or an actress clutching her Oscar, she didn't want this night to end and kept mentioning all the highlights to Lauren, who seemed equally hyped-up and Ed – not quite so much – and their taxi driver, who seemed surprisingly keen to hear all about the show. He'd even heard of PaigeP.

'She helped me to pick out my clutch,' Annie told him, waving the vintage Jacquemus about for his benefit, making it sound as if she and PaigeP regularly nipped out for a shopping trip together. 'But really, I think she's a bit of a Mean Girl.'

'I suppose she has to be in her job,' the taxi driver said.

'So... I've been asked to come for a meeting at M&S... they want to make me an offer I can't refuse...' she repeated once again to Ed and Lauren. Because it really had not sunk in and she thought if she said it out loud to herself just a few more times, maybe she would start to believe it. 'That is right, isn't it, Ed? I didn't dream that bit?'

Ed turned from the front seat to look at her and his face had that quietly amused look that she loved to see. 'Yes, you've got a meeting and they do sound very keen, so if it's the right thing for you, on the right terms... then, yes, it will hopefully work out.'

'Oh my God... I could be *never knowingly undersold*.'

'I think you'll find that's the John Lewis slogan,' was Lauren's response to this.

'Oh my God... what is the M&S slogan? I need to know this.'

'Is it still *dressing the nation*?' Lauren wondered.

'Oh!' Annie felt a little overwhelmed at that. It could be a very heavy responsibility, dressing the entire nation.

'But you know, when you go into that meeting, you need to keep *never knowingly undersold* in mind,' Ed told her, turning round to meet her eyes. 'Absolutely do not undersell yourself, because you really are amazing. What you put on tonight was stunning and raised so much money! And it wouldn't have come together or been nearly as amazing without you!'

'Thank you, babes... and I love, *love* my necklace. Thank you so much.' And as Annie put her hand over the gold heart he had put around her neck as her anniversary gift at the end of the show, she thought about all the people who undersold them-selves every single day and didn't have someone like Ed in their corner to brush them down, boost them up and send them back into battle once again.

And that was when she remembered that she *did* have a present for him. That crazed, late night, last-minute, over the Internet purchase that she really, really hoped was going to work out and not turn out to be some terrible scam. Taking her phone out of her bag, she looked for the right app.

Oh good grief, here were a flurry of messages. The delivery driver hadn't found her address... then it turned out he had... oh, yes! The delivery had been made, late, 10.45 p.m. this evening. Fingers crossed... fingers very, very crossed. For a moment, she wondered if she should tell Ed... but no, better to leave it as a wonderful surprise at the end of a wonderful day.

* * *

As the taxi pulled up, Annie glanced at the house and was surprised to see lights on in several upstairs windows and light peeking through the gap where the sitting room curtains hadn't been pulled tightly shut. The babysitter had planned to go home once the twins were fast asleep, leaving Owen and his now lightly bandaged hands in charge of not very much. Maybe he was watching TV downstairs, having forgotten to turn the light off in his room? But now she saw that the light was also on in the twins' room. What was going on?

The taxi was paid and the three of them hurried through the light drizzle to the front door, and into the warmth of the hall. Voices, laughter and the background sound of the television were coming from the sitting room.

'What on earth—?' Ed began as he opened the door to the room. Owen was sitting in the middle of the large, squishy, beaten-up sofa. He had that sort of harassed-happy look most often seen on new dads *or big brothers*, when they are trying to control a toddler riot but are also quite enchanted by it. Meanwhile Min, in her pyjamas, was standing on one arm of the sofa, while Max, also in pyjamas, was sprawled on his back on the rug, giggling like a mad thing.

'Owen!' Annie began. 'It's 1 a.m.!'

'I know!' Owen replied. 'But they won't go to sleep. I've tried stories, snacks, bribes, threats... they won't go. And I can't make them do anything,' he held up his bandaged hands.

'But why did they wake up?' was Ed's question as Annie scooped Min from the edge of the sofa, then sat down beside Owen and encouraged Max to come up for a hug. 'I dunno...' was Owen's first response, followed by a thoughtful, 'actually, there was this delivery guy. It was after Megan left, so it was pretty late. He was ringing the bell, knocking on the door. I finally heard him over my headphones. But I couldn't do anything.' Owen waved his mitts in the air again. 'Couldn't undo the locks, open the door or anything, so I was shouting through the letter box at him.'

'Oh God!' Annie jumped up, practically bouncing the twins from her lap. All this chaos going on in the house had momentarily put the anniversary surprise out of her mind, but now it was rushing right back in again.

'Urgent handbag delivery?' Ed asked, turning to Annie with something between a grin and a frown on his face.

'Where did he...?' she began, seriously worried about the whereabouts of the delivery now.

'Chill out, Mum,' Owen said. 'I told him to go round to the back and see if the shed was open. So, he did and it was and that seemed to put his mind at rest. I told him you'd be back soon. He took a photo of my face at the letter box and everything.'

But none of this was putting Annie's mind at rest. 'It's Ed's present!' she blurted. 'Ed's anniversary present! I have to go and get it. Right now!'

'OK...' Ed was looking at her with an expression of surprise. 'Annie, it is still 1 a.m. and it is still tipping with rain. If you don't want to go out to the shed right now to fetch my new designer suit... new designer guitar case... or whatever lovely, thoughtful item you have managed to find for me, even when you said we weren't going to do presents, that's totally fine. We can do this at breakfast tomorrow. I mean, everyone looks very tired. And when I say breakfast, I'm meaning brunch. I'm thinking no one should even consider leaving their room,' he turned to the twins, 'until the small hand is pointing to the number nine.' Minnie was nodding solemnly. But Annie was already at the sitting room door.

'Stay here, everyone,' she said, then changed her mind and asked if Lauren wouldn't mind just coming out to the shed with her to give a hand, 'in case it's heavier than I thought.'

'Set of weights?' Ed guessed. 'I mean that would be very thoughtful, but I might be a tiny bit offended.'

'Ha!' Annie said as she went out of the room, followed by Lauren, and headed for the door in the kitchen that led out to the garden. Outside, Annie took the wet path through the rain towards the shed, feeling a jangle of nerves and hoping that her big surprise was going to be OK. Her big surprise... it was something of a surprise to her. Had she really done this? She was suddenly so tired, she was just about delirious. 'I hope it's all right, I hope it's all right,' she worried out loud.

'Mum, it will be fine. No one is going to have crept into our shed to steal whatever big spendy thing you've bought for Dad from The Store.'

'No! It's not like that. I really, really thought about what he would want,' she explained. 'What would make him happy. This is definitely not about me. This is for Ed... and also everyone else. If it's what I think it is...'

'What?' Lauren said, pulling open the shed door. 'Was this a 4 a.m. in the morning online purchase by any chance?'

'Something like that...' Annie admitted, feeling very guilty. This was exactly the kind of purchase she should not have made on a whim, or in a fever dream, or by accident.

'Intriguing,' Lauren said, as they stepped into the shed and enjoyed the brief respite from the rain. The big cardboard box in front of them didn't give anything away, although it was perforated with small round air holes. And then came the tiny, plaintive miaow, such a heart-rending, little baby miaow that had Lauren dropping to her knees and gasping. '*No*! You haven't! Is it *really*...?'And Annie felt a little overcome by the conflicting emotions of huge relief that the little fur-baby was OK and almost immediate nerves and regret about what she'd done and what she was about to launch into her already quite full-to-the-brim family life. 'Thank God I'm moving back for good!' Lauren said, as she took hold of one side of the box.

'What?!' was Annie's reply as she took hold of the other. 'Yeah, I didn't want to steal your thunder, but I've been offered a new job too. Publicity and marketing with Clean Up Fashion.'

'That's amazing, Lauren, congratulations,' Annie beamed. 'And quite right too! Telling Svetlana all about them when the money was rolling in and she was feeling super generous was—'

'Genius! And... it will be OK, won't it, to move back to my room until I've saved up some money? I'll look after the kitten... and the twins. But mainly the kitten,' Lauren said with a laugh.

'Yes, of course.' Annie smiled at her daughter. 'Of course it will. It will be lovely to have you back. It feels like you've been gone forever.'

One out, one in – Annie couldn't help thinking to herself. And it would be lovely to have this sensible, grown-up Lauren back in the house for a while. Even if they did have a disagreement every second day.

'Can I take a peek?' Lauren asked, hands on the flaps of the box.

'No! Let's get the poor mite inside,' Annie insisted, as they each took hold of the box and began to carry it to the house. 'Do you really think Ed will like having a kitten?' Annie worried as they negotiated the back step.

'Are you kidding, Mum? He's going to love it, adore it! Remember when we first moved in with him and he had those two saggy old cats? He was so nutty about them. Even if they hated us and had to go to a new home. This is a lovely thing to do for him.'

'Good,' Annie felt a burst of happiness at these words, 'because I really do love that man. So, tell me about the new job.'

So, in just a few sentences, Lauren gave her the top-line highlights.

'Sounds amazing and perfect for you! And I think Svetlana and Elena are going to be fine about it, aren't they? Especially if you tell Svetlana tomorrow, when she's still on a total high about her raging success of a show,' Annie advised.

'*Your* raging success of a show,' Lauren said with a burst of laughter. How good it was to hear that laugh again, Annie thought. Lauren had been all sad and subdued, but she was coming round. 'Yeah, Svetlana and Elena are going to be fine,' Lauren said. 'They'll find someone new in a flash and they are going to be very busy with their Schiaparelli homage dress... have you heard about this? Svetlana cut a deal with Carina before the sale went through.'

'Perfect Dress is allowed to do a version of the lobster?' Annie asked, with everything going on, no, she had not heard about Svetlana's clever arrangement.

'Yes! A homage to the *homard* – which is French for lobster, by the way,' Lauren told her.

'Very clever. I am so putting my name down for a lobster dress.'

'No I'm putting my name down for a lobster dress!'

'No, me! I brought them that lobster!'

They were at the door to the sitting room now and couldn't help exchanging smiles.

'Fingers crossed,' Annie whispered.

'Oh! Ed and the twins... the twins are going to go crazy,' Lauren whispered excitedly.

'OK...' Annie called out, 'open the door for us and get ready for the big reveal.' She could hear Max and Min's voices, fizzy with excitement.

'What did Mummy get Daddy?' Minnie wondered.

'Maybe a new piano?'

'No, silly, she couldn't carry a piano even with Lauren.'

'Yes, she could,' Max insisted, 'Mummy is very strong!'

Annie and Lauren carefully carried the box into the middle of the room, setting it down beside the coffee table. Everyone was craning forward to look. And this time, there was no giveaway sound from inside the cardboard.

'Daddy opens this,' Annie commanded, as the twins approached with excitement. 'This is his present, so he's in charge.' Annie closed the sitting room door as a precaution against the kitten bolting out and exchanged a look with Ed. His eyebrows were right up in his hair and that bemused smile was on his lips again. Maybe he'd spotted the air holes, maybe he had a suspicion...

'OK,' he said, going over to the box and kneeling beside it.

'What has Mummy got me to say thank you for putting up... no, *sharing*, these glorious first years of married life!' He looked at her and gave her a tiny wink at this.

'Putting up with is fine,' she told him. He untucked the cardboard flaps and a look of such astonished delight passed over his face, that Annie's heart swelled and she knew she had done absolutely the right thing – which is how it usually turned out when you acted a little crazily but completely out of love and devotion to someone else.

'Oh... twins,' Ed said and his voice was all shushed, caring and low, just like he used to speak to them when they were babies, 'no rushing, no crushing, but in here, fast asleep is the most gorgeous little kitten you've ever seen.'

The shriek of delight and the thundering of toddler feet towards the box probably gave the kitten something of a shock, because now, it's tiny pixie face was peeking over the top of the box in surprise. The sight of this made Max and Min squeal with excitement.

'Shhhhhh!' Ed ordered. 'The poor baby doesn't know where he or she...?' he glanced at Annie.

'She... I think,' Annie replied.

'You don't know where you are, little poppet, do you?' Ed now had one twin peering over each shoulder. Lauren and Owen were standing over the box too now. Ed very gently stroked the kitten's head and made soothing noises. The kitten, to everyone's delight, crawled daintily out of the box, dropped straight into Ed's lap and seemed to pad around there for a few moments before deciding it was warm, safe and she needed to curl up and get straight back to sleep.

'Has it been a long day, little poppet?' he asked the kitten, as everyone crowded around to get in just a tiny gentle pat.

'She's so soft,' Max cooed, 'like a little feather.'

'Will she wake up soon?' Minette wondered, probably quite prepared to stay up all night if required.

There was no point in sending anyone to bed, Annie realised. Absolutely not one wink of sleep would be had until everyone had enjoyed some kitten bonding time.

'OK, people, snuggle up on the sofa and let's get her blanket out of the box,' Ed suggested. 'Then we can all take turns to give her a cuddle. We can see if she wants a drink and some food and when we're all exhausted, then we can go to bed.'

Turning to Annie, he asked a touch anxiously, 'Did you get any kitten food?'

'Oh yeah – and bowls, and a kitty bed and some toys. All organised,' she assured him.

'Can she sleep in our room?' Max suggested.

'Or we can sleep here,' Min improvised. 'Mummy can get our duvets.'

'What's her name?' Max asked.

'Good question.' Ed held the sleeping kitten in his hands up to his face, so he could have a good look at her. 'She's so pretty.' And this was totally true. She was a pale, sandy white with grey ears and a grey nose with baby kitten pink on the very end. 'A Siamese?' he asked. 'Like my other cats?'

'Yes,' Annie confirmed, 'a royal princess.'

'How about Pixie, because of her little pixie face?'

'Yes!' Max and Min chorused, while Owen grinned and Lauren agreed with, 'Love that.'

* * *

With Lauren's help, Annie brought down duvets, then made some hot chocolate and then her whole family tucked up on sofas and chairs in the sitting room with the kitten. Annie managed to find her own spot underneath Ed's arm, where she closed her eyes and felt absolutely worn out and completely happy.

'Best anniversary ever,' she told him. 'I don't know if we'll top this.'

'We will, every year,' he assured her. 'Thank you for inviting me into your very busy life,' he added.

'Thank you for agreeing to be in it.'

'Thank you so much for my baby cat,' he said. 'I have everything I could ever want.'

'Me too,' she said.

This made him laugh slightly. 'Mmmm... for the moment maybe.'

'So true,' she had to agree with him. 'Love you, love you all. But... if I'm going to be dressing the nation...' she began, 'I do think there may have to be a new handbag...'

Her entire family, even, she was convinced, the kitten, looked at her, groaned and rolled their eyes.

35

ONE MONTH LATER

New colleague Jasmine:
Cream cashmere jumper
Chunky pearl and gold necklace
Tan wide-legged trousers
Chunky brown and cream trainers

Monday morning, 8.30 a.m., Annie emerged from the central London Tube station, all set to walk into the M&S head office to begin her first day at her new job.

A job... a career... being part of the senior team, the executive leadership. These were all incredible new things and daunting new things. Goodbye to TV's *How to be Fabulous*, and hello to making her very best attempt at being fabulous in real life. If she said she'd just thrown on the first things she'd seen in the wardrobe this morning, she would be lying. Her outfit on this crisp November morning had taken days and endless conversations with both Lauren and Dinah to style from top to toe. She'd gone soft wool, pale grey trouser suit. Yes, trouser suit... because they were so bang on trend again. Weren't the Princess of Wales,

Victoria Beckham and Jennifer Anniston all about looking pulled together and professional in trouser suits these days? This trouser suit was accompanied by a silky white blouse, some strong gold and pearl accessory game on both the necklace and earring front and a pair of very up-to-the-moment trainers, as recommended by Owen. Then came a navy-blue trench coat, a sharp new haircut in brightest blonde, her favourite lipstick, and the touch of luxe M&S, a wonderful leather workbag, smooth and conker-brown that was this season's homage to The Row's *Devon* bag. Ha!

But if her appearance said, 'I'm here to do this job brilliantly,' her inward self wasn't quite so convinced. Despite her outward armour, Annie was feeling more than a little terrified. She was a personal shopper, a TV makeover minor personality, who'd somehow managed to be elevated to the M&S ranks of leaders.

How had this happened? How would she make it work? How could she possibly make it work? Even as she went in through the doors to the main shopping floor, which she had to cross on her way to the elevators to the top-floor offices, she really didn't have much idea about how this was all going to work out. But she walked through the shop, scanning left and right and taking some comfort from the autumn/winter collection out on the rails. Lovely woollen trench coat there, beautiful quilted outwear over there, oh and those knits were good, but oooft, those knits there, not-so-much. Already, the sequins of Christmas were in full overwhelm. And there were trees, robins and Santa hats everywhere. She powered on, until she caught sight of a woman frozen in front of one of the shop-floor mirrors. The woman was trying on a longer length blazer in deepest green and holding another jacket in chocolate-brown in her hand. She did not look happy at the sight of her reflection. No, she was wearing an expression that was probably similar to Annie's – mild panic.

Annie had some time. It was at least twenty-five minutes before her official 9 a.m. start time, although she was determined to be early.

So, she walked over to this woman and said a cheerful 'Hello,' with a big smile in place. 'I'm guessing important interview and you want a new jacket that is going to set you up. I'm Annie, by the way, and... I work here,' she tried those words on for size and realised she liked them.

'Oh... hello...' the customer looked at her a little warily. 'Yes... it's something like that,' the woman said.

'Would you like some hopefully helpful suggestions, or would you rather be left alone? Just let me know.'

The woman looked at Annie for a moment or two to gauge whether to trust her with this personal decision. 'Maybe a little help would be good,' she decided.

'Amazing,' Annie enthused. 'My favourite thing is to help people nail that crucial outfit.'

'So... the green or the brown?' the woman asked hesitantly holding up both jackets.

Annie shook her head gently. 'I'm going to say neither, babes,' she said in a low voice, making it sound like a secret. 'Both are too dark for your fair colouring. We're going to look for a soft grey, a French navy, something that's going to give you the seriousness you want but in the colours that you will stand out in. And we're going to go for a jacket that's a little shorter than this one, because that will emphasise the waist and make you taller and more authoritative,' Annie gave her a wink at these words.

'Sounds good,' was the woman's verdict.

'To be honest, it's my first day on the job here... and I am nervous,' Annie confided as she held up both the grey and the blue version that they had found on a quick tour of the rails.

'On the shop floor?' the woman asked, slipping her arms into the grey and immediately seeing how much better it suited her. 'You're so beautifully dressed for a shop assistant,' she told Annie. 'Shame to take that lovely suit off and put on the uniform.'

'Yeah...' Annie decided to agree rather than explain that, no, she wasn't exactly on the shop floor this time. 'This is nice fabric,' she told the woman, stroking the jacket sleeve appreciatively. 'A good wool to polyester blend. I love it.'

'Is your suit M&S? It's beautiful,' the woman added.

'Ermmm... no...' This was not the time to admit which designer label Annie had picked for her all-important Day One. 'But my bag is,' she held up the leather tote.

'Oh, that's beautiful. I'm going to get one of those... isn't it exactly like one of those very posh—'

'Bags from The Row,' Annie finished the thought. 'Exactly! You are looking lovely in this jacket,' she added. 'I'm thinking white blouse, nice necklace... try the blue on too, but the grey is really good on you.'

'Agreed,' the woman said, 'this is so helpful.'

'Totally,' Annie had to add, because this encounter was helping her too. This brief five minutes of going through the rails, inspecting the clothes and helping the woman to try them on was giving Annie all the inspo she needed for her new job. She would come down here every day for at least an hour at a time or more. She'd help people try things on, she'd listen to their feedback and get right in touch with what they wanted and how much they expected to pay for it and all this knowledge, that's what would make her great at her job.

'Annie!' She turned at the sound of her name and found herself face-to-face with her new colleague Jasmine.

'Hello, lovely to see you. Follow me up for the morning BAU meeting.'

Annie turned to her new friend in front of the mirror now

trying out the soft French blue. She mouthed the words 'BAU?' and shrugged.

'Business as usual,' the woman whispered back.

'Ah! OK... I have to go. Grey or blue, your choice, both look fabulous. Loads of luck in your new role'.

'Loads of luck in yours!'

Annie picked up her handbag, tucked it under her arm and set off with Jasmine in the direction of the lift to the head office.

OK, babes... you can do this, she told herself. *You have so got this.*

She touched the citrine ring on her bossing finger for luck – *brings energy and success,* Svetlana had promised.

Fingers crossed, babes, fingers crossed!

* * *

MORE FROM CARMEN REID

Another book from Carmen Reid, is available to order now here:
https://mybook.to/BrandCarmenNewBackAd

ABOUT THE AUTHOR

Carmen Reid is the bestselling author of numerous women's fiction titles including the Personal Shopper series starring Annie Valentine. She lives in Glasgow with her husband and children.

Download your exclusive bonus content from Carmen Reid here:

Visit Carmen's website: www.carmenreid.com

Follow Carmen on social media:

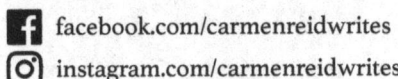

facebook.com/carmenreidwrites
instagram.com/carmenreidwrites

ALSO BY CARMEN REID

Worn Out Wife Seeks New Life

New Family Required

The Woman Who Ran For The Hills

Three in a Bed

Stuck in Second Gear

The Mum Who Got Away

Mum on a Mission

The Annie Valentine Series

The Personal Shopper

Late Night Shopping

How Not To Shop

Celebrity Shopper

New York Valentine

Shopping With The Enemy

Annie in Paris

How to Be Fabulous

Boldwood

Boldwood Books is an award-winning fiction publishing company seeking out the best stories from around the world.

Find out more at www.boldwoodbooks.com

Join our reader community for brilliant books, competitions and offers!

Follow us
@BoldwoodBooks
@TheBoldBookClub

Sign up to our weekly deals newsletter

https://bit.ly/BoldwoodBNewsletter